The Fossil Pits

The Fossil Pits

Tim Corballis

VICTORIA UNIVERSITY PRESS

VICTORIA UNIVERSITY PRESS
Victoria University of Wellington
PO Box 600 Wellington

Copyright © Tim Corballis 2005

First published 2005

ISBN 0-86473-508-1

National Library of New Zealand Cataloguing-in-Publication Data

Corballis, Tim, 1971-
The fossil pits / Tim Corballis.
ISBN 0-86473-508-1
I. Title.
NZ823.3—dc 22

Printed by Astra Print, Wellington

I would like to express my gratitude to Creative
New Zealand and the Randell Cottage Writers Trust
for my stay in the Randell Cottage, Wellington,
and to Creative New Zealand for their
further support of this novel.

The Alexander Turnbull Library, Wellington,
holds a sizeable collection of W B D Mantell's papers,
some of which I read. Thanks are due to
the staff there, in particular David Colquhoun
and Philip Rayner, whose suggestions for research
were invaluable in writing this book.

Thanks also, as always, to Ingrid Horrocks,
for her close readings, suggestions, and
presence-in-absence. This novel is dedicated to her.

In London

I was in London. The street curved away in a grand sweep of brick from its corner, and in a single tree birds—finches—occupied their place with a uniform high chatter, and from time to time one of them took a dive upwards towards an overcast sky, whose clouds extended downwards into the city itself as the fingers of a light mist.

I stood fumbling with folded papers: an airline boarding pass; a scrap on which I had noted some ideas during my flight; a list of numbers and addresses and other important information that I had quickly jotted to myself before my departure. Then, having consulted this list, spoken the street number to myself, refolded the small pile into its scrappy bundle and stuffed it back into a pocket, I hefted my suitcase, stood for a second slightly lopsided with its weight, and walked on, counting out the numbers under my breath as I passed them.

It had, as I expected, been a long and exhausting flight. Before I left, I had received no reply to my written request to stay a few days with Diane before I travelled on to Norwich, and though I had tried phoning her several times there had been no answer. I had retreated to my study in the evenings to work on my paper; it was the first time I had managed to pick up funding for an international writing conference, in this case a small one organised by a well-sponsored agricultural writers' group, and, although in the last few years I had grown heartily sick of dull, bread-and-butter writing for trade and industry journals, now the excitement at being offered an expenses-paid trip made the years of boredom seem worthwhile. All the same, I wanted to think about how I might begin again to write something of substance. As I sat in my study my thoughts turned from my paper to my real interests and back, but increasingly I was unable to concentrate on either, thinking as I was instead about Diane and her lack of communication. Finally, I had boarded the plane still uncertain as to whether she would be able to put me up, but without having arranged anything else.

Now, despite my lack of sleep and the sound of the plane's engines still humming in my ears, I felt newly alive from a breeze that blew along the road's bend and pushed the fine particles of mist into my back; I felt a determination to walk up to the address I had for Diane and ring for her, almost as if I were presenting a petition. I found myself imagining her as she was when I knew her years before, in the farmhouse, quiet and with, as I now remembered, the occasional distracted look to one side, out the window but with a focus which seemed to be on the glass, not on the view outside.

I pressed the button set into a weatherbeaten metal plate next to her name, printed faintly under yellowing plastic, and there was a long silence from the speaker. I was on the verge of turning around, kept there only by the uncertainty about where else I should stay, when Diane's voice answered, although at first it sounded like the barking of a dog, or a car skidding to a halt. I said, It's your nephew. I wrote and it's been a long time since I've seen you—are you there? . . . There was another silence. I said, Did you get my letter? . . . I wasn't sure whether she could hear me. I said, Are you expecting me?

The door buzzed open, and I entered through a tiled foyer into the stairwell which extended above me, both imposing and gloomy, and edged with shadows under the flights of steps which ran around three of the walls between landings along the fourth, and came up after four flights against a ceiling where, despite the darkness and the height, flakes of paint could be seen peeling from spreading cracks.

I had last seen my aunt at her husband's funeral at a small rural church near the city where I grew up, and at the farm afterwards; I remembered the hot wind that flicked the tops of the row of poplars running between the driveway and a shallow stream, and a bewildered small crowd breaking apart and re-forming in conversation around the silent central figure of Diane herself, who hardly uttered a word, didn't cry, but simply shook her head and squeezed her lips shut occasionally in response to some question. Her daughter Meri served drinks one at a time; I watched her walk from the house to the lawn and back quickly, her paces quickening more as I approached to talk to her, thinking I could see the sadness in her eyes even as she held her face gracefully firm and spoke briefly to each guest.

Finally I followed her into an empty kitchen. I said, Meri let me help you.

She said, No thanks.

Just let me pour some of these for you.

She stopped: Look, thanks, I'm okay, please ... She carried on past me out the door again. I wanted to hold her by her wrist, hold her head for a few minutes against my neck, and images of her father's coffin being lowered into the ground came to me while I stood waiting for her to come back inside.

How are you, Meri?

She said, How do you think? ... Then: I'm sorry ... She shook her head: I just want to ... With her back to me over a bench while she poured a cup of tea from a tarnished silver pot then, holding the saucer steady, walked out again as if feeling her way with her feet. I wanted to do something for her. She came past me again and again, each time taking something else out, looking at me as she walked past, as unapproachable as her mother until I came up to her from behind and put a hand on her back then held on to her shoulder; she shrugged it off, turned to walk away, and without thinking I restrained her with a hand on her upper arm, feeling no sadness myself, and she began to cry. I felt a surge of guilty happiness. We were not yet twenty. Later in the day, while my mother talked with Diane and some others in another room, Meri kissed me then pushed me away.

My aunt's apartment was on the top floor; she was waiting on the landing by her open door, leaning with one hand against the jamb. For a moment neither of us could take our eyes off the other; in the dim light of the stairwell

10

her face resembled her daughter's, at least as I remembered it, and in her stance she seemed like a teenager, at once unaware and aware of her body; she smiled briefly, opened her mouth, shut it again, and moved backwards a step before turning and waving at me to follow her inside.

The apartment was blinding and cluttered, spread out with low furniture, slim bookshelves packed with the familiar books, the books which as a child I had taken to be her husband's, and filled with a brilliance which came in through the lace curtains from the grey sky and was so surprising, perhaps after the poorly lit stairwell, that it seemed to be emitted from the fabric itself. We stood in the living room. When I asked her how she was, she said, I've felt better in recent years . . . She said, I think it's all right for you to stay.

I said, Did you get my letter? I did write and I wasn't sure whether it arrived?

She said, It arrived. Sit down there . . . She pointed me to a sofa. She said, I'm so sorry I didn't reply, please sit down, I'll make some tea. I couldn't decide, I haven't had anyone stay, and I haven't been in touch with your mother or—you're taller than I remember. How old were you?

I was nineteen. It was at Peter's funeral . . .

Yes, of course—and before then?

I can't remember. I'm sure I'm no taller than when you last saw me. Fatter maybe . . . She was looking at me as though studying me, and as though she were looking through me; I began to feel that I might suddenly become visible through a crack in my surface, and I was becoming aware of every muscle in my face. Then, gracefully, but with a movement so unfamiliar that it made me notice that she had aged after all—her hair was long and grey; her face appeared all at once to be pulled tight against the bone—she left the room. She walked unevenly, and from my seat I could see her back contract from the effort of bending down to empty old tea-leaves from a pot into a plastic bin.

I was looking through a red cloth-bound book picked up from a low table when she came in with the teapot and stood for a time next to me, looking over my shoulder at the engraved portrait of a man facing the title page: the man's face was relaxed and earnest, with each eye apparently looking in a slightly different direction, either straight at the viewer or into a misty landscape, and the mouth smiled comfortably but faintly. I started to close the book, but she leaned and put a hand on the portrait, keeping it open for a second before standing again; a long moment passed during which neither of us spoke. Finally she said, That's Gideon Mantell, surgeon and geologist . . . Under the portrait were the words Gideon Algernon Mantell, surgeon and geologist; the book was an edition of his diary. She said, I don't know whether you knew, I was writing a book once.

I said, Yes . . .

I did remember my parents talking about her attempts to write a book, a sort of history or novel.

She said, Anyway that's of no consequence. Here, I've made tea.

She was the same tall woman I remembered, changed, but at the same time unchanged, and charged and sparking with the stories I had heard of her since she left the farm after the death of my uncle, who was not my uncle but my mother's cousin. There were stories that she was a fascinating character, and even a genius of sorts with an encyclopaedic memory and uncontrolled passion for knowledge, but also stories that she was certifiably insane and even dangerous, or at least anti-social and difficult to get along with, and the stories contrasted with my own memories of the quiet woman on the farm with her husband and daughter. As it was, when she sat I had difficulty seeing her face against the glare from a window behind her, though I could make out her eyes with their faint gleam and I felt encapsulated by her look, held in place and chiselled out; hadn't there been the feeling that the face in the book had been sculpted, not drawn? I was feeling awkward, and was it from her words or the myths which had formed around her?

I said, How do you occupy your time now?

She didn't reply immediately.

In my memories she had only ever walked, from one room to another, making quick, bird-like movements with her head or hands, I thought, or from one paddock to another, or as often sitting perfectly still while her husband, my uncle, who wasn't my uncle, kept up a running chatter, a sort of boisterous commentary on everything as he shuffled about serving drinks or seeing to some other business. When I was a child he had delighted me, and even then, hadn't I seen that Diane was left behind, isolated by her husband's jokes and comments, as, perhaps, was I—and hadn't I been unsure whether to feel sorry for her or scornful? Even later, in my twenties, I felt the same mix of emotions towards her, long after her husband's death, when I heard that my father had tried to visit her; he had rung at her doorbell for a long time, only to be told in a croaking voice through the intercom that he should leave her alone.

She said, I do very little, now. I'm old. I read, and I sometimes write . . . She said that she would sometimes pull back the curtains to expose the street below to her gaze; the sound of the London traffic circled her the way the endless paddocks had begun to circle her with the sheep's cries; only on rare occasions would she leave the apartment, and she would see very few people—she was not used to making conversation. She said, Not like I used to be, when I was a right charmer . . . She smirked and hid her nose for a second in her teacup, which she then dropped back to the saucer with a faint clink that rang loudly in the room's silence. How could I sit here, facing her? She shifted in her seat and breathed in, dragging her chest upwards, then closed her eyes for a second and opened them once more on me. I picked up the book again, and turned it open again to the portrait, letting my fingers brush its glossy surface before flicking through the pages of the book itself.

She said, Mantell's an interesting character . . . She said, Sometimes his life seemed like a litany of losses—but he had amazing energy. That's the main thing about him, his energy. Finally, though, it broke down . . . I closed the book and left it sitting on my lap. She said, His son went to New Zealand, and his wife and other children left him—well he drove them out, finally, with his, you know—he would always be riding about the countryside visiting his patients and searching for fossils and he was so ambitious, that's what drove his wife and his family away. I was mostly interested in his science, not in his life, at least at first. But I did come across a good story about his wife, which fascinated me, as well as the son—it was the son mostly I became interested in.

There was another long pause; what could I say? She had paused as if expecting me to respond, and then looked down as if she also were at a complete loss. I opened the book once again for another look at the engraving there, showing its contradictory face, at once familiar and distant, surely a masklike face designed by either the subject or the artist to give nothing away and to draw the viewer towards the softly smiling mouth while the eyes disengaged themselves and, conflicted, seemed ready to look to one side, out or at a window.

I was about to make some observation, when she said,

I didn't know a thing about the son really. I didn't know much until once, when reading some book, I came across one of his drawings. It was a simple sketch of a landscape, a broad plain with the lines of a river, and over and above it the outlines of foothills and mountains ranked behind each other, with the caption, Sketch of an unknown location, W B D Mantell [1848?]. It said unknown but I had looked at the same location, the exact same view of mountains myself; I had stood and looked at the mountains and would recognise the view, from Peter's farm—well, it became our farm—anywhere. So in 1848 he had stood on the very same spot, the only small hill where the landscape opens out with a sense of perspective. It was interesting—the book said very little about him, just really a short description of his travels and his geological work. It seemed to bring a lot of topics together for me. I don't think I even have a copy of the drawing now, but I remember every detail.

In this way, almost without preamble, Diane began to tell me about the project she had once been working on. She said, Gideon Mantell was fairly well known to students of geology and palaeontology—I had come across his name even before I started again at university, when I used to read things out of curiosity. I am quite widely read, and well educated, even though your family forget that. I have a science degree and a teaching qualification . . . She seemed to remember herself for a second, give me a gauging look, before carrying on. She said, But his son was less well known. Gideon lost him to a whole different world, and he was devastated by the departure. Maybe he coped by hoping to discover something new, hoping to find some new discovery about the world which he really loved; he held on to a world behind the world, a faded, strange prehistoric world which he grasped and kept close to himself in the face of anything and everything else—at least that's how I understand him.

By now, Diane was frequently looking towards the window in the distracted manner that I thought I could picture from my youth, each time squinting slightly against the light, giving her the appearance of a bird sizing up its prey. She was speaking slowly and now she paused, her eyes focused on the curtains for a few moments.

She said, For some reason the term 'gizzard stone' fascinated me when it came up as an example of the fossil record . . . She said, I had an idea of how a gizzard worked in birds: the grinding action of stones and grit to break down food. I had no idea how a gizzard stone of a large, prehistoric creature might be different from any other stone found somewhere; what made a stone into a likely candidate for a genuine fossil gizzard stone. It seemed that everywhere I looked I could see gizzard stones, and when I was out on the property I would lean down and pick up a perfectly ordinary rock and weigh it in my hand before dropping it again. For some reason, this mystery was more interesting to me than the thought of actually finding bones or teeth, no matter how unlikely either discovery was. I did become stupidly obsessed with the words 'gizzard stone' and the word 'gizzard' . . . She looked at me and laughed, a sudden sound, letting her mouth open as if to take a bite out of something. She said, For some time I carried a stone which I had found on our driveway in my pocket, putting my hand in to feel its surface, and convince myself that its rough texture would be ideal for the action of a gizzard. Of course I didn't do this for long, and only when I was feeling especially—I don't know. Especially something. Though I never really had any strong feelings, even at the worst times. It was as though I was looking at the world from a distance: the hills seemed always to be on the horizon, on another continent. Or I felt as if, even though

I had all the space in the world, I was always inside in a small room and was looking out through the walls. Maybe I thought I could take my stone and throw it, and smash my way out of whatever I thought I could sense around me. I felt like I was looking at my feelings from a distance, and they never overwhelmed me; I never felt as if things were out of control.

I was beginning to think that she thought I knew her, and the more she talked the more I realised that I knew nothing about her, and even the memories I seemed to have of her became unreliable. While she was talking, I had been wanting to tell her that my family had never discussed her education. I also wanted to tell her that I had no part in this story, and that she was telling me things that didn't hold the slightest interest for me. I wanted to tell her that all I wanted was a place to stay, though at the same time I knew that I wanted more than that and was becoming infected by her speech, her language, the way her sentences had begun to fall out of her mouth, as though once started on a story she couldn't bring herself to finish. Even her silent look now was part of the story which I couldn't quite interpret, but which also didn't entirely pass me by. I was even becoming intrigued by the sound of the term 'gizzard stone', and felt an urge to repeat it to myself in the way she had while she drove back and forth between the farm and the nearby city, perhaps, for the duration of her studies, or while she walked amongst the paddocks.

By the time she began again to tell me about the Mantells and about the book she had once been trying to write focusing on the son, it was the next morning. I had shared a meal with her, and I had taken an evening walk around the neighbourhood, while the sun faded rather than set, and then slept on the couch which folded out into a narrow double bed. Over a breakfast of bread and jam she spoke to me about her interest in science, her interest in writing, about Mantell, that is to say the older Mantell whose picture I had seen in the book the previous afternoon. I felt the eyes I had seen in the picture stare out from her face now, and she let her mind wander with abandon as she spoke; it was as though she were letting someone else speak through her.

She said, I should tell you the story about Gideon Mantell and his wife Mary Ann; it's not true, but even so . . . She said that there was something about the story that made her want to believe it, but all the reading she had done since made it clear that there was at most a small amount of truth to it, though it popped up time and time again in textbooks and histories. She said that in more recent books it seemed to be told only with disclaimers. She said, I presume it was supposed to be on one of his long trips through the countryside around the town of Lewes, visiting his patients, sometimes sixty patients in a day. Mary Ann was supposed to have discovered an *Iguanodon* tooth on which Mantell's entire reputation was supposed to be based. It was early in his life—early enough in their marriage for her to accompany him from time to time on his rounds. He would have been your age, no, even younger, but full of career and certainty and ambition—his case was full of the leeches he applied in cases of illness or injury, his small saw for amputations carried out without anaesthetic. I can't help wondering if the medicine of the day helped anyone to recover, or simply took their minds off their ailments. While he was supposed to be inside attending to some medical case, Mary Ann was, according to the story, supposed to be outside, waiting by the carriage, wondering at the familiar countryside bathed, or so I imagined when

18

I heard the story, in unfamiliar light. The hedgerows and low walls seemed to hold secrets in their shadows. Why do I think she was normally a patient woman? In any case, not today, when the operation took its time, and maybe she could hear the patient's shouts coming from behind the walls of the cottage, and could almost feel the pain from bleeding or trephining until the woman fainted from loss of blood. She walked from the cluster of houses and into the road. She stopped from time to time to lean on something: a tree, or the wheel of a carriage left unexplained by the roadside, feeling faint, and feeling the confusion of the patient's screams, still just audible in her imagination; all this normally would not have bothered her but today it did. All at once coming over a slight rise a view opened up, down to the broad valley that stretched away towards Lewes, hidden on one side by the edge of a forest, the trees crowding the road, and leaning back against one, looking down at a pile of gravel at her feet, she saw a dark object half embedded in a piece of stone. She had already wandered quite a distance from the cottage, and she walked back while the feeling of standing both on the edge of the escarpment and the edge of the forest remained with her. Mary Ann knew something about fossils; she would have talked with Mantell about them and known the collection which he was already developing, and with the tooth in her hand, warming against her skin, she understood at least that she had found something interesting. Or something along those lines. As I said, it's not clear that any of this happened, or that she discovered anything significant: certainly Mantell had a tooth, and Mary Ann did find some of the materials in his collection, but it can't necessarily be said that she found *the* tooth. Mantell's own notes on this are inconclusive. But the story stayed with me, and I allowed myself to play it out in my imagination, with myself in the role of Mary Ann—

or with myself watching invisibly from over her shoulder, even reaching a hand to touch the top of her head, the way I always wanted someone to touch the top of my head as I went on my walks around the farm, though I am sure she would have been wearing a broad-brimmed hat or bonnet, and I would have felt only the lace trim.

Diane said, Actually I've come to hate the story. At first I thought only of finding the fossil tooth, the way I had dreamed of finding something which I could pick up and weigh in my hand then hold onto, a gizzard stone, or perhaps the way I held onto the story itself and carried it around with me. But the thought of the walk back along the road—the idea of Mary Ann walking back along the road to her husband, waiting now by the carriage, or so I imagined, her step infected with some urgent need to rush back to him as though she existed only for him, and in fact dropping the treasure into his hand to have him cast his surgeon's eye over it.

There was a knock at the door. Diane stood up quickly, with none of the stiffness that I had seen in her walk the previous day. She appeared transformed, lightened, and at the same time startled, and she cast me a glance which seemed like that of a shop-lifter. The door opened to a woman in her late forties. At once the air was pulled tight—the woman said nothing, and Diane simply stood to one side, as though wishing the two of them to be presented to me as a tableau. I stood up and, after taking my jacket from the living room, left the apartment, understanding from the woman who had arrived that this had been arranged, that the two of them had something to attend to—though I had quite a different sense from Diane, who had become concave, and only looked at me once as I left: a quick discharging glance.

I traced the steps I had taken the night before to the

edge of Hampstead Heath and then further into the heath itself, where it seemed for a time that a carriage might pull around at any minute from behind the stands of oaks, or a pair of horses whose riders were Gideon Mantell and his wife, his face looking severe, his eyes unfocused, and hers hidden under the shadow of her bonnet—in fact her whole face an invisible dark blur. Or, I imagined Mary Ann's face to be that of the open-mouthed woman who had stood at Diane's door (hadn't she been holding something in her enclosed fist?)—I imagined that the visitor had in fact been Mary Ann, somehow arriving, expected, even summoned, proof that people's death is never final, that what seems to be a conclusive end is never conclusive, that time only repeats and that the past rises up again and again. For a moment the oaks were growing almost visibly in front of my eyes, the initials carved in their trunks ageing as I looked at them and ran my fingers in their grooves—next to one name on the spreading roots of an enormous tree, the date 1897. I was unsure how long I should spend wandering in the park, and exploring the city beyond; I was shocked by a sudden view of the telecommunications tower. I walked in a curling route, reluctant to leave the heath, wanting to return to Diane, feeling homeless and now cut off from the woman whose stories were beginning to take over my imagination and make me want to tell the very same stories myself, as if they were mine.

Narrations (1)

The high-ceilinged room, lit with lamps placed in brackets
and atop some of the cabinets and bookcases lining it, had
been his father's study; the row of cabinets was broken there
by a window, and at the far end by another that looked out
at street level on darkness, obscured just now by curtains that
Richardson drew before it as he made his way around the
room's edge. Some of the collections were in here now, but
the space had been opened up into a small lecture room, with
seats placed at angles to one another, and at its end a lectern

by a long presentation table. The men in the room were the small aristocracy Gideon had been courting with his science for as long as Walter could remember, unfamiliar faces that nonetheless looked on his own with familiarity, that leaned across to one another to whisper briefly, even while keeping their eyes on him or letting them close for a time as he began the short lecture. At one side and to the back, with his arms folded and his eyes raised attentively but with darting looks at the others in the room, with a wink and a faint smile, was Gideon, and next to him Richardson, standing alongside and now leaning slightly on a low display case, his face frowning, his eyes also engaged, following the movement of the fossils as they were picked up from the table and passed from hand to hand.

Fish teeth, small *terebratulae* and other fossils, some still in the chalk that had come out of the cliffs near Chichester with a soft resistance as of congealed tar, and that hardened around them as it dried, scraped clean of a yellow-green layer, still damp and greying in its crevices. Behind Walter a mild ocean had ebbed back and forth at the rocks of the beach. Somewhere a ship had been passing, its sails letting out a distant snap as of a footfall, but on turning towards the sound he found the narrow strip of coarse sand and rock as deserted as when he had made his way down to it from some way along the coast, and the ship, until it passed out of sight, was his only company. Clouds rolled sedately off the top of the cliffs and broke free, progressing across a pale blue sky to obscure the sun then let it break out suddenly and allow the cliffs their brilliance, drawing his vision sidelong along the coast, along the rise and fall of the cliffs' upper edge and their ranked shoulders, exposed in series by their curves vanishing away into the rising, and for a second equally brilliant, then faint, sea mist.

Out here, had he come closest to a sense of the geology of the region? The long views, the undulation of the downs subdued and finally cut off by the abruptness of the ocean—wasn't the proof of the theory of geological catastrophe that he had discussed with his father, or rather listened while his father talked—wasn't the proof here, in this catastrophic landscape, as if the gentle rolling country had been all at once torn away by a great flood? And still, in the face of the resulting cliff was evidence of a more gradual development: the small details, fossils buried under millennia of soft stone. As he chiselled them from the chalk, he let them warm for a moment against the skin of his hand, and only reluctantly put them in their case.

Now, as he talked, he again kept a small prize in his hand: a lump of chalk, a stone containing some small fossils and overall small enough that, after he had passed around the other samples, he could palm it, keep it in a closed fist, without the audience noticing; or did one or two of them look down at his hand and its chalk stone now as he talked? What now of his father's frown? And of Richardson's soft-eyed look? When the room had been an office his father's desk had been where he now stood lecturing; it had been side-on to the door, so that if Walter had interrupted him at work in his study he would be presented at first with a profile leaning over the letters, accounts or writings that occupied his time, lit by a single lamp on the desk, and he would wait a painful moment before his father turned to him with, was it the same frown as he saw now? And on the desk, after all, an account book, its columns filled with a spidery close handwriting of figures, his father's grip on the pen tight as his own on the small rock. The house, which had then been their family home, seemed to echo about them now, empty but for the museum and his father's new room and study and

Richardson's room, the whole bearing down with its bones and empty space.

Later, with the patrons and other guests gone his father said, You've been finding time outside your apprenticeship for good things! I've got high hopes for you. Come with me—come on, Richardson, you come along too. We're going out. I've been waiting for your visit for this, Walter.

What is it?

You'll see . . . He took one of the lamps and they went out into a night that was alternately dark and lit dimly through gaps in the cloud by a slender moon, a light that gave the buildings faint highlights but wasn't enough to cast a shadow. Richardson trailed behind them a few paces, characteristically silent but hurrying every now and then to catch their words. They discussed Walter's apprenticeship to a surgeon in Chichester, his fossils and his lecture at tonight's *conversazione*, the patrons of the museum and the local notables who had been there. His father said, There are some good men here . . . He said, We're creating a science! It's a shame I need to put up with the nobility—they sweep in and make their comments and look over the collections, always saying the same thing. But I'd never keep the museum without them, and I tell you it's more than pleasant to receive their invitations—a society I never thought I'd keep!

Walter said, I'm sure one of them was falling asleep while I was lecturing.

No doubt! No doubt they were all nodding off with their liquor inside them. Now, Richardson, this is strictly *entre nous*, of course—and that goes for you too, Walter—but if I could do without them I would rid myself of them without hesitation, take only their funds but turn them away at the door . . .

Richardson laughed, and Walter also smiled to himself.

His father had already, after the *conversazione*, lost the stoop and slight limp that he had noticed with a mild shock when he arrived from Chichester, and was walking with a springing step that Walter knew well. He pictured him at the hall of the Old Ship Hotel stepping up in front of an audience, what, two years previously? The assembly room had been packed and charged with a continuous exchange of whispers and the bending of necks and tapping of shoulders even while his father had lectured: how shells got inside solid rock and how wood changed to stone; how the bones of fish and animals had been entombed in stony sepulchres; his mother sat with her hand across the bridge of her nose and her eyes closed, then opened them to the room and sat straight, if distracted, letting her looks stray to her children but also to the wider audience and their small movements. His father told how the Weald of Kent and Sussex had once been the delta of an ancient river, and that what had happened since was a matter of some contention; about Cuvier and Lyell and how the latter's theories required us to think of times, of histories previously unthinkable, of histories so long that the removal of the smallest pebble every year would be enough to destroy an entire mountain many times over; this was the world that, just maybe, science was beginning to show us.

Out, afterwards, on the streets—the same streets where now they were walking, lit by lamps and accompanied by others and to one side now the ocean, taking a slight occasional silvery charge from the moon—the crowd had come to his father in twos to shake his hand briefly, and then they had walked quickly, his father taking the lead and turning with half-sideways steps to look over his shoulder at them, Walter, his mother, brother, and sister, as if to reproach them for not keeping his pace, or just to encourage them to keep up, to be infected with whatever had taken hold of him in front of the audience and which sparked his eyes into a vision of the town, its people, its buildings, the coastline winding upwards out of town over its cliffs, as mere specks in a greater time, one in which what mattered was the encasing of things in stone. Had he been speaking occasional half-sentences at them as he walked, small continuations of his lecture that trailed off into mere gestures, and gestures that became increasingly hunched until, when they arrived at the house—the now-museum—he had gone straight to his study, informing the maid that he would sup there?

The people on the street seemed to be the same ones that had filled the audience room on that occasion, and others. A mild rush of voices from around them, and hats tilted in their direction—in his father's, but with a gesture broad enough to take in Walter and his father's employee—and the crowd on the strand proceeded with an orderly grace broken by the rushing of a child or a shout from somewhere, at which everyone stopped for a moment, then took up again in their same direction. Walter put a hand into his pocket from time to time to feel the chalk stone and feel its surface's slight give as he pressed it. It left a residue on his fingers, oily and grey–white; he imagined feeling the shapes of the few tiny *terebratulae* on it but could not be sure of them against his fingertips. Behind them and beside them people stood on the beach and somewhere a violinist was playing. Groups stood and walked along the Chain Pier, flickeringly lit along its extent and casting a spreading and retreating pool of its light around itself at its end, where a few boats were tied up and shifted as though resting on a bed of rising, luminous vapour, curling itself around the hulls and sending up surf and congealed sparks. The road turned inland and up a small hill, dark here again with houses behind a wall to one side, and on the other the expanse of a park forming a black space loosely continuous with the sky except where the shallow outlines of trees impressed themselves up into it, silver for a second with the emergence of the moon, lit from underneath also by the faintest orange from his father's lantern interrupted by the shadows of legs passing through it. For a moment they were alone, and Walter again squeezed the chalk stone and thought about its form in his hand, in his pocket. Then in front of them, from behind another wall that curled in towards the road from the park, there were more lanterns held by others approaching and behind them lights as from a miniature town, organised into shapes and lines and buffeted by the sounds that hit them as they walked: laughter; the cry of a woman's voice, at first unintelligible.

He said, Travelling showmen?

His father said, Yes, they've been here for a few days. They had booths set up on the strand, and made an appearance at the Old Ship. But we can ask for a private audience.

An audience with whom?

You'll see.

Walter knew his father's enthusiasm for various curiosities and wonders: the learned pig; a man with no mental abilities save an extraordinary memory; a native of India— a fine physical specimen—who juggled knives and met the onlookers' gazes with fierce pride, as it was told. Walter could now make out a familiar look on his face: eyebrows raised, his mouth pulled down into an grin that threatened to break open and reveal his teeth but stayed closed; his walk remained quick, even quickened, the lightness and ease of his step carried him now half a pace ahead of Walter, who trailed along with Richardson. Over his shoulder, half turned now and then and sending a gesturing hand back at Walter, occasionally at Richardson, he said, These people are real scientists . . . He said, The showmen have the curiosity and

29

the drive that we need, and it's no bad thing that they exploit their discoveries for financial gain—how else will they continue their explorations? . . . He said, Even if we have to put up with a certain shammery. You can learn from them—you too, Richardson. These men bring us the wonders, the strange peoples, the New Hollanders and the things from the strange ultimate ends of the earth. That's no bad thing; it's no bad thing even if sometimes we might not agree with the manner of their presentation—and remember the New Hollander in his pen is given a better wage than he could earn in the uncivilised parts of the world . . .

The woman's shouts were comprehensible now as a constant harangue, an attempt to interest passers-by in the roast nuts at her feet; before they approached she stopped, heaved a sigh and, with the boy who had been standing with her, folded her wares inside the blanket on which they were piled, then carried the whole bundle away from the road. Caravans and tents were set up along one side, and small crowds of people, fishermen and farm workers mostly, moved under the lanterns, some of which were being hooked down, the groups breaking apart and re-forming, moving to the ends of the lane, lingering for a minute in the remaining glow and beginning to disperse along the road in either direction.

The woman who had been selling nuts re-emerged from behind a tent. She said, You're a bit late. Everyone's going in.

Gideon Mantell said, Tell me, where could I find, is it Harold?

Har-*ald*. The gentleman in question is from the Continent, sir.

Ah, I see . . .

His caravan has his name over it—it's just further down.

They knocked at the door of the caravan with the name

over its door, and decorated with a crude painting of a top hat out of which spilled a chaos of dominoes. After a minute, during which there was a scuffing noise from inside, a faint rocking of the structure and a quick shout, a face emerged, lit from one side by the flickering of candlelight.

Well?—oh, it's you, sir.

I was hoping for an audience with Harald? If it isn't too much trouble.

No, no, just give me one minute. There's no charge for you and your colleagues, of course, as a matter of scientific principle. Can you just give me one . . . The door shut again, and there was a further scuffing and scraping, a soft repetitive sound, a clatter, and again the man who had addressed them emerged, then turned in the door and dragged out after him a small, low table. Having placed it in front of them he nodded, turned and brought out from the caravan a small box. He said, I suppose you were wanting to play dominoes? Or were there other scientific enquiries you were after?

Dominoes will be fine. And do let us pay you . . .

I wouldn't dream of it . . . He turned once again and, standing in the doorway, had a brief whispered discussion with someone inside. Then, after he entered fully, there was the clink of metal and from the doorway came a lean short-haired dog; strapped onto its head with a thin ribbon, and forcing its ears down to the side and slightly forward, was a tall hat. The dog jumped to the ground, reared up and placed its forepaws on the table, squatting back on its hind legs. The man said, A fine example of animal intelligence . . . He said, Harald has his ancestry in the dogs of the Royal Kennels of Denmark, fine animals known for their powers of reason. His father was a learned dog that travelled throughout the Continent and to America . . . The man came around behind them and shook the dominoes from the box into the table, laying out around half of them in front of the dog, face up. He said, But you won't be interested in his history; you'll want to rely on your own observation. Go on.

Two or three others came up behind them and stood close, so that Gideon Mantell, Walter, Richardson and the dog's master formed the front rank of a small crowd, all silent as Gideon put down a domino and the dog, after looking up at them one at a time, meeting their eyes, leaned down with his snout and pushed a domino forward with short pushes of his head, looking up again between each one, sometimes stopping to let his tongue roll out of his mouth and look to either side in a repeated, seemingly habitual gesture.

The man said, Good, good, Harald . . . He straightened the domino slightly. He said, He of course lacks some of the finer dexterity that our limbs are graced with.

The game proceeded, with Gideon and the dog, assisted in these finer movements by his master, making alternate moves. The crowd was still silent, watching the dog's eyes and his curious head gestures, and in the game's routine the air seemed to settle about them, the light from Gideon's lantern and one over the door of the caravan delimiting at its edges a small world, strangely serious, as if there were money or something greater on the outcome. Walter watched the dog's performance, keeping his gaze on the eyes as if they were human, even trying for a moment to fathom something of the dog's thoughts from the expression, the shift of his head from side to side, the flicking of the eyes from one viewer to the other and lingering there as if in search of something, the strain almost visible in the ears against the weight of the hat, which shifted slightly on his head with the repeated movements, almost as though he was—was he?—trying to flick it off. For a second the dog's eyes looked into his own, the ridge above them pinched upward towards the hat's rim in a sort of blinking expression of effort or pleading, and he lifted a paw off the table towards him, folded it down towards his chest before, after a look away, placing it back where it was. Still, his eyes returned for a second to Walter before he ducked his head, wrestled it once more from side to side and pushed a piece from his pile towards the centre of the table with a quick snuffling breath.

After the game's conclusion, the man said, Do you not get a sense of an almost human intelligence? . . . He said, He is constrained only by his physique, and sometimes I get a sense of the tragedy of such an intellect trying to find expression for itself, but unable. Come, Harald, shake hands with the gentleman and his colleagues . . . At which the dog came around the table, stood again squatting on his hind legs and raised a paw. While his father was holding the paw, almost earnestly, Richardson met Walter's eye for a second.

His father said, Now, do let me give you some money. Not for you, of course, but something for the dog himself? A piece of—something nice for him to eat?

Well, since you put it that way, very well . . . The man accepted a few coins from Gideon. Now they looked up to see that their small group was the only sign of life left in the collection of makeshift homes; the farm workers who had stood behind them made their way into the darkness, commenting briefly to each other on the spectacle they had witnessed.

On the road, and some way from the tents and caravans, Gideon said, What did you observe?

Walter said, Observe, Father? The dog did seem to play a good game of . . .

Yes, yes and what else?

Walter thought of the dog's look, the momentary indication of pleading which, in any case, he was inclined to disbelieve; wasn't it after all a mere beast? It would be rash to impute human motives and causes, though of course its master had been, or had seemed, certain of its higher intelligence, trapped as it were in the body of a dog and forced to demonstrate itself through the act of playing dominoes with all-comers. He said, Would it have been interesting to try to test the dog's understanding in other areas? After all, the game is hardly evidence of higher knowledge . . .

No, well, maybe, but I'm thinking of something else.

Richardson said, Perhaps there were signals given by the master from over our shoulders? The dog was reading and responding to his master's wishes as any dog might? I think young Walter has a point when he suggests other tests.

No—what else?

Richardson said, Well, I did notice—

Gideon said, I'm thinking of something to do with the master . . . A pause, during which their footsteps grew louder on the road's gravel, echoed on the wall alongside until they emerged at the shore, now almost deserted but for the melancholic sound of a singer on the beach, mildly competing with the wash of surf, its regular advance and hissing retreat and the knocking of something in time with it—the oars of a boat pulled up and tied, but left to be swayed by the ocean's movements? He said, When we left, he was standing taller than when we arrived . . . He said, We did him a favour. He was delighted that the 'famous scientist' paid him a visit, and with two colleagues. Certainly the dog performed well and may even be, for all I know, the very thing his master says he is—frankly I wasn't observing too closely, but I wouldn't be inclined to be overly critical. Why not, Richardson? Isn't it such wonders that drive us in our search for new knowledge? The tales we hear from those who have been around the globe are hardly less fantastic, and the tales we ourselves tell about great floods or about times so distant they can hardly be imagined, or about enormous lizards roaming this very landscape? We needn't be so suspicious about a dog who plays dominoes. If we should discover that indeed there is a higher intellect in this dog, we should welcome the knowledge. And, yes, by all means devise other experiments . . . He walked a few more paces in silence, then stopped and faced them. He said, But science needs its audience, and it needs its peers. That's what we're building—a science! You took part in that tonight, Walter, when you gave your lecture. You can do all the digging you like, but if you don't write your discoveries to your peers, if you don't give your results in a lecture to an audience, there's no science, only a lonely individual tapping away at the chalk; you're only someone with an opinion. We gave that man an entry into the world of science.

Walter felt again for the lump of chalk in his pocket, wondered for a second what had made him want to hold it back, an unremarkable stone but for the few small fossils clumped on its surface, which he now scraped at with a fingernail. And there had been the dog's look, as if it were also holding something back, but not voluntarily; its discomfort with the absurd hat that had, he thought, weighed too heavily on its ears, and its final image, standing on its hind legs, offering a paw to his father.

Gideon turned again and started walking, but now more slowly; they caught up and walked alongside.

Richardson said, I did make one further observation.

Yes . . . ?

Harald was a she—a bitch.

Oh, he was—a—why did you . . . ?

I simply happened to notice.

*

35

Diane had said, I wanted to leave something behind. Now I think I won't. I haven't spoken to my daughter for five years—I've disappeared from her life. She hasn't disappeared from mine; I think about her every day; she is as present to me as she always was. Could you help me with this?

With . . . ?

With writing this. I could never be a writer, I realise that now—all I have are piles of paper, false starts, spectacular failures, half-hearted research. I should admit I was thinking about this even when I got your letter and I couldn't decide how to put it to you. You happened to put me in mind of it again when you happened to pick up Gideon's diary . . . We were in the living room once again as the day faded, maybe the second day I was there with her, with the lights still off in the room giving it a dusky flatness that seemed to cover the surfaces with a grainy layer, punctuated by her eyes and their movements like the movements of insects ducking up and down, to meet mine and look away, catching a glint at their edge each time she did so, each time also she leaned forward towards me and put out a hand as if to touch me but let it drop at the elbow, leaving it half outstretched as if waiting for me to give her something, or as if clutching at something, missing it, and falling away. She sat back finally and said, No, it's true I put the book there for you to find. Listen, I've got notes.

I said, I don't know . . .

She stood and was already moving towards the hallway. She said, You could put your name on the cover.

I said, Wait . . .

She stopped. She said, Just look at what I've got. I've got a lot of notes, research material, and quite a lot of writing already complete. Well, it's false starts, but it's complete, it's there—look it over. You could make something of this the way I can't . . . She moved to the door again, but this time only to flick the switch next to it, turning on the lights, cancelling the remaining glow from outside, reducing the room to its walls and its barrier of curtains.

I'm not sure where I would find the time.

She said, There's so much work done on it already! It's practically finished, practically a book already. It wouldn't take any time at all . . . She took a step towards me, somehow a repeat of her earlier reachings, then back, and turning in the door frame she left the room. I closed my eyes and the room spun itself into its small noises: a ticking, a hiss, something constant from outside and the noise of my own breathing.

When she returned I said, Thank you, it's really nice of you to offer this. I mean, I'll have to think about it, and maybe I could work on what you have before I think about getting it published.

She looked at me for a few seconds as if startled. She had a package under her arm, a tattered yellow envelope that, as she sat next to me now on the couch, she opened and dipped a hand into, looking down her nose and along the line of her wrist to sort through papers, pulled out another envelope that had been contained in it and from this further envelope pulled a pile of photocopies.

The top sheet was a page of handwriting, darkened at the edges by the copier, in places reduced to only a slight tracing and dominated in the centre by three sketches: three birds' skulls, with the names Dinornis, Palapteryx and Notornis in bold capitals alongside. The heads were really just outlines, overlaid by old rings from a coffee- or teacup laid out in rough approximation of the symbol for the Olympic Games, and seemed to stare out though the eye sockets that were in no case clearly discernible; cross-hatching indicated areas where the bone seemed to have disintegrated altogether.

One could imagine the cavities and smooth surfaces of the beaks. The rest of the pile was a collection of handwritten and typed pages—the handwriting seemed half-hearted, like absentminded though densely drawn doodles with no meaning, and each of the words was at first impossible to make out; a tight concentration of letters differing only in length, with here and there a long loop rising above the level of the writing and representing the spine of a 'd' or the curve of one or another capital.

She said, These are diaries and letters between Walter and Gideon, and various other notes. When I first tried to read them I kept staring, trying to make out words, but I find now I can read them, or any of the dense sloping scrawl which seems characteristic of letters of the Victorian era . . . She said that there was a point at which, all of a sudden, words become clear, like an intake of breath. She said, At first single words would make themselves out as if they were being written before my eyes; then I could understand or make a good guess at the content of a sentence; and finally the sense of whole pages seemed to open up—I found myself hooked into this slow unfolding of meaning, though as often as not the writing concerned the most trivial matters. I have more, and I've used some published sources. I have more on computer disks and some of my own writing—this envelope here is all original material, copied original material.

I looked through the pile of notes, and some further material that Diane fetched for me, without, at first, making much of it. I kept them in their order, although she assured me that there was no order to them and that they had accumulated as they took her interest—some items found their way to the bottom of the pile simply because she had found them uninteresting, and for no particular reason. The notes contained, in addition to the copies of original material, her writings, her notes to herself, her doubts, her thoughts and her imaginings and seemed to contain something of her hand, of her voice, as if, as I looked at them closely and got closer to the pages, she could be heard speaking from them.

The next fragment of writing that presented itself, in something like a chronological order, but one disturbed by interruptions, confusions, interrupted by Diane and by myself at times as I tried to order and interpret what I had of the material—did something of the material resist this and resist any way of ordering it?—was set on a gently sloping lawn by a courthouse, and bordered on its far side by a stream that wound between two low hills in whose gap could be seen the masts of a ship, as stationary as the land. Mantell stood amongst sheets laid out with bones and fragments, momentarily inactive and watching two boys carefully pack the items, labelled and numbered, into cases, carrying them now with exaggerated stoops and occasional looks towards him. At Waingongoro, where the deposit had been found, fragments had been broken underfoot by excited natives, lifting one find carefully from the site only to demolish others in their run towards him, and now, the memory made him uneasy, over-watchful, as if these boys might repeat the clumsiness. They knew it as well as he did, and were being careful already; they carried on their task, exchanging glances, even grins, with each other.

He turned away from them and away from the narrow sea view, looking up inland then down at his feet at more bones, then up again at the middle ground in between. A man approached, from the direction of the barracks, raised a hand at him: Mantell! . . .

It was the Governor. Mantell said, Your Excellency. This is an unexpected visit?

This is quite a collection, Mantell.

Yes, of course. I'm very pleased with it.

What are those? Egg shells? . . . Grey moved past him, stepping around the edges of the sheets and bent down. He picked up one of the larger fragments, cradling it in his hands and stood with it.

Shells of the moa's egg, Your Excellency.

Yes, very good. I'm sure Professor Owen will be very grateful to receive such a collection.

Mantell said, I'll be sending them first to my father.

Well, of course, and I feel sure that he will also be happy with this. He has such high hopes for you. I dare say you're living up to them . . .

Were there one or two syllables hanging from the end of the Governor's sentence, unspoken? Mantell opened his mouth but was caught for a moment in a kind of waiting, as if for him to finish, to avoid interrupting but also to hear the sentence's final qualification. Finally he said, Nothing would please me more . . . And with this he held his hand out, almost involuntarily, for the shell fragment in Grey's hands. He said, I only hope they arrive safely; I would hate for them to—

Grey said, Yes, this is excellent . . . He dropped the piece into Mantell's outstretched hand, suddenly, it seemed, with less care. He said, You'll do well . . . Mantell leaned quickly down to put the shell fragment back in its place. The Governor said, I expect good things from you. This collecting of yours can only get you a good audience at home, and a good audience for your father too, though he hardly needs it . . . Grey looked over the collection, towards the limited view of the ocean, seemingly picturing something more than could be seen there. Mantell remained silent for a moment, until Grey said, Well, I just came down to see this. I must be on my way, Mantell . . . He cast another cursory glance over the collection, a look that took it in quickly, before shaking Mantell's hand once again and retreating towards the barracks. Mantell stood watching after him; from behind Grey lost some of his bearing, reminding Mantell somewhat of his father, or at least the father he knew as a child, before he had slowed, developed the stoop which had transformed his appearance and made every action seem slightly laboured—it was as if the air around him had, sometime during Mantell's apprenticeship in Chichester, thickened.

Surrounded now by the collection being packed away, and with Grey's figure receding from him, he thought of the closure of his father's museum in Brighton. Walter had made the trip along the chalk coast. On that occasion the three of them had opened the display cases and carefully lifted the smaller fossils out one by one; the crates around him now reminded him of the task, of packing away his father's collection into boxes to be moved into the British Museum. At first his father had been concerned for the fragility of some of the items and had carefully supervised. In the original museum room, which had already housed the Maidstone Iguanodon twisted and splayed out on its slab of rock some years before when his mother and siblings had still lived there with them, his father stood with his back to the window that overlooked the street, in the posture of an overseer, giving instructions and sometimes a quick word, almost a shout of caution as one of them, it seemed, was about to mishandle something. After some time, he simply stood and watched, mute, as the items were packed; then, he turned to the street and watched there instead, moving his head slightly from side to side as if following the progress of people as they walked or the rattling passage of a cart or carriage. Finally, he turned back to them, sighed, and instead of watching over them he now got to his knees, not without some difficulty, and helped with the packing himself. They moved throughout the house, cataloguing the items and packing them where possible in the rooms where they were displayed. With a few boys from the foundry helping, they carried the crates and the large items downstairs and onto the street, there to be loaded onto carts. The boxes stacked next to each other—and now, in New Plymouth, remembering this, the completed boxes placed to one side, in rows on the grass by the stream ready to be packed on board a ship bound for London—seemed for a second to combine as units in a game, clicking easily together in their different arrangements. And where—as he thought this he copied the remembered movement of his father, kneeling to help with the packing of the moa bones and eggs—was this game's audience?

The Governor was now out of sight, and a wind was beginning to rise off the ocean, doing no more than pulsing the leaves of grass emerging from the mossy lawn, the leaves of the trees that remained standing not far distant, back and forth in gentle motions, a sort of slow rhythm noticeable only in the smallest details of his surroundings: here and there, the edge of the sheets on which the bones were laid out flicked up. The wind and the rhythm made him look up again at the landscape: the mountain and the edge of forest, partly cleared and farmed, seemed suddenly harsh, seen in comparison with the English countryside and its towns, the painted buildings lining the sea-front at Brighton, its streets. His father's new London practice was in a dark building, heavily wooded—as indeed was the old house with its museum, but the former had at least the comfort of childhood memory—and the cottage where his mother now lived had a sense of impermanence that seemed to emerge again in the very view he was faced with now. He had a strong, sudden and childish sense that if he could return anywhere—if he had any home—it would be an impossible return to the Brighton house as it was: that is, still a house, inhabited by the whole family but still with its museum room. And wasn't it the museum room within the living house that most drew him, drew his imagination to its cases and mostly to the big Maidstone fossil over which he would stand, in the half-darkness of dusk, and follow its disappearing contours with his eyes?

It had been eight years since he left, and now Mantell felt the passing of that time as if in an instant, as if he had just stepped off the boat onto a beach whose only shelter was the tents and huts they had brought with them, or the village of the natives, or, in fact, the ships they had come on, anchored in the harbour, and where they still slept for some time. The time, the landscape seemed to have a sense of betrayal about it—perhaps his own betrayal? He had all but forgotten the training as a surgeon; in the intervening time, he had worked instead as postmaster of the new town of Wellington, and then as a superintendent on the roads, but also there had been times of inactivity, desperate times when, without income, he had drawn money against his father's name, funds that were honoured, he imagined, with the same pained reluctance with which his father received the news that he was to leave for the colony. Grey had said that his father had high hopes for him: perhaps this collection might, finally, justify them? Or what did it matter?—his father now was a world away.

Of Diane's papers, one of the first complete letters in the set described Mantell's journey back to Wellington from Taranaki, where he had discovered and unearthed the deposit of moa bones. He reported in his letter, written to his father, that past Wanganui there were new signs of civilisation: at Horowhenua a young chief met him and was dressed entirely in European costume, with black boots polished deeply and reflecting two points of sky at their tips. At Otaki, the party stopped at another's house and sat to dine at a new table, with chairs, knives, forks, plates and tea from a shining new pot. Further down the coast, a broad, slanting white line marked the new road which was to lead from Paekakariki to Wellington or the Hutt, or both, the road being built by armies of natives, with a European supervisor to each ten men, and a superintendent to each party, the parties ranging from fifty to ninety and the shouts of the whole mass audible long before Mantell could pass and look into each man's eyes, and shake the hand of a number of the natives who recognised him, and the supervisors and superintendent also.

Then he arrived in Wellington itself which was, as always, watched by three or four ships, rung around with the sounds of new building, and pressed under a light mist which obscured the tip of each of the harbour's hills. The harbour was bounded on the east and west by hills; on the north by a broad flat valley which narrowed and sloped upward towards the mountain range frequently, in winter, whitened by a layer of snow; and at its southern end was almost closed off by the tip of a sunken mountain and the strip of land which joined it to the mainland on the west—from most outlooks, and most points by the water's edge, the harbour seemed in fact to be a lake, situated not at sea-level but high in one of the mountainous regions of the world; couldn't it in fact be Switzerland? The feeling grew with the not infrequent mist or haze which settled over the water's surface, obscuring the far shore, making the settlers yearn for a horizon which they knew, in any case, would never be visible.

Mantell once again accepted a job on the road being built on the shore of the Porirua Harbour; this harbour, not as enclosed by the hills as Wellington, opened to the west, and frequently had a choppy white surface as winds blew in past the flat, steep-sided island at its entrance. Some weeks into the job news came via the barracks from Government House that his department would be the first to feel the effects of retrenchment as the situation in Europe worsened, and supplies became scarce. He was asked to reduce his party to thirty-five men, and the overseers from seven to one.

The men assembled between the rows of tents next to the beach and Mantell addressed them.

He said, We feel Europe's wars here ... He asked for volunteers to leave, and each of the natives looked at the person next to him or behind him for a second and, after a minute, two men approached Mantell and shook his hand before sitting down, some way off, talking to each other, touching shoulders on the beach with the edge of the water on the toes of their boots.

One of the children accompanying the camp joined them, and, with the sound of a steady murmur, in twos or at most threes, groups of the workers came to Mantell and took his hand briefly, as though he himself were being dismissed, and joined the group on the beach. Some took down tents and carried them as they left the encampment stretched along the road; others began to stand aside before they left and give short speeches, or, when they arrived at the beach, stood behind their companions and spoke to them from there. There were speeches about the war in Europe—one made the observation that it must be a huge war indeed if its effect were felt even here. Mantell paid less attention to the words than to the sky and their faces; there was a light drizzle, and the colour of the water slipped into the air and vice versa. The sky became slowly darker and more and more natives left the encampment, until Mantell began to fear that those departing would include the whole gang—it wasn't clear which handshakes were to signal farewell and which to signal a renewed commitment, or indeed whether the whole sombre ceremony covered a mass walkout in protest at his announcement. Signs of discontent had begun in the speeches: a young worker stood and said that the roads were paved with their bodies and bones, that they were expendable as if they were supplies bought and sold. Nonetheless, Mantell and the other supervisors were included in the ceremony even as they stood to one side of the natives, discussing amongst themselves which of them should stay.

When, only a few weeks after the numbers had first been reduced, an officer arrived, signalled in advance by the crush of, I don't know, gravel, under the horse's hooves, ringing about more loudly than a person's footsteps (and in that distinctive rhythm, speeding and slowing to a lightly tapped-out halt as the rider addressed Mantell from behind)—or perhaps sliding less audibly in clay, only whispered pops and sucks of approach—Mantell wasn't looking at his nearby men but was looking down from the horizon to the ground at his feet.

The officer said, Mantell? I can't say I'm sorry. You'll be free of this employment after the 31st. Mr Compton, your replacement, is a better man than you are, and he knows what he's working for here. I won't have to look at your grin any more, God willing. But it was good that you volunteered to leave the job to Compton on account of his wife and family. I have to say that, and thank you for it. So the time has come: after the 31st you'll be gone . . . Then the horse's backside retreated into the drizzle and the red back of the captain's uniform. Two of the enormous, tiny-headed pigeons crashed into a bending branch and opened their beaks at him. Mantell had the feeling (as he occasionally did) that he had hardly been in this colony, or that the colony had hardly been a place at all, and that in the midst of the changes and new beginnings since he had been here (from the leaking building which served for some years as 'his' post office, to the diggings in Taranaki and the roads) he was still waiting to catch a glimpse of the new land. To the horse's retreating buttocks, he said, And I won't have to deal with military baboons, men known only for the thickness of their brain case.

In the last few days in the job, Mantell took every opportunity to sketch the far shore, with each layer of low hills more dissolved in the mist than the last, until behind and above the visible landscape there seemed to be another landscape, the same grey as the sky and delimited only by its upper edge, a faint jagged line which had disappeared the next time he looked up from his sketchbook. Finally, with Compton and Rogan, a man from the barracks, accompanying him, he left the camp late in the morning. The natives were working in two groups, each on a point at either end of a broad bay. As he approached the first group—they were just knocking off for their dinner—they stood around him and, one by one, shook his hand and said a few words of farewell. Then, walking on the sand (not the newly constructed road) away from the natives who, he was sure, must now be sitting down while their food was distributed, he heard behind him a loud cheer, and turned to see them lined up and watching him walk with his two companions. With the second group, the same shaking of hands and, as he left them behind, the same cheers, and still more cheers as he came to the end of a further point beyond which he would disappear from sight once and for all.

He stopped, and Rogan and Compton stopped a few paces on. He was looking down, avoiding their eyes in case they should see his expression, for a second on the verge of tears; he looked away then turned to the work parties. He suddenly felt as though he had hardly been their supervisor but instead had been welcomed into their fold, learned their language, and had been excused the physical labour only by their generosity; he began to feel as though he had in fact been in their power, and almost thanked them for their forbearance; the landscape, all of a sudden scarcely scarred by the new road, came into focus for him, and he saw himself in it as if for the first time.

Then pulling himself straight he raised the broad-brimmed hat from his head and bowed deeply. To Rogan and Compton he said, Well, this will be good practice for my time as Governor—taking my hat off to the adoring crowds.

In Wellington he stopped directly at the house belonging to his friend Moore. It was dark, and he arrived on his friend's doorstep soaked through from a rain which had grown heavier throughout the day and pooled over the surface of the road, joining what would have been isolated puddles into a sliding mess of mud, some of which now thickly coated his boots and the lower parts of his trousers. It was a small building with Moore there alone and the walls thin and punctuated here and there by gaps.

He said, To be honest it doesn't feel like the end of an era. Mostly I'll miss my friends in Wellington, and even the few decent people at the barracks. Moore, the Ngati Toas gave me a magnificent farewell, a thundering applause! I can't get it out of my mind. I'm not sure if I should be ashamed of it, but I've grown very fond of them.

Moore said, They're still Te Rauparaha's people.

I know, and a lot of them still worship him. But now they're very much on my mind, after their farewell. They surprised me. By making such a fuss they made my departure seem unimportant—a strange thing.

An offer still stood for Mantell to act as the New Zealand Company's agent in New Plymouth. They discussed what ships might be going there and when; Mantell would need to send a note to the agent and soon enough travel there himself—he would make enquiries tomorrow. Moore's room, in a state of disarray—books of accounts and other papers, two crates stacked in one corner by a table and writing desk, and Mantell's swag dropped against the wall by the door—seemed to grow darker around them, though the lamp mounted on the wall was still lit and the stove added a slight flickering glow. A comforting darkness, it seemed to draw the walls closer to their backs until the sound of the rain, and somewhere—inside the house?—a regular drip which occasionally doubled itself, lost its rhythm then began again, became part of the texture of the house or part of its insulation. He had, while working on the roads, sometimes suddenly felt the tent's flimsiness, as the evening quietened into night, its quiet seeming to express only a desertion of the land as if the rest of the road team had sneaked off and the tent stood isolated, porous, invaded by the emptiness of its surroundings, and he had had to walk out to the beach and along—the feeling remained, despite the view of other tents and huts around his and the groups of natives seated in circles. In fact sometimes their presence had only increased his isolation, and in his walks he felt himself trying to stretch out, to find something else.

Mantell said, It isn't the Ngati Toas themselves, but the fact that yet again I'm taking my leave. What's to become of me?

Well, the offer from the Company . . .

You have your shop—you've been here for years now. Maybe I should find a house to stay in once and for all

49

. . . He looked around the room in his friend's cottage, at the floorboards that didn't quite join. He said, Even one as miserable as this.

Miserable . . . ?

Oh God, Moore. Listen to me. Do I need to settle down once and for all in New Plymouth? Like you have here? Buy a section and build a house, devote myself to life as clerk to the Company's agent? Find a wife? Though you don't seem to have done especially well at the latter . . .

Not for want of trying.

Mantell said, You know Moore, I might now be a practising surgeon in England, a respected scientist, up-and-coming, as my father intended—

There was a knock. The door opened to reveal a boy's face wet from the rain and reddened about the cheeks and eyes. The boy said, I was told I might find you here . . . He handed Mantell a letter. He said, It's from the Lieutenant Governor.

Mantell stood, received the letter, which was addressed to him at Porirua; he read the page, looked at the messenger, then over his shoulder at Moore, who was now standing behind him. He said, Thank you, I will call in to see the Lieutenant Governor when I am back in Wellington . . . The messenger blinked at him. He said, It will surely take some time for me to come to town, don't you think, Moore? It's quite a journey from Porirua.

The messenger looked at him impassively, nodded, then left.

Mantell said, I've been offered employment. It seems the Lieutenant Governor has employment to offer me. Well!

What form of employment?

To start immediately. But he doesn't say anything more. Of course I won't get this note until tomorrow, no doubt, and then it will be a good day's travel—so it will be Wednesday before I can see Mr Eyre.

I hope you make it to Wellington safely. I look forward to your company . . . Moore bowed to Mantell, took off an imaginary cap and held it for a second against his navel and straightened up, before the two of them took their seats once more.

Mantell said, The men may refuse to let me go, and keep me prisoner in the camp, so enthusiastic are they about my company—

But what form of employment, Mantell? Are you to be Mr Eyre's clerk now? And will you accept? Will you be working at Government House?

I may refuse. I can't refuse! The Lieutenant Governor! One of the great class of idiots trying to run this place. I used to see them scraping about at my father—who used to scrape right back. What else is there to do? Well, I don't know what the work is, do I?

So much for New Plymouth, Mantell, and your plans to settle.

I may yet . . .

For more minutes, they sat talking while the sounds of the rain melded into a lighter hiss, a sheet-like noise wound around the walls of the cottage. Moore put a kettle on the stovetop for tea, and stood for a minute poking at its fire. Before he re-seated himself the door opened again, this time without a knock: the same boy.

He said, Mr Eyre understands that Mr Mantell is already in Wellington, and would like to see him immediately . . . The messenger left, before a response could be given.

Mantell said, Ah. Then I shall have to turn down your offer of tea.

Moore said, Wait . . . He left by a door to the back of

the room and moments later re-entered carrying clean, dry trousers and a coat jacket; then, leaving and entering once again, he presented Mantell with a clean and polished pair of boots.

Mantell walked quickly up the slight hill to Government House. Outside, the rain had eased; from one of the ships in the harbour came the sound of a hurdy-gurdy, its melancholy notes constant alongside the sound of harsh wavering voices; faint lights from house windows shimmered in a curve along the edge of the water; and from somewhere the sound of footsteps and breathing magnified by the low cloud so as to seem only yards away—or were they his own?

Eyre received him across a large desk. The boy who had brought the message stood in shadows in the corner of the room, looked at Mantell, then left. Eyre sat straight, then leaned forwards on his desk and looked to one side out a window, through which was visible only the darkness of the night sky then, once more, he sat upright, and Mantell had the impression he was kept rigid by the uniform, as if it had been fashioned from wood. He paused for deliberation often as he spoke. He said, Mr Kemp, the Native Secretary, to whom was entrusted the purchase of the Ngai Tahu district in the Middle Island—and the allotment of reserves to the native inhabitants—has, unfortunately, partly neglected his duty: he hasn't allotted a single reserve for use by the natives. Mr Kemp has fixed the 12th of December for the next instalment of the purchase money, and, Mantell, it will be necessary to appoint a commissioner to remedy the omission before the payment is made. Governor Grey has instructed me to offer you the position. You speak the natives' language well; you are said to have a rapport with them . . . Once again the Lieutenant Governor looked sidelong out the window. He said, And you'll be perfect for the job, Mantell: you're young enough, and still fit, and have the necessary skills. It's practically unexplored territory. You will have to cross several dangerous rivers, and here the timing of the payment is unfortunate: the rain at this time of year is likely to be almost constant.

Mantell wondered about the Lieutenant Governor's frequent looks out, through the darkened pane of glass with the highlights of water on the outside. Though he had been speaking in a deliberate, rehearsed manner, there had been an edge to the words, of some emotion, emerging with the occasional overly forced syllable, and with it his eyes would narrow as if he were staring out, not into darkness, but into a remembered sun. Eyre had, notoriously, been involved in exploration of the Australian wilderness some years earlier; was he wishing he could withdraw the offer from Mantell and perform the expedition himself? It could have been an edge of regret, and a slight over-excitement at the difficult conditions that Mantell and the surveyor to accompany him would encounter. For a second, he paused and looked at Mantell, seeming to shiver slightly.

There was, of course, no option but to accept the position. Once he had done this, Eyre became businesslike, pushing across to him a sheaf of papers concerning the deed and the requirements for the reserves, and instructing him to return the next day to meet the surveyor. Finally, armed with the instructions—a pile that seemed too thick—he took his leave and went out, once again, into the night.

The journey began some days later. Under a sky that seemed to lower itself down to the surrounding water, the ship leaned and came out past the heads, near a thin thread of smoke that wound upwards from one of the coastal villages near the harbour mouth. Mantell leaned on the railing amidships, always his favourite place on board; when the ship was on course, and the pace of the crew slackened, he stayed as long as he could by this railing. The *Fly* cut its way along the coast; outcrops jutted upwards, and there were patches of water of different colour which could have meant rocks just under the surface but which would, sometimes, suddenly dart away: schools of fish. Here the colour was so different from times in the open ocean, with only sea and the subtlest gradations of grey or blue water. A shouted greeting came from a whale-boat which was picking its way in the opposite direction, closer to the shore.

Mantell wondered what had become of the surveyor, Wills. The two of them were to travel together and Mantell had met him in the most official circumstances in Wellington, at Government House. The surveyor had said, standing for a second on the balcony overlooking a harbour which appeared and disappeared with rough sweeps of rain, that he hated getting wet. Then later the two of them made the arrangements for equipment and food to be purchased and loaded. This morning Mantell had seen him, late, running towards a boat waiting to take him out to the ship; but he had not appeared again after, having climbed up over the side, he raised a hand quickly, and with his other hand on his hat rushed below. In the meantime the coast turned away to the north leaving the ship in open water; the view along the land's edge was one of fading, diminishing cliffs and, at their base, the haze which extended upwards from the retreating and advancing arms of waves, and which rose to join with a layer of cloud broken only at a narrow blue line above the differently blue horizon. Mantell could have easily taken this scene down in his sketchbook in two or three lines— converging for the cliffs, parallel for the horizon and cloud edge—but where would the human figures fit? In a ship (yes, this very ship) breaking the horizon with its patchwork of sails? The Middle Island was in view: a dark field the colour of a bruise over the water with the clouds above no longer the uniform grey of the rest of the sky but textured in sweeps, bright–dark like tensed muscles. Behind him a man shouted at one of the crew; a slurred order, and incomprehensible to Mantell; the man approached and slapped him on the back: the Lieutenant Governor.

He said, That's yours Mantell—treat it as yours . . . Eyre indicated the island in front of them whose southern limit was lost as if simply dissolved in a strong, salt-laden wind. He said, Grey sets great store by you. He thinks you will do an excellent job. I dare say he's right, but you've got your work cut out for you . . .

Eyre might be talking to him like this all the way to Akaroa. The Lieutenant Governor was to accompany them that far, and now that he was on board this ship his uniform seemed not out of place; it seemed as if he might, at any minute, take over command of the ship altogether. Mantell said, The whole of the Middle Island just for me, Your Excellency?

You know what I mean, Mantell.

Indeed . . . Mantell felt a shiver like an exhalation and a momentary deep revulsion for the man standing next to him, who was now silent, closing his eyes against a wind which rushed off the sails and eddied around the level of the railing; his lower lip was extended slightly outwards in a child's pouting grin.

Eyre said, I've done similar work, Mantell. I know what you're getting into. It gives me pleasure simply to be here on this, minor, part of the journey. But don't think I can't advise; my experience in central Australia is considerable, and I've already had a chance to talk to the surveyor about it, to offer him something of my opinion about the conditions. You'll have to be fair to them.

Of course.

He said, They shouldn't give any trouble if treated well . . . Then: I understand your interest in geology. You've already done good work there, so I hear?

I hope so, Your Excellency.

It is always one of my regrets that I wasn't able to do more in the way of science. Make sure you remember it. Of course, you will have other things to think about; but it would be a shame if you had the same regrets.

I will of course be considering my job, first and—

On my long expedition into the Australian wilderness we took time, though there wasn't much, to gather samples, in as far as we could without neglecting our duties—but this is an important aspect of any expedition. As we travelled, we thought less and less of science; we collected almost nothing from the second half of our time. It wasn't easy to keep our minds on it.

There must have been other difficulties to—

Yes—difficulties aplenty, with the simplest aspects of living, and with the natives . . . He shook his head, looked down for a long moment. He said, And to make it worse, when we shipped our collections, such as they were, to Adelaide, they never arrived at their destination.

Never arrived?

It was the collections from the first half of the expedition, and we had carried them with us painstakingly for months, with such attention.

What can have—

Leaving very little, leaving really very little of our efforts. I don't want to overstate this, but take good care, Mantell.

But—lost? How?

Eyre said, How? Oh, I've no idea. It hardly matters now. Of course, it was out of our hands at that point. There's the thing, that you can take all the care you wish and still, once it has passed to someone else's responsibility, there is nothing you can do. I suppose they were stolen and sold to private collectors . . . He stopped, appearing distracted, sighed, and turned so that his backside was against the railing. He said, Well, if you want to ask anything further, I'll make myself at your disposal.

Mantell tried to catch Eyre's eye, but his gaze was directed firmly over the deck and southwards, set against the cold wash over the water's surface, squinting slightly at it.

I—thank you, Your Excellency . . .

Eyre waved a hand in acknowledgement as he turned and moved away.

Later in the day, having moved around the points of numerous tongues of land and islands each covered down to the shore in thick forest, though even here echoing across the water the sound of someone cutting wood would be heard from time to time, the sloop moved slowly through glassy water: over the top of the water and reflected in it were the shapes of distant snow-covered mountains to the west, across a broad bay. On the other side of the ship, the nearby shore and forest responded to the ship's disturbance with the sucking of small waves against the rock. To the fore, a group of marines who had gathered, at first only with curt greetings, then in silence, and then with low conversation, at last began to sing. One of the songs was a modified folk tune with words explicitly praising the native women; the group broke into harmonies of two, three then four parts even as they sang the crude lyrics. Mantell felt blood rush to his ears as he walked from fore to aft keeping abreast of the land— the ship was moving slowly and the sails overhead beginning to collapse and emit loud, startling snaps as they flicked back and forth—and he felt a buffeting wind, but from where? They were practically becalmed. And, yes, rounding painfully slowly into a shallow bay with the town of Nelson already in sight with buildings like pieces of coloured glass under the still ominous sky, the cry went out to take up the sails and to drop the anchor. At the very aft of the ship he turned suddenly towards them, as if he might shake the marines' song from his head, their voices now obscured by the sound of the anchor chain and the shouts of the crew, but somehow it seemed directed at him: a solitary figure, he alone out of uniform. No—there was Wills, close to his elbow, as if the surveyor had followed his walk down the length of the ship, just out of reach, and a fluttering hand outstretched for the whole distance to clutch or tap at his shoulder. Wills said, It'll be all right, won't it, this trip?

I don't know, Wills. What do you mean?

Just the sea voyage. You don't think we'll be blown out of our way, lost in another miserable dreary dark ocean? I've heard of ships unable to get into the southern harbours thanks to an unfavourable wind, and spending weeks tossed about in huge swells before . . .

God, Wills . . . He closed his eyes for a second.

Wills said, This ship's seaworthy enough though, and the crew seem to know their business. Don't you think?

Mantell sighed. He turned to Wills, looking at him face to face for what seemed like the first time—perhaps it was? Had they only ever been side by side for the last few days, looking at maps, drawing up lists? The look in Wills's eye did not seem like that of a surveyor: a determination not to look at the view around him but instead to focus on Mantell or alternately on the back of his own hand.

Wills said, You're pale. You're not a natural sailor either,

Mantell? . . . By now the group of marines had moved away, dispersed and become individual faces moving one by one below or about the decks. He said, I mean, heaven forbid that I'd ever do another big sea voyage. I nearly stayed ashore, when we stopped at the Cape on the way here—I don't know what inspired me to return on board and come to this place. Yes, I can swim well enough, but I'd never choose to, would you? It's only a relief to me that on trips like this the shore remains in view . . . In the midst of his speech Wills had turned away from Mantell and was looking aft; Mantell still faced in the opposite direction, leaning back on the rail, while above them the sails were furled and members of the crew climbed up or down the rigging and Captain Oliver stood where the marines had been, looking past the far point of the small bay, set within the great sweep of the larger bay that extended around under the ranges visible against the glowing clouds to the west, and now the water was dead flat or moved only with small ripples that seemed to curl over and under each other from the ship's edge.

Listen, Wills. You've been in this sort of country before. Will we be able to cover the area we've been instructed to?

Wills was looking at the water's surface. After a minute he said, Yes . . . Then: The rivers will only be half the problem. For all his talk Eyre doesn't know much—the rivers come down from the chain of mountains in the centre of the island and are snow-fed. They're highest in the summer with snow melt, and spring, and should currently be manageable with the help of the natives. The swamps are difficult—again, the natives should know ways through. You end up swinging from tree to tree, in fear of falling through a hole hidden under the opaque water and once something becomes wet in a swamp—your blankets, your food—the smell doesn't leave. We will have to warn them at Akaroa to have fresh blankets in store for when we come back through. You've dealt with the natives often enough and I'm sure they won't be a problem. It will be cold. After a while it will feel like we have never set foot on anything solid.

And will we cover enough ground? Will you have enough time for your work?

Yes. I'm sure of it. I'm sure we will be able to. Besides which, we'll just do what we can, and no more. We'll do a good deal more than Kemp did—we'll have reserves surveyed, even if they're not final, even if they have to send down another party after us, and another. We'll have done our job.

We're only human . . . ?

Quite . . . Now the man-o'-war sat unmoving, and could have been a building with foundations deep in the soft sand of the bay. There was a pause, a lull in the ship's work, and more sound seemed to come from the shore and the single building—a low cottage with a shallowly sloping roof that Mantell noticed tucked under a headland nearby—than from the half-whispered furtive conversations of the groups of sailors as they settled about the deck: a chair scraping and clacking across a rough wooden floor; something or someone shuffling through the forest's leaf litter. Wills said, Still, I wouldn't like your job. I'm glad it's you, not me, responsible for the natives' acquiescence. I think you'll do well, from what I know about you.

What do you know about me?

Oh, I've heard a few things . . .

Wills fell silent. What was it—the marines' song? something in Wills's voice?—that made him remember the night, over a year before, when working on the harbour road, a cold night with the harbour's smell faintly washed up over the beach—work had been wet and slow, weighed and interrupted by

60

showers that blew suddenly from the south, catching at their skin with its freezing points—and the sky clear as if scoured, with stars brilliant against the darkness? Wills now slapped him lightly and awkwardly on the back, moved off, nodding to him and leaving him to himself. Mantell had walked, as he sometimes did, away from the harbour mouth, inland, along the route to be taken by the road but which soon became rough, coarse beaches interrupted by rocks, short promontories, or trees whose roots enclosed between them small caverns of darkness—there: a sound, sibilant, faintly whispering, and he stopped to look carefully at its source. It was late, and the workers had, in general, lain in their tents and blankets, and were talking or sleeping already. A figure, silent now, was sitting on a root that extended almost to the water, or—it was hard to tell in the darkness—it was a rock that the root gave way to, winding itself around and into its small cracks. It was sitting heavily, small, wrapped in a cloak pulled up over its head against the cold. The figure sniffed, looked up and saw Mantell only paces away, and the cloak fell to reveal a face that hardly seemed to register him before she jumped up, let herself fall down the other side of what was now more clearly a rock, took steps backward and stumbled. Mantell said, You don't need to—wait! . . . With his arm outstretched, and he took some paces forward.

She said, in English, It's you, e te rangatira. I'm sorry, I was just sitting for a minute.

It's—don't worry. It doesn't matter. You speak very good English.

I was just now going back to the camp.

You may sit out here as long as you wish.

She said, I should go back now . . . She stood still, looking at him, with the rock in between them, then, despite her words, climbed back onto the rock and stood, still facing him, looking at him. She said, I shouldn't be here, should I?

Well, I dare say, neither should I. Is your husband one of the workers?

She said nothing.

He said, What is your name?

Again she said nothing. She shook her head at him but remained otherwise still.

He said, What can I call you?

Why do you want to talk to me?

He paused. Then: Please, forget I'm the rangatira. It doesn't matter—you have no reason to be scared of me.

I'm not scared of you, I don't think. You gave me a surprise, just now . . . Then: But I'm going back to the camp . . . She moved at an angle to him, to come past him, and almost involuntarily he took steps towards her and, as she quickened her pace, he ran a yard or two and caught at her, holding her arm. She shrugged at him, flicking herself sideways until, still held roughly by the upper arm, she was facing him again. He let go and turned his head away for a second.

Why do you want to talk to me? I should go back.

Don't go back.

Is that an order? . . . Then: I'm sorry. I didn't want to spit out at you. I want to go back to the camp.

Not yet.

Why?

He didn't answer. Instead, he took half a step backwards, away from her, to get a better view of her. He couldn't remember having seen her at the camp, but the workers' wives tended to keep to themselves, and, now, there were none whose faces he could call to mind. He said, Maybe it can be a secret between us. Being out, away from the camp, when we should be in our beds.

After a moment, she said, I don't have a name, not here.

I beg your—

You asked me my name. But if it is really a secret that I'm here, if no one's going to know, then I don't have a name here. I'm no one.

And I'm not the rangatira, if you like. We can both be nothing.

Both?

If you like.

I'm not a Ngati Toa. And you . . .

If you like.

Then I can speak to you how I please . . . Again she fell silent, watching him. She said, Why shouldn't you be here, rangatira? You can do what you want.

I have my employers.

They wouldn't like you talking to a woman. That's it?

Well . . .

She laughed, briefly, then looked down.

He said, Well, here, since it's a secret, I have no employers.

She laughed again, meeting his eye for a second—though in the darkness it was only really a flicking up of hers, a quick almost invisible smile—before again looking down.

Can I call you something?

Call me what you want. Call me a name if you want. Call me after your mother.

Mary Ann.

She laughed, still looking downwards.

He said, What will you . . . He stopped short, looking again at the woman huddled against the cold, the cloak or blanket pulled up again over her head so that her forehead was obscured, her face a scarcely visible outline of nose and chin. He said, No, what are you called?

I'm called Mary Ann . . . Her laugh now was little more

than an exhalation, and they were both silent for a minute until she began to softly sing or whisper, in fact so softly that it was barely audible over the faint rush and breath of the waves. He felt that he could walk away from her now as if they hadn't spoken, but still, he stayed, watching her, his body tensing and relaxing, his mouth opening once more then shutting, before he lowered his eyes to look at the ground between them—a dark and faintly glistening sandscape, dug roundly with a few footprints left from her approach. Her feet, under the blanket, he imagined, were bare, and the whispers of song came from a body now entirely invisible, her head bowed further until she raised it, exposing her face and throat once again to say, It's cold, Mr Mantell. I am going to go back to the camp.

She walked and he put a hand out to her as if to grab at her again, without thinking, and she ducked and flinched so that he only brushed her gently on the head. She stopped as if she had been restrained, immediately, straightening up as if against his grip and rearing slightly backwards. He said, No, wait.

Why? . . . She was looking at him, leaning away, then her body relaxed again.

He said, It's nice to be nobody for a time . . . His hand was still outstretched but no longer touching her, having dropped back at the elbow, leaving him as if he were about to receive a gift from her, something small placed into his palm—a stone, a piece of rubble from the beach, covered over with tiny encrustations of extinct life—and, yes, she reached for his hand and held it, briefly, giving it an almost curious look, feeling with her fingers as far as the wrist. Quickly she let go.

She said, What do you want? . . . Then: I'm sorry.

No . . . It seemed, though she hadn't moved, that she was

going to start off again, and Mantell said, Tell me, wait, where did you learn such good English?

It was from one of the whalers. I used to talk with him.

He said, I see. And you're here with . . . She shook her head. He said, What is your name?

Mary Ann.

What is your name?

Mary Ann. And I'm going to call you Jack.

Jack?

Now you're really not the boss, Jack . . . She took his hand again and ran hers up inside the sleeve, a little further, looking this time at his face. She said, I might be out here again some night, Jack . . . She stepped away from him and started walking. She turned after a few steps and said, Please don't follow me?

He said, Who is Jack?

She pointed at him, then turned again.

It was an absurd name but it had stuck, he thought; it was surely the name of her whaler—but wasn't it too much, too obviously a whaler's name? Mantell thought, on the deck of the *Fly* as the dwindling light gave highlights to the mountains to the west, of this meeting and the others that followed. Sometimes he would seek her out along the coast, leaving his tent as if suddenly disoriented or abandoned and taking the route of the still unbuilt road; she would not always be waiting for him, but sometimes—often enough—she would be there, or would arrive after him. Didn't he have some of the same feeling now? Faced with Wills, with the marines, with Eyre, the captain, the sailors and even with the evidence of some quiet industry ashore in the cottage—didn't he want someone to vouch for him, even simply to register his presence but make no demands on him, expect nothing, give nothing but a look or a nod?

Finally, the next day, they made it to Nelson, a tidy town spreading out on its broad plain towards the arms of the hills. They dined with Bell, the Company's agent there, and Eyre, walking through the streets to and later from the house, almost broke into a run, averted his eyes and kept his arms stiff by his side, possibly to avoid petitioners who in any case didn't seem much in evidence; he was recognised by a few of the townspeople, who only nodded to him. Though only a few inches taller than the agent who stood with him in the dark, waiting for the ship's boat to come ashore, he seemed to lean over the other man and cause him to cower. The mountains on the other side of the bay seemed to emit their own light, and even light up the night sky above them—or was that simply the light of a moon that had risen behind the town? The sky was as clear as the day's had been, scattered with stars, and the air had the same invigorating bite. Wills and Mantell stood some distance behind them, Wills having looked sidelong, put an arm across Mantell's path.

Wills said, It is his giving of orders. He wants his hand in everything, every step I take. He's been the same with you?

Mantell said, Yes. My directions are only too clear: I have to conquer, not only for the colony but for the glory of the Lieutenant Governor. He won't allow himself to be embarrassed again by the sort of incompleteness embodied in Kemp . . .

The man's insufferable.

There, look at Mr Bell there hastily nodding, cowering under the fearful gaze of the great—or I guess that's how Eyre sees himself. The embodiment of glory—the very limb of our Queen . . .

Mantell had turned to face in the opposite direction, towards the line of buildings that had spread along the foreshore's dirt road, so that his words and his face would not be noticed by their employer. His past week had been a sort of headlong rush, without time to consider his task, quite aside from the opportunities for geology that it should afford him. His head was ringing with instructions, written for him and spoken to him at every opportunity.

Wills said, So, God willing, we will escape all this when we leave Akaroa. I'm looking forward to the relentless, exhausting trek . . .

Well, if it gives us respite from—

Mantell . . . Wills touched his arm, gently turning him back towards Eyre, and, leaving his hand on Mantell's coat-sleeve while Mantell caught Eyre's eye, turned on them all at once. He said, Maybe we should go up.

Eyre shouted across: come up, you two . . . And when they approached: what were you discussing?

Mantell said, Details to do with our work, Your Excellency. There is so much to consider.

Nothing to discuss that I can't hear. I might even have some advice for you . . . Then, turning: Come on, let's get aboard.

The ship sailed around the peninsula, and they were met by bays and inlets and cliffs smeared with the faeces of birds, before, for the turn into the Akaroa harbour, Mantell clasped his fists tight, and the water surged around the heads with a sound of tearing fabric; the ship leaned to starboard and the crew all took a stumbling step, even as they moved, dancelike, towards the rigging. There were small settlements on either side from which smoke stood against the scrubby hills. The snapping of sails echoed from the slopes; rock outcrops at the top of each hill seemed like watchers. The crew were hushed, and at length the town itself came into view set in cleared land on the eastern side, no more than a group of houses but, when they looked again, there seemed to be more than they first noticed, with a church and a fortified building by the shore. Mantell went below to meet with Eyre and Wills in Eyre's cabin; above, the clamour of the crew, the anchor-chain's clatter and was that the sound of voices from the town itself?

Eyre was to leave with the ship in a few days' time. He said, But what about a drink to our endeavour now? . . . Mantell met Wills's eye and nodded in response to the Lieutenant Governor's suggestion, still looking at the surveyor.

Wills said, Quite, Your Excellency.

I envy you going into this untried territory . . . Each received a tumbler of liquid, a harsh whisky that reflected in gold the light from the window. He said, I have been preparing more instructions for you, Mantell; I should have some more notes to give you before I leave.

Thank you, that will be just what I need.

For a minute there was a silence. Wills held his drink close to his face and shut his eyes tightly, trying, Mantell thought, to conceal a laugh, his head inclined towards his chest; Eyre watched the two of them carefully, but looked away soon enough. There were no other sounds from the ship, save for a sudden clack and a few softer repetitions, like the tapping of a drum—a boat had pulled up alongside?

Then, Captain Oliver stood in the doorway to the cabin. He said, Listen, a whale-boat has come with some of the chiefs. They're asking for Kemp. I told them he's not with us, but they insisted on coming aboard. I've let them. Will you see them?

A small group of natives stood at one side of the deck. The crew were still lined up along the yards overhead and the ship rocked faintly and slowly with a circular motion, tracing out scribbled lines in the sky with the mast points as they looked up climbing the ladder from below, and emerged onto the deck, over which a bird—a pigeon—swooped with the movement of a piece of cloth blown in the wind before carrying on its flight across the harbour. The sailors' eyes were focused on Eyre, Mantell and Wills one by one as they climbed up and stood in a line face to face with the group of chiefs. Mantell translated their speeches for Eyre: They are greeting God, greeting us, greeting Kemp, whom I think they still expect to be on board Your Excellency . . . He spoke in response to the chiefs, before turning back to Eyre: I just acknowledged them, greeted them in return and announced once and for all, I hope, that Kemp isn't with us. But I've indicated that you're Kemp's rangatira, that all questions can be addressed to you.

The natives took turns to speak again, and again Mantell translated: Your Excellency, he says that the land north of the Waimakariri should remain with Ngai Tuahuriri. He says that he never signed a deed or agreed to give up the land to which he has rights, that north of the Waimakariri and as far north as their pa, or an even greater area. He says that others would claim, as he does, continuous rights even as near as the Opawaho . . . Another native took up speaking. Mantell said, That what one person has given away might not be theirs to give, Your Excellency, and that Te Rauparaha has sold land belonging to them. He's talking about Te Rauparaha's campaigns here, his incursions as far south as Kaiapoi, and saying the invasion is still too fresh to accept that it has ever been Ngati Toa land . . . For a short time Mantell fell silent, even while the natives were speaking, and, looking at them, he sighed then looked down. Eyre clutched at his shoulder. Mantell said, It's much the same; they are simply repeating each other . . . Nonetheless, he took up the translation again:

He says that we have already been sold land that belongs to them and that they do not wish to part with; he says they will keep that land, that although some of their number signed the deed as God is his witness he is quite clear what has been sold and what hasn't, what the deed includes and what it doesn't; he says that with respect while some of them might be stupid not all of them are, and that he knows that they can have our respect; that they can't give us rights they don't possess, that they leave that kind of deal to their enemies, I guess meaning the Ngati Toas. He says their land runs from the Waipara south and that he knows we can acknowledge their ownership.

Eyre said, Well, of course we will respect their ownership. I've no intention of doing anything but the honourable thing . . . He was looking at Mantell and hesitating slightly between each word. He said, If that's what they want we'll give it to them—what, the land as far as the Waipara?

Mantell said, That isn't possible, is it, Your Excellency? What of all my instructions? You were very clear on this point, that we can't renegotiate the boundaries . . . He hesitated and looked up at the group of chiefs who stood watching the short exchange, as if with curiosity, or with doubt, and talking quietly amongst themselves while still keeping an eye on the Lieutenant Governor.

Eyre said, Go about your business! . . . He was addressing the sailors and marines who were gathered watching and listening; he waved a hand at them, circling around: Go on!

Mantell lowered his voice further, certain in any case that the natives couldn't understand. He said, It's a huge area and would certainly be an impediment to the Company's settlements. And we can't alter Kemp's deed except for the addition of reserves—surely that has been made more than clear in your directions to me . . . He was still looking sidelong at the natives: one turned to another man near him, whispered something and turned back, meeting Mantell's eye with a long steady gaze. Mantell looked suddenly away from the chiefs and at his own body. Wills cleared his throat and Mantell felt a lump in his own and once again, looking at the chiefs, he felt their gaze as if it might immobilise him, as if it would stay imprinted on his vision.

Eyre said, No, you're quite right. No, of course not. What was I thinking? Mantell, tell them it's out of the question. Tell them we won't finalise anything now, but that you'll simply be responsible for negotiating the reserves.

Narrations (2)

In the midst of the house, a hot damp kitchen whose walls, unlike the other dark rooms, were white, holding within themselves smells and the heat of cooking. Her first memories were of returning to this kitchen, or, before this return, of being handed across fences from her father to one of his workers or being asked to sit in the truck while they worked on something where she might be in the way. Her mother stayed largely inside, or made her way out to the garden, itself surrounded by a fence, not wire but a cracked and peeling white row of vertical pickets, and here kept herself covered with broad hats or headscarves against the sun which, when it was too bright for her, gave her headaches or migraines, or simply made her squint so that when she returned inside she complained that her face hurt. When out—this single word was how her father referred to the farm, to his work on it—he would say to her, sometimes: Are you going to help me with this, Di? . . . Instead of helping she would run away to the truck and there stand with an arm and half her body in the door, casually left open by the men; she would peer around it while he and his workers laughed in her direction, perhaps gently, keeping their smiles when they took up again whatever task occupied them. She loved and hated the land referred to only as 'out': against its simplicity and blankness the weeds—thistle mostly—grew up against fencelines giving it a rough edge; in a gully a pocket of bush only became visible when the truck edged itself down a steep track at walking pace. Occasionally she watched while he removed the body of a sheep from the stream nearby, hardly connecting this dead animal with the live ones above on the gentler slopes of the paddocks. While she was wrapped in oilskin and wool that carried with her something of the kitchen's condensation, her father stripped to a shirt and rolled up its sleeves.

In the kitchen: She's not a son.

Her father said, She loves it, don't you, Di?

It's not the place for her out there.

The air will do her good.

Diane herself had no place in the conversation—how old was she?—but stood by the steamed-up windows unable to make out now, with the light failing in any case, anything of the view. In fact she loved returning to the overly hot house; here the air seemed almost liquid and her body became heavy with it, in contrast to the constant breeze that seemed to accompany the smooth roll of the land outside, that chilled and exhilarated but at the same time made her feel fragile and served only to emphasise the difference between her and her father whose skin seemed impervious to it. This contrast made her tentative when she was out, blown easily from side to side, and at times she would look down at the grass mosaic, a shimmering of blades overlapping one another, play games with its form—see in it shapes of animals, but not the ones familiar to her from the farm—before looking up and finding herself alone with only the sheep, at some distance: where was he? ... Until his torso appeared over the rise of a nearby hill, or from behind the truck's bonnet, staying her momentary reel. She had the same feeling of smallness even inside the house, when the workers who lived from time to time in the rooms out the back of the house came in, as if they were bringing the farm with them, for dinner or a cup of tea; though they made her laugh, touching her gently on the belly button, and even when they had become as familiar as her parents, she felt shy around them, unable to speak above a whisper.

Looking back, she pictured herself perched in one corner of the kitchen, comfortable and semi-oblivious to her mother's movements, breathing easily down into the space formed by her arms and her chest around a book. She was seated atop a high, white wooden stool with her knees up on a strut, and like this, able to observe but in fact not doing so, able also to speak but not in fact speaking, she was at her most content, at least until she began to wriggle and had to twist herself down, leaving the book behind on the seat.

She couldn't quite believe in anything other than the almost abstract simplicity of the landscape of her childhood, after she had left home and moved to the city at the southern end of the island. She felt as if under the city's hills were the hills of the farm, bare, and whatever grew here—pines, or, visible from some of the city's vantage points, the rough scrub around its suburbs—all this growth was, to her, an afterthought, and the farm landscape named 'out' was the truth of all other places, an originary featurelessness that gave the houses, the buildings in the city centre, the roads the feeling of the same fragility she had once felt in herself. What would come and reduce it to its green nakedness? What was obvious about the city, and often commented on—its precariousness, the fact that the houses might at any time slip away—was to her also something of the city's lie, and reflected her own suspicion that the buildings were false. Surely, under here, as its truth, was rolling green country, occasionally scored by fences and windbreaks.

Her hostel at the city's College of Education was functional and bare, different from the boarding school, wood-panelled and decorated in its halls with portraits or other markers of achievement, where she had spend a large part of the last years, but it echoed through with the same ring of voices. Her friendship with Theresa, a fellow student at the hostel, began, in a sense, in the boarding school, where she had seen Theresa but never spoken to her. Theresa was some years older, but was now in the same year of teacher training as Diane, and it was initially the strangeness of the reduced age difference—the face that had struck her, years before, as older and fuller—that made Diane wonder about the intervening years, and made her stop Theresa once outside the building.

You were at my school.

Oh—really? That's . . .

You won't remember me.

Well, I'm sure I will . . .

No—I was younger. I only left last year. But I remember your face. Theresa?

76

Well, and you remembered my name!

Theresa said that she had spent the years since she left school as an optician's assistant, and described her work in a suite of rooms upstairs in the city's centre where she served as both a secretary and receptionist and a helper in the workroom, assisting in the fitting of lenses into frames or standing by while her employer dealt with his customers. Now Theresa was slightly shorter then her, if still possessed of the same solidity, a density that would transform itself at once into motion, that Diane thought she remembered. The hostel was set in a broad valley, a cold suburb of the city, and now the sun was leaving its upper floors, darkening still further the small forecourt where they stood talking, each remaining interrupted, Diane from going in from a short walk, Theresa from heading out of the building to some destination; now each of them had halted and had no thought of moving, until finally they entered together to sit in the hostel's common room.

After some time, Theresa said, Of course he felt me up.

Who? He what?

The optician—my boss. He felt me up—he tried to put a hand up my skirt once, but normally it was only my tits . . . Diane laughed, then caught Theresa's eye, itself amused but at the same time looking at her sharply; Theresa said, I've never told anyone that.

You've only just met me.

I know.

God, what was it like?

What, the . . .

Him, with his . . .

Oh, I don't know. He touched me a couple of times, more than a couple of times.

Diane said, But was it horrible?

I don't know . . . There was a silence, perhaps for the

first time between them in the hour or two they had been talking. All at once Diane couldn't speak, caught in the fear of what Theresa might say next, and still she couldn't imagine Theresa in a workroom allowing herself to be touched by the optician, who was—what was he like? She was certain of his ordinariness, and Theresa hadn't described him. Now Theresa was in front of her looking to one side then the other and somehow reduced though she sat straight, straighter than previously and hemmed in as if by something solid around her. Theresa was a different person entirely from the one she had pictured at school, and was this transformation already something of the city's work, its hiding of the foundations of things, its resistance to penetration, a resistance that she thought she could see, simply in the hills, impossibly in the very view from the top floor of the hostel, as if a landscape could mean anything whatsoever? Theresa had been in the same boarding school, which was placed as if it had fallen there from the sky in amongst fields. Had the move to this new place, a move that Diane herself had only just made, had an effect on Theresa, covered something of her, that was now almost visible in the gap in the conversation where Diane opened her mouth and closed it, ruffled her face and shrugged and made some small noises but came up each time against something like Theresa's blankness or blindness, as if Diane were simply not there? Theresa was also a mess of small movements, but each of them was directed to one side, in the manner of someone on a footpath unsure of the side on which to pass an oncoming stranger, whose eyes she couldn't quite meet. It was surely only for an instant that they sat there like that and their movements, small shufflings, seemed like a negotiation or like repeated moves on a board between them, jockeying for position, and in the years following, this instant was not remembered, as such, but seemed to sediment itself as something, a glue between them or an understanding, holding them in a grip. Then, the instant was broken by Diane:

What was he like, your boss?

He was over forty.

But was he nice?

He was over forty. What else is there to say? . . . She laughed, looked fully at Diane now, and her laugh broke out compulsively, suddenly into laughter from both of them. After a moment Theresa said, It was a game. There was something stupid about it . . . Her smile was not yet faded, the words came out through a barely suppressed giggle: After a while he'd come up to me and I'd make some excuse to leave the room, and he'd come after me again, making some excuse again to follow me, so I'd have to go to the toilet. He must have thought I had a terribly sick bladder. He never followed me in there; he had his self-respect, of course . . . And again, after another pause: God, you know, Diane, I think he was desperately in love with me; I'd catch him looking at me sometimes, and each time I ran away from him he had these big eyes that—he'd look at me with his mouth open in this way that was, God, it was really very funny. He had this desperate look, and I had to feel sorry for him; well, not that sorry for him, but I wondered about his—he was married with children! I don't want to ever pass him in the street; or I do, I want to pass him in the street where he can't do anything and I'll ignore the bastard, walk right past him, but he's probably got some other poor girl now, some other love of his life to torture, to rub himself up against, and he's probably forgotten I exist. Well and good. I was there for more than two years. It's hard to believe now—two and a half years, and it was just a routine I went through. It's amazing what you can put up with . . .

Diane's sense of something hidden in Theresa, something which she had perhaps had a glimpse of in this first conversation but which was forgotten or remembered only as a hint of itself, was something she sometimes had the sense of herself chasing in her friend, wishing for a re-emergence, as if something had shone, or rather, came briefly to light, or was awakened but only for the moment that Diane was catching her breath and forgetting to look. Mostly in their time together Theresa pointed things out and talked about things, even her intimacies, as if they were not her property but simply happened to be nearby. It was different only when she talked about the city and its history—she was training to become a history teacher and would bring facts from her courses back to Diane, or complaints: the history she was taught was dry; what she wanted was something under the surface, something to give life to the present day, to her surroundings, to give depth to herself as if to give herself a genealogy and even, she said once, to connect herself to the place, even to this city where she lived only for a few years.

She said once, It all seems so grey and lifeless, this place . . . They had already known each other for almost two years. She said, I'm sick of dreaming of bigger places overseas. I want to dream about here. I don't want it to be the dry diggings of this place, I want it to take me away from the present and its boredom. God, I'm bored! After the summer holidays I didn't want to come back. You're the only thing I like about being here.

Diane said, Me too . . . In the instant she said it, it was true. Was there also something in Theresa's interest in history that reflected her own experience of the city as something slightly unreal? Didn't she also want something that would take her away from it, and at the same time make it appear all the more clearly? And wasn't this no more than the fact of their boredom, the city's grey, windswept nature and its geography that only hid damp corners? She was simply homesick—no; the farm held nothing for her but a familiarity that seemed to underpin her experience of anything, but at the same time was blank.

In the plates of a book that Theresa had, a collection of texts and artwork from the earliest European settlers of the city, the drawings offered, sometimes in a naïve, childlike hand, something like an alternative view, a city not affected by anything, not underpinned by anything, blank in a different way: new, untouched, open for even the worst artist to try their hand at a sketch, away from the weight of culture. The drawings showed people, so it seemed, simply living, and living in a way that now seemed impossible, even here in a city that was hardly less isolated than it had been then, at the southern tip of the island. It was impossible to look at the drawings and not wonder at the dirt prevalent in all of them—everything gardenlike, dug up and planted—but now gone under layers of asphalt that reduced the city, not to its foundations of dirt, but to the dust that blew along its streets. Even in its isolation the city had been thoroughly covered by its change, so that only the views over and across the harbour were recognisable from these drawings, and then only by looking away from the buildings themselves or ignoring them, seeing them as an afterthought to the land's form, and thus ignoring the very history that the contrast seemed to promise. It was this sort of recognition that most excited Theresa: she would point out, in the pictures, what could be seen of the hills that they knew well from the skyline, naming them; and here, there were clues to the names, of hills, of suburbs, from the events of that early period or the names of the settlers that had farmed them. Such details brought things to life. Mostly, however, though she didn't say so to Theresa,

Diane thought that the pictures and the texts in the book and others presented the early life as something, if rough and improvised, incompetent and ad hoc even in its organisation—the attempts to add the weight of government to a crowd of newcomers milling on the beach—that was essentially polite. There was little to give the impression of anything deeply troubling, and what troubles there were seemed to be met with flippancy, drawn lightly and the drawings annotated with exclamation-marked phrases. Although Theresa loved the drawings, Diane sometimes felt in herself a sudden hatred for them.

She said, I don't know if I can do this. You're so good at it—you've got a real, I don't know, interest in the history.

Do what, Diane?

Diane didn't reply for a second, during which Theresa stopped and seemed about to repeat her question, but in any case looked at her with the same sharpness with which she'd asked it. Diane said, Teaching. I find it so difficult; I hate it.

No, you don't. Do you?

Yes. Yes, it's too hard.

You're fine. You've never said this before.

I hate it. I only do it because you're here . . . This sounded false on her lips, though she had meant it; she understood how ridiculous it sounded; she said, No, I mean . . .

If you hate it so much you can stop it.

No . . .

Look, I'm your friend. You'll see me no matter what you do, love.

That's not it. I feel like crying whenever I'm in front of the class.

Well, but you don't? You're fine, Diane—you'll be a good teacher.

You can do it; you're older. You're good at it.

What do you mean, older? That's got nothing to do with it. It doesn't matter how old I am or how old you are. Age isn't important; it really doesn't matter. And besides, you'll be older yourself, soon, in a couple of years, if you really think it matters.

No, I won't. I'll never be old enough for it, like you are. We both know I'm right.

That's stupid. That's just stupid—you can't say that! You can't talk like that. Come on, love, why are you looking so—what's got into you with this? You'll be just great as a teacher. You'll be brilliant. You'll be fine. Why don't you tell me what's the matter?

God, I don't know. It's suddenly become too much for me. I'm not like you. I can't do it.

Of course you can.

And if I think about the other things—I couldn't do one of those other jobs. I can't imagine being felt up by some optometrist, him touching me. Then: Oh, sorry . . .

Theresa laughed through her lips, a dismissive expression: Don't be.

It's just that I have to perform in front of them; every time I move to the window to look out they are watching me and it has to mean something; everything has to mean something. I'm sick of standing up in front of them. I never got used to it, not like you.

What makes you think I find it easy?

You do. It's obvious. You've always got something ready to say; you've got things always hidden up your sleeve . . . Theresa opened her mouth but said nothing now; in fact it seemed almost as if she made several false starts simply to prove Diane wrong, to show that she was floored momentarily by the observation. Diane said, I don't even have anyone to marry.

Oh, Diane.

I just can't quite see how I'm going to get on.

Love, you never seem to care about these things . . . ?

I have no idea. I mean I have no idea . . . There was something she was reluctant to express, a sense of struggle, a disbelief in the very politeness that seemed to be expressed in the representations of the early settlers, and seemed still to overlay everything; a sense that under all this was the struggle of living or of making a life or even something so simple as remaining alive, a struggle taking place secretly in everyone, and didn't she in some way want to force an acknowledgement of this out of Theresa? Instead, she found herself slumped in front of her friend, letting her head fall to a level below hers, despite her greater height, and letting Theresa's hand sit, comforting, on her knee. She almost said: It's not me, it's not just a problem with me . . . She found the words, the argument, circling in her mind while instead she stopped, Theresa stopped, and they sat for some moments more—how many moments?—the book open on Theresa's knees.

It was some time—some days, perhaps weeks—later that Theresa approached Diane with a suggestion: I know what I can do for you . . . Since their conversation, she had had a new, sidelong glance for Diane as they met or parted company. She said, Why don't you come out with Glen and me? You can . . .

Glen?

Yes, my boyfriend. You can . . .

Your boyfriend?

Yes, I've been with him for . . .

Why do I never really know a thing about you?

What, Glen? You must have known about Glen?

No. No, I didn't. You kept him good and secret.

Well, I just thought . . .

You keep so much secret. How can I not even know you had a boyfriend?

Listen, come out with us, you can . . .

For God's sake, Theresa!

You can meet his friend.

Well, that all sounds very nice.

Come on, Diane, I'm sorry. It just never came up, I guess.

Never came up!

Theresa said, Oh, by the way, did I mention my boyfriend? Did I mention that I've got a boyfriend? I've got a boyfriend now. Lovely. Let's have a cup of . . .

You could have told me; if you were excited you would have told me.

Maybe it was none of your business.

God! . . . She reeled for a second, stepped from side to side and looked away from Theresa whose hand was still hanging forward, half in its outstretched greeting from the beginning of the conversation. Now Theresa looked at it, and it dropped. Diane said, Okay . . . Then: It is none of my business. You do what you want.

Yes.

And with whoever.

Yes . . . Diane lifted her hands and let them fall again; she began to move away, on the way to her room. Theresa said, Please come with us some time? In the weekend?

For a moment I looked at the surface of the water and the fingers of breeze which for a second blew across it then faded, leaving inverted branches of the trees opposite; what had seemed like a still harbour was in fact only a pond on the heath, navigated only by ducks and surrounded by park benches thinly occupied by single, preoccupied people such as myself. Hampstead Heath felt like a quiet, familiar place, the one place where there wasn't a frenzy of walkers and drivers. I had with me a note pad and pencil and sat next to the ponds trying to make sense of what Diane had told me and shown me over the previous two days, and my hastily scrawled confused notes with their unfinished sentences, imagined scenes and descriptions and fragments of history and memory. I shook my head, hearing Diane's voice and confusing it with Mantell's and wondering at the hidden effect of Gideon's eye on his son's view of the new colony: the bones under the surface of the land, and at Diane's own interest in the same bones.

A surprisingly hot sun was etching shadows from trees and benches into the grass around me, black empty spaces which only became blacker when I stared into them and, when I closed my eyes, still took on the shapes of shadows in the after-image. I noticed a woman sitting, like myself, on a bench across the water, reading intently—was it the woman who had visited Diane on the day I had arrived? The notes I took seemed to start and stop at random, to be a messy collection of confused stories. I was having difficulty distinguishing between what Diane had told me and what I myself imagined; I was having difficulty remembering and noting down correctly what she had said, and what separated her ideas from my own ideas; for a second I wanted to shake her voice from my head, and considered throwing the notes in the water or dropping them in a bin. I stood up. I needed to walk, not sit and take notes—I had been sitting and taking notes in my mind for the two, or was it already three, days since I had arrived, and was at the same time still fighting off the exhaustion of jet-lag. I would sleep better after a long walk—after a decent amount of exercise. I looked across towards the woman sitting opposite. I was sure it was the same woman, but her face was in shadow, and it seemed all at once as if a cloud had passed across the sun and put everything, the pond, the trees, and the passers-by, under the same shadow, or under a harsh frown.

What would I say to her when I approached? Nothing. I turned and walked along the edge of the pond, and kept going away from the woman with her book.

The colour of the grass was dampened by the dust which seemed to emerge from between its roots to cover every blade, and also to dampen the colours of other surfaces. Before I had left the apartment to walk on the heath Diane had been talking about a recurring dream—was she aware of the dangerous implications of giving too much importance to dreams and reporting them as part of a narrative? She had told me the dream in the same tone she had used when telling me her stories of Mantell—was it all in some way implicated in a greater story? And did this story therefore take on the quality of dream? She said that Peter approached her but seemed to hesitate before talking. This was strange, she said—Peter never hesitated, at least not an open-mouthed, doubting hesitation. Instead, if he took some time to speak, once he had decided to speak there was no stopping him. Then, she said, I see that he is not talking to me but to our daughter Meri—I am all at once outside the picture looking in at them talking and agreeing and then turning to look at me. Then they're on a boat on an ocean that is also a bleak landscape, and I'm there on the boat. No—they're on another boat and I'm following them, looking at them through a telescope at the horizon where there is a city, and they're climbing a tower; she's crying—she's afraid of the height. A staircase with no railing runs around the outside of the tower. He's dragging her up the tower, and I don't know whether it's an act of love or an act of cruelty; he had with him a case of brass instruments. The crying was real—the first time I dreamed this, when Meri was only three years old, I woke up to her crying; her real crying had entered my dream from the next room. In the dream, the horizon that I could see through the telescope—the city and the tower—never came any closer. But in any case I was fixated on something else, on the mountains behind the city . . . She had watched me while she related the dream, and I had the sense that she was watching to make sure I copied down its details correctly.

By this point, my notebook had begun to fill up, not only with notes relating to Diane's Mantell project, but with details of another life: Diane's own. I understood that her watchfulness as she told me the dream was the same as her watchfulness as she told me things relating to herself—if there had been a loose contract, an understanding between us that I would help her with the book on Mantell, or at least look seriously at its material, then these looks signalled a testing of the boundaries of that understanding, forcing more and more into the agreement until I was to find myself writing about whatever entered her head: not only the Mantell book, but her dreams, her thoughts on her relationship with her husband and her daughter Meri, her thoughts on everything, her thoughts on the price of groceries. All the while, road works of some sort, having started some time after I arrived, had been going on outside the window, and she winced at each new noise of the pneumatic drill or whatever other machine. Maybe, I thought, it was just the racket that was making her nervous? Or wasn't there in her voice a hidden edge of aggression? Now, I found myself walking faster with the thought of Diane in my head, wondering what I had got myself into and how I could back out of the project before it expanded out of control, and before I disappeared into it pure and simple. At the same time I still found myself thinking back and forth over what she had told me, thinking back and forth over the notes I had taken, ordering them and trying to make something, not only out of Mantell's story, but out of hers. Perhaps it was too late, and now that I had been exposed to her talk, her confusion of fragments and starts, there was nothing for it but to order them, try to simplify them, if only to keep them from buzzing uncontrollably in my mind. If I had entered into some sort of contract against my will—and I baulked at the idea, and the idea of her waiting back at her apartment for me to return—then, I thought, didn't the contract hold nonetheless?

It was in Peter's car, newly bought and still with a smell of polish, on a Sunday, sunny but with a wind from the east; Theresa drank in the breeze; she laughed and Diane heard the rhythm of her laugh in time with the engine and the wind and in time with the shadows of trees which fell across the windscreen, her talk drawing them together, except for Diane, who, on the car trip out to the rocky beach to the west of the city, found it difficult to say anything. Peter was a friend of Glen. Diane winced when the men looked over their shoulders at them and when, with Peter driving and looking at her, the car seemed to steer itself. The valley swung around; clouds were raked out over the tops of the hills in unravelling fingers which only obscured the light for a moment before disappearing altogether; and finally the stream they had been following turned away from the road, ran hard up against a headland at the far end of the beach where the waves—once they were out of the car and standing on the shingle—chewed up the pebbles with a sound of loose bead necklaces swaying against one another. Diane felt the sound in her abdomen, buoying her up from there; suddenly impulsive, she grabbed hold of Theresa's hand and Glen's: Who's for a swim?

The others looked at her and withdrew their hands and put them in their pockets or folded them against the spray and wind that hit them face-on. Peter looked at her, wide-eyed and smiling, and shook his head: Well, you're a live one, aren't you!

We didn't come out here to swim, love . . . Theresa also smiling at her and Diane felt herself blush before she turned away. In fact the thought of a swim horrified her and she could hardly believe that she had suggested it; she reminded herself suddenly and surprisingly of her father with his jocularity and determination to throw himself bodily into any situation. They walked for some distance along the beach as two couples, Theresa and Glen lagging behind and then, when Diane looked over her shoulder towards her friend, she noticed that they had silently turned back and were walking now away from them. Theresa leaned her body towards Glen's and matched him so closely as to appear, for a second, little more than his outline.

Peter stopped and said, Well, look at those two. They're off. There's no holding them back . . . Then: Are you really going for a swim?

Do you want to? Do you want to walk into the hills, like them? . . . Diane was aware of her breathlessness in asking.

Is that a loaded question?

I don't know what you mean . . . Theresa and Glen were already some way towards the far end of the beach, the sliding crunch of their footsteps somehow reaching Peter and Diane through the sound of the sea. With Peter beside her unmoving, she stared after them. Once Theresa turned her head as if to catch her eye, though she was by now too far away for her eyes to be made out clearly, and gave a gesture that could have been: follow us—but at the same time seemed to be: stay where you are.

Diane turned to Peter, took his hand, pulled him towards the waves, let go of his hand (he allowed himself to be pulled, then stopped) and, with a single movement, though it felt utterly ungraceful to her, Diane slipped out of the dress she was wearing, dropped it, looked down at her body, turned away from Peter and ran into the water with a look over her shoulder that she imagined emulated Theresa's look of a few seconds ago. The shingle sloped down steeply; a wave caught against her thighs and pushed her backwards for a second like her own amazement at herself, which pushed at her sternum and her neck, made her want to double over and made her want to stand straighter. She clenched her fists and imagined the stretch of the land on the farm. At the next wave she dived under; she felt encapsulated by an unfamiliar muscular energy; the water's surge, the roll of pebbles and their feel under her feet all combined with the feeling of endless sky, so that she felt at once stormy and stretched out. Looking back, she saw Peter take off his shirt, slowly; she felt a pull under her feet and, all at once, a panic in her stomach which spread out and made her raise, first her elbows, then her arms towards him. Then the water drew back and she was standing, scarcely up to her waist. A smaller wave pushed then pulled at her and without looking behind her she walked out of the water.

Oh, now. I was just coming in.

You're too late.

He shook his head, stopped, laughed easily. He said, You're ... Then his expression, broad, his head thrown back and to one side, faded: I don't get it ... He seemed for a second thrown, his arms raising slightly at his sides then falling back, his eyes squinting then blinking once, before his face took on once again an amused expression that now, all the same, seemed forced. Diane felt pushed now not by the waves but by something from him: an awareness of his upper body, bare and bulky, held uncomfortably all of a sudden—his shoulders slightly shrugged?—and in front of it hers, also almost bare, also with a new, unaccustomed bulk. She crossed her arms, a stranger to herself, wondering how she could have thrown herself into the ocean, what part of her had suddenly emerged nervous from her gut and as soon disappeared. Now he was grinning widely, almost as if pained.

She said to him, I'm only two-thirds your age.

Slightly more.

Well, we know each other's ages already.

What else do you know?

You work in the same insurance company as Glen.

He frowned: And . . . ?

That's all. Maybe that's quite a lot since this is the first time we've met . . . Then, shaking slightly, wondering if he noticed the shivering of her chin (was she simply cold? She was still standing in her underwear, facing him with his shirt off, feeling the water's feather-trickle in drips down the sides of her torso), she said, You don't like the work. You don't like to be in an office.

She thought, still somehow it was she, who even then preferred to stay indoors, who rushed into the ocean; what was it that made people change into their opposites?

He said, Then there is something we have in common.

What?

You don't like the teaching, do you? Neither of us likes what we do.

She told you . . . ?

What do you want to do, Diane?

What did she tell you . . . ?

Don't you dream of something else?

I don't know.

You've got to have something you dream about?

I don't know.

Diane moved past him, almost ducking under the level of his armpits as if he were there to present an obstacle; she picked up her dress and turned back towards the sea and towards him. He had also turned towards her and was unbuckling his trousers and slipping off his shoes without undoing the laces: Come on, Di, come on into the water again. It'll be good for you.

She stood with the dress in her hand, looked to the side and saw no sign of Theresa and Glen; instead two fishermen were walking along the beach, each carrying a small wooden crate. They laughed and looked away and one hoisted his crate under an arm and onto his hip and touched the other briefly on the back. Now Peter was standing in his underwear; he approached Diane and took the dress from her, carefully folded it and leaned down to place it on the ground where it had been. She was moved by the sight of his hands (and a sudden memory of their softness when, earlier, she had taken hold of one) and the dress folded by them into a square stack of fabric with one hand underneath and another on top, spread out flat; a feeling that her own hand would be tiny in comparison although she was tall and long-fingered. Briefly, while he was still bent over—it seemed to be expected—she touched his back at the base of his neck, where his shirt had previously covered the few raised points of vertebrae. His shoulder blades slid together towards her palm as he straightened slightly and he said, Thanks . . . She wasn't sure what to say. She suddenly felt as if she had noticed him for the first time, didn't have to put on an act for him and pay attention only to herself. When he stood her hand stayed for a moment on his back, but then it raised past the level of her elbow and it began to seem as if she were reaching up to him and she pulled it back as from a fire and stepped away. Without looking at him she walked towards the sea and into it.

He dived under and swam out further than she had been. She felt herself once again pushed back then forwards by the waves' stacking-up, advancing and draining. She dug in her feet and wondered what she was doing here—in the water, at the beach, with Peter, or even in the city. For a second his head was visible as the dome at the top of an approaching wave in silhouette against the water (which had become fire with sun along its upper edge), then it fell back some yards away. She ducked, let the surge wash over her head, let her feet slip slightly and dig themselves further under the gravel, and stood up straight again. Peter was nowhere to be seen. She shook her head: why this? He would of course emerge from the water at some point—closer, further away—but still she felt the requisite fear, began to imagine the worst, sensed his body somewhere under the surface (which, for a second, was flat and visible, it seemed, all the way to the horizon, before the surf once again raised itself like the water's many shoulders lined up behind each other) and imagined him dead; that is, the thing which would brush against her legs would already be his waterlogged cold body, which would make his grasping, the thought of his touching her, the thought of her touching him—running the same hand dispassionately down his back and counting the bones—at once violently revolting. Though she could see him coming before he grabbed at her ankles then let go and shot up with his arms in the air, still she shouted and stepped back—not from surprise.

She said, Why do people always have to play these games?

Again she walked back and up onto the beach.

She put her dress on over her wet skin. The sun was hot enough and the wind hotter still. He followed and sat beside her, still in his underwear. He said, Did I do something wrong?

I don't know what you mean.

Did I do something wrong?

How could you do something wrong? . . . Then: No, you didn't do anything wrong. This is just . . .

The sea-smell hit them with each of the water's advances, and Diane once again felt amazed, now sun- and wind-warmed, that she had been not only near to, but had crossed, the water's edge. She rubbed a hand over her eyes. He looked at her and touched her awkwardly on the cheek, then rubbed her earlobe. She said, I'm not normally like this.

All right. Maybe we should start again. Just be you.

She said, I can't . . . She said, I don't know who I'm doing this for.

Doing what?

She shifted backwards so that she could see him more easily, then twisted her back and neck towards him. His face was motionless, even at first when she kissed his lips—they were soft, closed, his jaw quivering slightly. Then they opened and, when she received a kiss in return, she pulled away. She said, You do seem very nice.

He smiled. His mouth opened in a quick expression like a gasp, then he laughed and said, Thank you . . . He laughed again, stood up, sat down, and after a minute said, So do you, Di. Well, I know you're not normally like this but all the same . . . He turned to her now and kissed her again.

*

95

Peter surprised her once outside the foyer of the hostel and said, Come for a drive . . . They walked out towards his car, into a day of swaying trees with their leaves rattling and a wind that picked up papers and dust and deposited them with violence against the sides of buildings and in hollows and the corners of walls, until, as they walked, a light rain began and weighed everything down. The landscape opened up for them from time to time, a view across to the west and the hills with each shadow darkening, with low cloud spelling out its trajectory above and, it seemed, radiating towards them. It was already months since she had first met him, and she knew him well enough to understand that he had something to say; he found it easiest to say something serious when walking or driving, though when the time came to speak he might take a few quick steps ahead of her, turn and stop. Now he walked absentmindedly, making a noise from time to time like a sigh and paying little attention to where he was going. They walked together out of the hostel grounds and onto the street, then turned and turned again before finding the car. He said, I'll always remember that first time I met you. Would you like to come to the beach again quickly?

Yes, all right.

She let him drive in silence and with his head tilted forwards and his shoulders hunched so it looked as if with each turn of the steering wheel he shrugged; he tapped the wheel as if beating out time to a song. She said, Yes, Peter, it was lovely, that day . . . She put a hand across onto his forearm and he blinked several times and his mouth softened and fell open slightly. She said, I won't go swimming this time . . .

He laughed.

In fact she did remember the day of their first meeting, their first kiss and their second, as a lovely, thrilling day, although she had not forgotten the nervousness, the feeling of being thrown suddenly into something and the small starts and reversals of her conversation and her actions that still made her blush to think about them, her confusion when faced with him—a confusion also that had not entirely gone, even today with him sitting next to her, a confounding presence—but all this added to that day's mix and amounted to a shock that could only be positive and exciting, because it forced something into existence that was different from what she came, quickly, to think of as her 'other life': the classes, her fellow students and the life of the college and the hostel.

At the beach the rain was still sparse and blowing in with small misty drops, and surf constantly spread itself along the shingle, which was dark with the water and seemed to be covered with a solid slippery sheen. The few houses seemed to hunker down, and tussock on the hills whipped back and forth as if enraged, while waves at the headlands threw themselves up and fell back on the rocks with spray that merged with the rain. There was no one in sight; the beach was an empty landscape to be filled, Diane said to me, with their own thoughts or dramas. With Peter, holding hands, she walked past the headland at the southern end of the beach and up a slope into the farmland. At the top of the hill where the paddock flattened against a sudden cliff they closed their eyes against a wind that seemed to be filled with ice; he leaned down to kiss her and she let him. He was warm; she enjoyed his presence beside her and enjoyed also his momentary quiet as she looked away from him and out to sea where there was no horizon, only a cloud that rolled then fractured, spread itself in the distance against the water's surface and seemed to tear up water into itself then release it again as rain. Water was entering the neck of her coat; her hair was wet and clung against her face and neck and she felt pulled down by it, and pulled to follow Peter, who, equally wet, continued walking away from the beach and along the cliff-top, leaving her behind for a second.

He turned and proposed to her and, hardly thinking, she said, Yes.

They looked at each other, still now, and the sounds around them seemed magnified. He said, You accept?

Yes.

You do?

Yes.

I thought you'd put up a fight. I thought I'd have to really twist your arm before you'd . . . Now he took her by the arm and pulled her into a quick stride in the direction they had been taking, only faster. He said, I wanted to ask you the last time we were together but, still, I'm glad to ask you here, you know, where we started. God I was so sure you'd have nothing to do with it. I've been sleepless thinking about it, asking you.

That night, Theresa sat across her small room in the hostel and reacted with a slow smile that spread and eyes that seemed pained. She said, Married? Listen, love, that's, it's great news.

When I've finished college. We haven't got a date yet but it'll be some time after that.

Theresa said, I'm in shock. I didn't think it would happen like . . .

I'll move into his new flat with him. You know, he's living in a new place.

Then: Is it what you really want?

What do you mean?

Oh, Diane, you're so, you're a good girl and, did you know Glen asked me to marry him too?

Diane raised her eyes to Theresa's face now from their focus on the floor between them. She said, But you've hardly seen him lately.

I told him to bugger off . . . There was a silence for a few seconds, then she said, It felt wonderful. I even said it just like that, and it felt so good . . . She began to laugh and Diane also began to laugh in time with her, feeling her forehead rise and her whole face rise; then she shook her head and looked down. Hadn't there been something about Peter's quick turn to keep walking, after she had said yes, that was too sudden, making Diane feel like she had no choice but to follow his steps, strangely deflated, or simply confused by the repeated assault of the new when of all times, dripping, half-running then actually running with him down a short slope as if, with the water under her coat and the expansiveness of their movements, she were diving once again under an ocean's surface, of all times she was supposed—wasn't she?—just to be simply elated?

Theresa said, I thought he was going to cry, it was awful, I felt so sorry for him . . . She forced out a few more laughs and Diane's face was still frozen in a smile. She said, But I couldn't do it, I just didn't want to spend my life with him. I felt like I'd used him up.

Theresa! That's . . .

Isn't it? He was okay; he didn't know what to say but he'll be fine. I've even seen him going about with some girl in town, you know, and they look to me like they're already married, and I see them together and just feel like I've escaped something dreadful.

I don't know why you're telling me this.

Theresa said, I didn't want to end up like my parents; they just fight all the time . . . She was looking at Diane and she began to laugh again. She said, If I think of the photo of them when they were married, they still keep it on the mantelpiece, and they looked so hopeful and, well, they looked like beautiful people. They've made each other ugly. Stupid old . . .

That's not funny, I, my parents are fine together. And Peter's . . .

He's what?

Why are you talking to me like this when you should be happy for me? I thought you'd be happy for me; it's good news. I . . .

You what? . . . Then, after a pause: Look, I'm sorry. It's great news, it really is, love. I just hope he's right for you. Well, I introduced you to him so I hope it works out okay.

I can't wait around for ever, Therese.

You're so young.

No, I'm not. Don't talk to me like that.

God, love.

You know I haven't got a choice. But I want to marry him.

Sorry, Diane, I didn't mean to upset you. You'll be fine with him. You'll be fine. I'm really happy. And if you need anything . . .

Yes . . . They sat together in silence for another minute before Theresa stood and walked across the room in two steps and, reaching to the wall, flicked on the light against the increasing dusk which had been finding its way into the corners, throwing shadowy light against the west's red cloud and the darkening contours of land.

Narrations (3)

The harbour water's slap on the sides of the ship with its slight tilting movement, and the cries of gulls which echoed in question and answer across the harbour, ringing through a porthole which was occasionally darkened by their passing shadows—these sounds were interrupted by Eyre's distinctive knock on the door.

Mantell? The natives want to have another discussion . . . Entering the low room with a stoop, he peered at Mantell from under a creased brow. He said, I think you should talk to them, since you'll be dealing with them from now on. There are more of them; they've been arriving for the last day or two from the surrounding country.

Mantell said, I should talk to them?

Yes, Mantell, that makes sense.

Very well.

Taking a copy of Kemp's deed with the associated plan, and accompanied by Wills, he took a boat ashore. The natives had been gathering in camps at Akaroa and staying at Opukutahi across the harbour, and now assembled in front of the town. A larger crowd faced him this time; more of the Ngai Tahu from further afield were represented. Wills and Mantell listened to their greetings and speeches in silence.

One of the chiefs, a new arrival from down the coast, confessed to having signed the deed, but said that this placed him in a minority. Indicating the map of the deed area with its lines stretching all the way to the west coast of the island, he declared it to be a fabrication, declared that none of them had seen the map at the time of signing, and that in any case the land on the other coast was not theirs to sell—that, while the Crown had bought their land to the north from others, now it had bought others' land from them.

Mantell said, Kemp, Eyre and Grey are all perfectly satisfied with the deed, and it only remains to survey the reserves outlined in it . . . When the chiefs asked to see Eyre once again, he said, Eyre is on board the ship. In any case you will have to deal with me from now on.

Again, one of the chiefs said that the deed was a lie, and that none of them had ever seen the map attached to it.

Mantell said again, Eyre and Grey are satisfied with it, and they understand it to be the area sold. And in any case I'm in no position to discuss the map with you. Kemp isn't here, and I am only here to set aside reserves for you. I can't do anything about the extent of the purchase. Eyre won't speak to you now.

To Wills, after the crowd had reluctantly dispersed and the two of them remained for a moment on the shore: Why are they managing themselves in such a belligerent manner?

Don't ask me, Mantell. I'm only a surveyor; I only deal with the land.

The land! That's exactly the problem. What do I know about this map? Damn it, Wills, what do I know about any of this? For all Eyre's instructions, his repeated instructions—this much land for this many people, the reserves concentrated in so many areas—I have no idea what to do when faced with them . . . He signalled to the sailors by the boat to wait for a few minutes more before they returned to the *Fly*. He said, On board the ship Eyre was about to give it all to them, half the land included on this deed. Maybe I should have let him, and just translated? He is the Lieutenant Governor after all, though I dare say Grey wouldn't have been so pleased.

I couldn't possibly say, Mantell.

I've begun to worry that they understood me when I stopped him.

Oh?

The town was a small collection of buildings and fenced-in yards; the muddy spaces which passed for streets were deep with footprints of people and livestock, and overlooking everything the rock outcrops which topped each hill. Wills seemed for a second as uncooperative as the natives; then he seemed simply tired, caught permanently in a shrug or a yawn.

Two days later, at the end of Green's jetty, looking back along the town, Mantell saw Wills tighten his jacket around him on the beach under the hill with its church and stop to talk to a man half a head shorter than himself. The papers

103

Mantell held in his hand flapped in a wind that brushed into the town from the north-west: Eyre's written instructions, trying to pull themselves out from his grasp and, one by one, like the gulls that flew past and circled to the beach or to land in flotillas on the turbulent water's surface, take off and lose themselves. Instead he held them tight, crumpling them slightly and flicked them over each other to skim their words once again, hearing Eyre's voice in his head, though now the Lieutenant Governor was, with the ship, well past the heads at Takapuneke or further, outside the harbour, beginning to make its way up the coast. The haven was empty but for some whaling boats belonging to the settlers and a few to the natives set up in camps at the far end of the beach, from villages and pa around the harbour and peninsula. Now Wills moved away from the stranger and began to walk further from the town, now and then heavily waving his hat to one or another of the people he passed before looking back at his feet, and Mantell couldn't help wondering at the curve of his back, perhaps curved against the very gaze he was directing at him or, oblivious to Mantell, it was simply the half-finished gesture of a conversation with himself held and interrupted and resumed as he walked.

Like him, Mantell shrugged to himself, felt pinned down by Eyre's expectations, sat with his boots six inches from the water's surface and quickly sketched out the lines of the town, including Wills, who was less than a pencil smudge at its furthest extreme now.

Mantell walked back to the hotel; there, the owner was sitting outside talking to a group of whalers who sat in a circle around him listening to stories of his own whaling exploits. The owner himself cast an eye in Mantell's direction, winked in mid-sentence and carried on as he entered the building—Mantell pictured the men behind him slapping the ground with their laughter, mouths hanging open even after they had become silent. Upstairs, in the room overlooking the shore and the group of men from under a steep gable, he sat by the window and now began to sketch the view from it, including the men's faces, then, turned towards him, the face of a native woman who sat just outside the circle. Then he put down the sketchbook and began to wonder about the following days. It was one of the whalers in the group below who had agreed to take them to the head of the harbour with the Ngai Tuahuriri chief who would guide them. Wills passed the men, and the native woman who sat as if she were owned by one or all of them. He awkwardly raised a hand to them but without looking up and, a minute later, during which Mantell heard his heavy footsteps on the staircase, joined him by the window.

He said, It's getting windier, Mantell. I was talking to a man who was worried about losing his livestock on the hill—he said he wanted to keep his cattle inside but there wasn't enough room in his cottage. There's a life for you. He approached me and started talking, just like that. I think the arrival of our ship was quite the event . . .

Mantell said, Yes? Well, I'm sure.

I think he was German, from his accent. He just walked off when he had finished, and he realised I had nothing to say on the matter. Did he expect me to give him advice?

I imagine so, Wills. He will have seen your thoughtful countenance, and said: There's a man who knows about cattle.

God, these people. Who'd set up a life here? Things must be less miserable than this in Germany, or France, or even England? I still remember Pall Mall, lit up magnificently, and the carriages and people in their finery. This all seems a half-hearted attempt at imitation, where the most imposing buildings are this hotel, with its drunken captain at the helm, and that dark little church . . .

Mantell said, Well, what are you doing here, Wills? In the colony . . . ?

You know: adventure, a new life . . .

The new Jerusalem?

God forbid. Who'd want that? Everyone thinking they're starting something new. New this, new that . . .

Quite. Maybe that obscene lot down there are the way of the future. Who do you suppose the woman is . . . ?

It'll be one of their wives . . . Mantell caught Wills looking at him; he raised an eyebrow, then looked at the window frame. He moved back and sat on a chair that occupied the far corner of the room, in beside the door, then leaned it back against the wall and closed his eyes. Mantell remained seated by the window, looking out over the heads of the group that was now starting to disperse, some coming with Bruce into the hotel, others heading away in the direction of the jetty. Wills said, They all take native wives, don't they? The whalers?

Yes, of course, you're right . . . Looking down again, he was unsure which direction the woman had taken; she didn't seem to be walking with the small group, three or four of them, along the shore. Had she entered the door almost directly under this window? Mantell wondered at her name, wondered whether she had a name, whether she had taken on an English name as many of the natives did. Now, as Wills remained silent, his breathing become steadier as if, impossibly, he had fallen asleep in his tilted position on the rough, somewhat precarious chair, Mantell fell into a memory of the woman he called Mary Ann. As their meetings continued the name was shortened to Ann, which felt altogether more comfortable on his lips. They had been

106

on the beach on the Porirua harbour with her walking one or two paces in front of him, as was her habit; she had turned towards him; only a faint sliver of moon cast highlights curved, like itself, onto the edges of things.

She had said, My husband knows I sleep with you.

Mantell had stopped and taken a step back away from her.

She said, I told him when he was angry with me one night; that shut him up.

It was the first time she had mentioned him, though Mantell had known of him, and it was as if this mention broke onto the beach bringing the camp, the work teams, the road with it.

He said, No. I can't see you any more then. He can't . . .

He does. He'll keep working. He wasn't happy about it but he won't say a word to anyone. He's in on the secret now . . . Holding onto his upper arm, she said, You're really his boss now.

Stay here. I don't want to hear this . . . He turned and walked away from her, but heard her footsteps behind him. He felt her warmth, although she was not touching him and there was a breeze which blew across the harbour and in between their bodies. He walked more quickly, looking down, seeing his moonlit shadow delineate the sand's contours with its edges, a silhouette of himself which became grotesque then minuscule as it dipped into a shallow ditch. Her own shadow hung about his knees, a head bobbing and lunging at him.

She said, He doesn't want anyone to find out any more than you do. I know that you don't want anyone to find out but nor does he. And I haven't got anything to lose either way; the worst he can do is kill me . . .

Mantell stopped.

She said, Don't worry, he wouldn't do that. What you

must think of us natives! You're as stupid as the officers—

He choked and turned and raised a hand involuntarily and brought it down towards her, and now in London in the sun I couldn't think this through; I couldn't quite believe it. I stopped walking in the direction I had been taking, down a slope which led gently towards the city centre, where I didn't in any case want to end up, and turned and began walking in the other direction. She was standing in front of him on the beach and her face angled downwards again, shocked or simply passive; she took a step back and stared at him for a second and put a hand to the side of her head. Her eyes widened and he took a step towards her, holding out a hand—she took one or two tripping steps back.

She said, Sorry rangatira, sorry it was a stupid—

He said, I'm not, I don't want to be—

Who else can I turn to?

It's okay. I wasn't thinking.

After two or three deep breaths, during which she frowned and looked away and nodded, she seemed to come to a decision. Was there a slight shrug, or a movement of surrender, a downcast look to her eyes? She reached and put a hand on his chest, moved it slightly so that the fabric of his shirt slid against his skin. She said, He can't touch us . . . Her hand slid, somewhat testingly, around to his back; her other hand also and she pressed her body against his, familiar, and he felt the small of her back underneath the shirt she was wearing, stiffened his face and shoulders then let them relax again. Something in her pulling now seemed forced, with little of the calm that he felt had developed between them and between their bodies. He kissed her but held something back, his mind going over what she had said and his own shock of anger.

He said, There's no reason to be afraid of me . . .

108

No, I won't be.

I don't want to be the rangatira.

No.

In the silence between them, he thought of her husband, who sat unmentioned, almost as a presence, as if he were watching them. It would be impossible to bring him up again—why had she in the first place? With the silence about him something returned to normal, as if he had never been discussed, but it gave that normality—the almost regular routine of their meetings—a new meaning; as if the honesty that had seemed to grow between them were revealed as a lie.

It was—wasn't it?—the last time they had seen each other. Some days later an officer arrived with a reprimand from Kemp, in his capacity as Native Minister, delivered in whispered tones to one side of the camp; and, after this, the woman never again appeared on the beach. He looked sidelong, given the chance, at the women accompanying the workers, and did he see her face, once or twice, amongst them? He frowned at the thought that he might not recognise her—almost as much as at the thought that she might be gone.

Now there was a knock and Bruce, the proprietor of the hotel, entered the room accompanied by the clattering of his boots and the scrape of the poorly hung door on the floorboards: Is there anything you need? The sun's getting low. We must be expecting the magistrate at any minute to join us for a meal. Come down . . . Without giving them time to answer he bowed, straightened and left.

The room was growing dark in its corners, anticipating the darkness outside which was coming up from the valleys and the water's surface when it wasn't broken through by a wave, sending across it a quick reflection of still light sky. For a time there seemed to be a brief lull: Wills had awakened, or at least now sat with his eyes open and his face staring flatly out the window which, from his vantage point from the other side of the room, must have afforded him a view only of featureless hillsides across the water. There was no sign of life in the town or elsewhere outside except, there, a whale-boat making its way in from the harbour mouth, some way from the town and not obviously headed in its direction: more natives?

At supper the magistrate sat with one of the local cattle farmers at the end of a table set in a sideroom; next to them Wills, his face contorted and waxen in the light of the lamps; Mantell was hedged between Bruce, who held position at the table, allowing himself to spread his arms wide as though claiming territory on its surface, and the captain of a shore whaling station who leaned across the corner, across Mantell, to talk to Bruce while Mantell, at least to start with, remained relatively silent, suffering the introductions, forgetting the names as they came at him, seating himself in a manner that seemed overly delicate in the circumstances, making him narrow and, he half-hoped, unnoticeable. For some time it seemed to work: conversation revolved around everything but their visit, instead focusing on the work life of the place, the whales that were towed ashore to the beach station west of the harbour mouth and the trade in the oil extracted from them. Slowly, however, the conversation seemed to implicate Mantell in his silence; it was being performed for him—surely the landing of the whales here was not news to either the captain or the hotelier, so what other reason to discuss it but for the benefit of their audience? The conversation turned, as if planned, to the subject of the workers, many of whom were drawn from the surrounding tribes. Then, abruptly, the captain leaned further forward and said, They don't know what they want. They don't know who owns what. We're doing them good just by being here, don't you think, Bruce?

Bruce said, They'll sell you something at one minute, then say the price was only rent the next. I've seen that sort of behaviour countless times . . . Bruce, though responding to the captain, was looking at Mantell.

The whaler said, I don't know what I think about his being here, do you? How many times do we have to buy the same land only to have the government take it off us?

Mantell turned towards the whaler and said, And where was your land again? I must make sure it's confiscated forthwith . . . He sat as if to jot down the details in an imaginary notebook held on his lap.

Damn you!

Bruce laughed and the whaling captain also grinned, if reluctantly, the expression narrowing his eyes. Mantell said, I'm just here to set aside reserves for them. I'm not here for any other reason than that.

See that you don't give them . . .

—and I've got strict instructions as to what I should lay aside. The whole thing will follow the correct procedure and be done—

Correct procedure! Look, they're good workers, but they don't understand any such correct procedure! Bruce? If it weren't for us they'd still be eating each other and—

Listen, I think—

They need to be told. I mean we've done them good, don't you think, Bruce?

Mantell said, I think we should get ready for tomorrow, we've still got some work to do before we leave . . . Then: Well, I'm only here on instructions anyway, from the Lieutenant Governor. He's quite clear on what he wants me to do. I haven't got any say in the matter, so if you want to take your complaints to Wellington you're most welcome to do so.

Mantell caught Wills's eye—he glared back then nodded, winked, and looked down at his food with disgust. The room was small, dark, and the smell of whale-oil combined with the smell of the meat, and was that also the smell of their companions and themselves, huddled together with their backs against the walls so that the serving girl—the same woman who had been outside?—had to press herself against them to set down plates and pots of wine and take them up again. Now moving flat against the wall she let a hand brush against Mantell's neck. Bruce leaned towards her, or towards Mantell. He said, They're good people, Mantell, don't get us wrong. They'll work like mad. They do have their own ways. They're not like your Ngati Toas.

My Ngati Toas?

They're altogether finer, if you ask me. They're good people.

The shore-station captain said, And we've been here a good deal longer than your Lieutenant Governor, haven't we, Bruce?

Bruce was drinking now and looking away as if he hadn't taken part in the conversation at all, and he breathed in deeply as if he might take in what little air was remaining in the room. The shore-station captain also looked away as if Mantell wasn't there. All at once Mantell felt a stronger need to stand up and leave the room, and even, though this was impossible, to leave the settlement that very night and cross the hills to the north on their way to Kaiapoi. He remained seated.

He said, Quite . . . He pushed his glass away, wanted no more wine or food and listened while the captain began to describe an incident: some years ago, at the time of the massacre to the north that had shocked the settlers and led to an increase in the town's fortifications, a Ngati Toa worker on one of the stations had been suddenly killed by the local natives. As Mantell let himself listen he felt increasingly ill. Finally, he said, Excuse me, I think we have some last preparations for tomorrow . . . He stood up, reached behind the whaler and tapped Wills on the shoulder; Wills looked away from the magistrate and towards him, also stood up, and together they left the room and climbed the narrow staircase—almost a ladder—which led to their rooms.

At the doorway to Mantell's room, the one where they had sat earlier, Wills held Mantell's arm for a second and whispered to him: What insufferable people! They wanted to tell me, endlessly, what to expect, how to do my job, how to do *your* job, how to treat the natives. And their endless stories of how they purchased their land!

I had the same treatment, Wills.

I stopped caring whether they were right or wrong.

They said the same things to me. They think we're going to take their land away from them.

How very tempting, Mantell.

Mantell laughed quietly and ducked into his room.

The next morning, the whale-boat lurched upwards on choppy water and Wills looked down at himself then up quickly, then fixed his stare down again at his body. As they passed the headlands north of Akaroa the more prominent trees swayed, a tearing sound accompanying their movements—or was it the water finding its way under the boat's hull then sucking out again as they were thrown onto the top of a wave? Then the head of the harbour, where they waded ashore with their guide and another native who was to accompany them, and where there were more natives waiting, so that accompanied by a group of eight they ascended a long sloping wooded hill ending on the north side in a very gradually sloping wooded flat. There, they were surrounded by trees, a combination of silver leaves and dark spaces in between, the whole somehow pointing downwards as if dripping with heavy rain—though today they were dry, and the wind whipped up air from the soil to meet each imagined raindrop. The forest, sparse, gappy, seemed to contain even in its gaps a wall; easily passed but resisting passage, gently asking to be overcome and brushed aside; each branch that projected out onto the track, pushed aside then flicked back, or the newly sprouted plants, all added to the friction. Although it was a well-travelled track—cattle had been driven over here some years before—with their passage Mantell felt as if they were discovering it anew, rendering it empty and simultaneously finding it again. One of the natives moved from behind to walk beside him. He was silent for a few seconds, and Mantell looked at him, and suddenly recognised him: his face was not tattooed, and he wore the clothes of a whaler; he had been in Wellington some years before. Mantell remembered coming out of the small cottage which served as both his living space and post office, and being met by this man, his trousers muddy as if he had been kneeling in the street, and demanding the mail addressed to him. A companion—a settler, or more likely someone from one of the whaling ships—stood at some distance. His name was George William Metehau, and Mantell had seen him around the town from time to time thereafter and each time wondered if he was drunk. Now as he walked his face seemed calm, smiling slightly, and he nodded.

He said, in English, You've come a long way since delivering the post, Mantell?

Have I just?

Tell me what your mission here is. Are you here to finally solve all the difficulties we had with Kemp? I've got rights to the north, by Tuahiwi. This is my real country. With the mountains on the horizon, always reminding me of themselves.

Mantell said, Kemp didn't set aside reserves for you—I'm here to do that.

Metehau said, Kemp didn't do much. He stayed on his ship and fed himself. So you're here to finish up his job.

Through the trees it was possible now and then to glimpse the bays to the north and the broad sweep of coastline above them, past which they had sailed on the way to Akaroa. Mantell stared into a dry wind, blinking and trying to make out the lines of landscape that reached into the sea-haze, ultimately overlapped themselves and became lost. Metehau said, Of course, Mantell, I never sold my land. I'll be pleased to have you as a guest though.

Thank you—you're so kind . . . Mantell didn't know what to say to him. He looked away to his right, and up to a view of the high cloud stretched across the peninsula. He owned land here? It seemed wrong; the flat country visible to the north seemed featureless, a faint smudge, hardly habitable, though of course he knew that people—Ngai Tahu and settlers with native leases—lived and worked there. He had trouble seeing the land as a place for rights; he had trouble seeing Metehau as a landowner; he stumbled slightly and carried on with the man at his side.

Metehau said, The berries of this one . . . Crouching and running a hand over a dense shrub at his feet, he said, You can eat them. They taste like juniper . . . Then: Of course, I've never tried juniper . . . He laughed. He said, You'll have to come back in spring to try them. And soon we'll come out of the forest—there's a better view from there, to the north, down into Wakari and beyond. The truth is, Mantell, I don't want you to feel unwelcome. I know that if we're reasonable with you you'll be reasonable with us and see our side of things.

All the same, Mantell didn't now want to have the man's company, though he seemed to be a different character from the one he remembered in Wellington. He said, Of course I can be reasonable. I'm here to be reasonable.

Metehau said, Good. Then there's no problem, is there?

Mantell laughed and shook his head.

Again Metehau said, Good . . . He said, I've heard some unflattering things said about you, but it doesn't matter. I don't believe them.

What unflattering things? . . . Now Mantell was aware of Wills close behind, listening to the conversation.

It really doesn't matter, Mantell . . . He smiled and touched Mantell lightly on the elbow.

By four o'clock they reached Mr Hays's house and crossed to visit the native settlement on the east side of the bay. Around thirty were gathered there and they remained listening to the speeches on the Ngati Toa boundary to the north until the light fell. At the head of the bay, or so they saw on the return trip to Hays's house, the water swept up along a muddy inlet, finding its way to the shallow extreme of a creek surrounded by a stand of trees. The next morning, struggling against daylight and the wind at their foreheads, they passed Mrs Sinclair's cottage; they climbed the hill, in forest, which separated Pigeon Bay from Port Levy. At the top, after some time on level ground, they emerged from the bush. On a grass hill they descended to a small kaika; from there they crossed in a whale-boat to Heaphy's house. These settler's houses with their pasture and gardens were nestled under trees—small cottages which, inside, tried to reflect something of the order of the civilised world, but still, where they had floorboards at all, were marred by muddy footprints. At night the water in the port was pushed back and forth by a heavy swell; waves that seemed to want to take the land with them, that seemed to copy the shape of the hills above and, when Mantell stood for a while before returning inside to his bed on Heaphy's floor, themselves seemed to stand still for a second, the points of white at their tips, thrown up and backwards with a peak of turbulence, reflecting the great rocks at the tips of the mountains. All this visible in the highlights which a narrow moon cast onto the darkness. The house smelled oily, and of hair, like the smell of someone's scalp.

Mantell, Wills and the natives accompanying them, after a Sunday's rest at Heaphy's house in Port Levy under a gale which continued out of the north-east and blew the harbour up against its shores with the overlap and crunch of breaking waves, took a boat across the water, now flattened with the new day, to Rapaki, and after counting the inhabitants and hearing some speeches continued up to the summit of the last range separating them from the plains. There, the lines of two distant fires swept across the view in front of them, glowing more brightly here and there for a second and sending up a pall of smoke that thinned and tore outwards, stretching over the land like a soft wash of watercolour, then puffing out and up before their eyes, dulling edges, giving the horizon with its glimmer of snow-capped mountains a feeling of obscurity. Their day's destination, Putarikamotu Wood, was a darker patch amidst the glowing water of the swampy plain with its rivers feeding into and out of the swamp, cutting across in a narrow, winding thread before opening to the sea. Gradually, as they descended a shallow, grassy slope towards the plains the view shortened, the mountains appeared to launch themselves into the sky so as to be suspended over the flat land and a swampy stench hit them then seemed to disappear, no doubt as their noses became accustomed to its presence. Wills walked with his shoulders hunched in front of Mantell, preceded by several of the native men, the two of them followed by more men and women in a line of single file, though there was plenty of room even on the sometimes awkward ground to walk two abreast, skirting cabbage trees, matagouri, and rocks that leaned or piled against each other or simply leaned into a gap beneath and beside themselves. At the edge of the swamp, where a moat ran around the base of the slope, Metehau and some of the other natives waded in, picked their way one by one up onto the drier land some metres on, and called back for Mantell and Wills to follow them.

Wills hesitated and turned his head away from the brownish, stagnant water; Mantell gave him a short push from behind, but hesitated himself; it had come no higher than the knees of their guides but the bottom was invisible, or was at most the suggestion of a surface under the surface, a further brown under the brown. The water filled their warm, already damp boots, sending the shock of its cold up through their bones and making them close their eyes for a second and breathe in sharply. Their feet dragged through the mud then stones at the moat's bed and they emerged onto mossy ground whose surface subsided with each step, allowing brackish liquid to fill from the depressed sponge into the hollows around their feet. At points where there was surface water, their guides kept them close to the trees and shrubs, which seemed to hold the ground solidly around them. In the spaces between, the water sat rippled by the wind but only a few inches below its surface undisturbed and, or so Mantell thought to himself, devoid of any life save for the occasional intrusion of their footsteps.

At a river the water came up to their hips and tugged slowly but heavily on their legs with each footstep, insistently flicking the material of their trousers and eddying away downstream. The shingle banks, solid after the spongy ground of the swamp, gave way to broad pasture, grass and the native scrub and ferns chewed down to harsh stumps by cattle, which sat in groups at some distance from the party. Finally, coming around the eastern edge of a stand of forest, they reached the small cluster of buildings separated by fenced-off yards with the forest edge nearby to the west; here the native pines each seemed to stand alone as if leaving a gap between itself and its neighbour, each reaching a different height and only coming together in the diffuse shadow that merged under their branches in the overcast light of the afternoon. Metehau, who seemed to have taken the role of liaison with Mantell, said in English: This is Putarikamotu. The Deans brothers are here and some of our hapu work for them.

A voice from one of the farmhouses—in fact only a small, four-roomed cottage—where a man stood under the shade of the verandah: Mantell! I was thinking you'd get here about now.

Are we expected?

The man said, I've got Mary to make us a meal. Come in. The natives can set up their huts and tents out by the bush ... Then: Of course you're expected. I'd heard you were in Akaroa, and coming this way.

Wills and Mantell followed William Deans, the older of the two brothers—Mantell remembered his face from Wellington and the stories told of him since his departure years before—into the farmhouse where a table was waiting and beds had been prepared for their arrival. Wills said, Thank God, a good meal. Thank you, Mr Deans—you will live on in our memory ... He bowed, stepped backwards, doffed his hat; his trousers dripped onto the floorboards, clung to his legs, and when he straightened pulled away from his skin audibly.

And Mary will dry those for you in front of the oven. Come on, get changed, and we will eat.

The brothers were, despite the difference in their years, almost identical—except that John, the younger, kept his eyes in contact with Mantell's almost constantly as if watching him, suspicious, hoping to find something out. William made expansive gestures and looked at the two guests only long enough to smile at them or nod and solicit the same in response from them: You've come to paradise! Of course, it's the paradise of the hard-working, but paradise nonetheless. We live a better life than anyone, in the old country or anywhere else.

The younger squinted at this and frowned slightly, then nodded as if only agreeing on condition that he didn't share his brother's enthusiasm. He said, We've hardly been disturbed for years. The natives come and demand payment for our tenancy, or sometimes they come to gather food or perform some ceremony—and then there's quite a feast. We employ some of them. But there's almost no one through apart from yourselves; we're on an island.

Wills said, And still your success is famous.

We make it work here because we keep it small. But of course we've got to sell our produce to someone.

The older brother said, And we make it work because this is the best land I've come across. After the meal I'll show you what's here.

Later, John Deans disappeared into one of the other buildings; the light had faded to a faint glow, casting the shadows of the trees towards them and sending, through the gaps, illuminated shawls of the faint mist which rose from the ground. Wills and Mantell, with William Deans, walked outside, the two guests choking slightly on the cold air. Deans said, This is the best water I have ever tasted . . . They stood for a second on a bridge which led over a stream to a stockyard, a shed and other buildings; beneath them in the water they could only see the occasional reflected highlight as if coming not from the stream but from a sky, visible beneath them through a gap in the land and shot through with silent, half-hearted lightning. Deans said, suddenly, downwards and almost to himself: John's heart is somewhere else—he won't talk to me about it . . . Mantell and Wills stayed silent; they searched out each other's eye in the fading light; Mantell wondered whether he should put a hand on the farmer's back as if to comfort him, or as if to steady him. However, Deans turned, apparently without the need for steadying, waved his arm around once again—how often had he made that singularly possessive, proud gesture?—then, walking away from the bridge, said, Even the natives know this place as a garden: the streams are full of eels, trout, crays and other fish; there are shelducks in the swampland; the forest is full of pigeon and kaka, quails, wekas—when I first saw this forest I knew it would be the place for me. I would die here.

Wills, following some paces behind, let out a whispered exhalation.

The sunburst from the wood had disappeared save for a single ray above their heads seemingly emerging from one of the trees—a particularly tall native pine whose foliage was confined to some branches near its very tip—and which, as they stopped and watched, extinguished itself and left them in what seemed like a sudden complete darkness, except that it led their eyes upwards to the grey–blue–violet gradation in the sky above, nearing black at its apex. The wide gestures of Deans's arms, the silence hardly broken by the footsteps of stock and the sounds of the natives whispering amongst themselves in their nearby camp, gave a sense of a literal island, as if the swamp had deepened and filled with ocean fish, its bed pushed down by the onset of night, its small rivers and currents, the occasional belches which emerged from the mud now merged into the swell, the spray thrown from the wave-tips, all of which had formed, along with the horizon only visible from the highest wave crest, the content of so many of Mantell's dreams since the first, long sea voyage: a dream ocean that was at once a bleak landscape. While he looked out into it he also wondered at the life of the settlers here, and the natives: the fertile pocket of forest, the source of so much food; and still the stale smell from the swamp—destroying the deep-sea illusion—swept across from time to time with its feeling of entrapment. How easily could a sheep break through its fence and make its way out, picking through the surface water, then fall and, finally, sink, letting its bones be preserved covered with a shrunken layer of skin?

He said, Have you heard of anyone studying natural history here, Deans? Has anyone ever come through looking for bones . . . ?

Yes, you're the moa man, aren't you, Mantell? I don't remember hearing of anyone interested in digging for bones around here. I'd ask again in Akaroa—might be the best idea . . . Then: Here, the orchard. Here, apples, peaches, plums, cherries. We also grow every kind of vegetable with success, and crops of barley and oats. And here, the forest provides more than enough wood for all our needs.

Deans stepped into the space between two trees at the forest's edge where tussock grasses came up over the level of their knees and, above them, groups of ferns came higher, brushing against their waists. The sound of talking, louder than before, echoed from the native camp in a long monologue. In darkness that seemed almost complete the leaves of the ferns and tussock were visible as grey sketches; the small cluster of buildings, the orchard and fenced-off yards and gardens, and the tents and huts of the native camp all had the illusion, in the dark outlines that presented themselves to view, of a quiet solidity, an impervious but moreover natural feeling as if they had sprung from the earth like the forest at whose edge they stood, undisturbed, eternal, unassailable. When Deans finally excused himself—he said, I must attend to some of the day's final tasks; even here, there's money, paper, accounting to do . . .—leaving Wills and Mantell leaning in silence each against a tree, side by side, surveying the small settlement in front of them and listening to the sound of the natives' talk but without making out their words, Mantell said, It is an attractive life.

I didn't believe a word of it.

Mantell said, I must say, I was convinced. It seems like a real Garden of Eden. Maybe this is what I imagined when I first set out from Britain—this kind of life. Don't get me wrong, I don't think I could do it. I'm not exactly a farmer.

Don't like the hard work? . . . Then: Why was he so determined to show us around like that? Something more than just pride, I can't help thinking. Is he trying to convince us of something?

Mantell said, Why are you here, Wills?

Just a job.

No, I can't help wondering, why *are* you here in the colony? Is there anything about the place that you enjoy?

A pause, then: It *was* just a job—I was employed to come to the colonies as a surveyor. I honestly can't remember what I expected. I guess the same things as everyone else—a break from the miserable existence of Britain, from poverty and the constant fear of cholera. Or it was just that it seemed like it was somewhere to go. And why not? Why not be anywhere? Why not be somewhere else? Nothing ties me to Britain. Nothing even to our gracious Queen.

Come, Wills, I know you carry her miniature next to your heart . . . Then: Will you stay?

Nothing will make me go back.

Nothing, Wills?

I have no attachments.

I know.

Wills started walking towards the native camp and the farmhouses beyond it, and Mantell followed, at first placing his feet in the other man's footsteps, then catching up and walking at his side.

Wills said, I suppose I used to want to explore, to survey the new land. Now I only do it because I'm told to and they pay me. All the excitement of the place has left me, if I ever had it. But you—you're here for other reasons, aren't you, Mantell? Governor Grey was impressed with your moa bones and he knows your father. And you're sending them back to him. You've hardly broken your ties. You can't tell me you've no attachment to the place.

I want to return as little as you do. I understand only too well your lack of attachment to Britain.

Wills said, Really, Mantell? . . . Then he threw up his hands, turned away again and continued walking.

In the native encampment the light from a fire reflected highlights of the faces arranged around it, threw out sparks and a circle of light that widened and shrank and yellowed the tents against the blue night and the deep spaces between them, while a flurry of movement surrounded them under their feet from behind and ran on, ratlike, towards the fire before darting to one side and into the tussock: a pack of weka running with slipping strides. Around fifteen people sat together eating from small flax baskets and one of them raised his hand, offering them food.

Mantell shook his head: We've eaten.

When they offered again, he again shook his head and waved his hand in a dismissive gesture. Two standing figures moved towards them as they walked past; one carried something large under an arm and walked awkwardly, swaying slightly; the other held the first by the elbow: Mary, the servant, and the younger Deans brother. They had been talking to another figure, a native who sat down completing a now silent circle, when the two Europeans left to join Mantell and Wills.

The younger Deans said, Mary likes me to accompany her when she deals with the natives. We were bringing them out their meal.

She said, Seeing as my husband laughs at me when I say I'm scared of them. Do you think that's stupid? John's good to me.

Their expressions were invisible, their forms mere outlines and the tray under Mary's arm glinted suddenly with light reflected from somewhere—the natives' fire or a whale-oil lamp lit in the window of a farmhouse—and the four of them walked towards the cluster of buildings. John Deans said, I hear you were asking after the bones of the moas—William told me. I tell you something: I talked to someone at Akaroa who'd seen a live one. Even the natives won't believe it, but I do.

A live moa? Around here? In the swamp?

No. Down south. He'd been inland from one of the southern whaling stations, God knows what he was doing in there, said he saw a huge footprint, then another, then another, and so on. It was in swampy country somewhere, some muddy hole in the mountains there. He said he'd followed them out of the swamp and into a forest—thick overgrown forest by the way he told it—and before you know it he startled a huge bird, taller than him. He said he'd left his shotgun with his camp and went back to get it, and by the time he returned the bird had gone off.

When was this? Where is he now?

Deans said, I couldn't tell you. He was coming through on one of the trading ships. He wanted to get a party together to go and hunt the bird, but as far as I remember the ship was heading northwards. I wasn't interested in going with him—that's not my sort of thing. You know, he was drunk but his story was true. He had this look in his eyes which I believed.

Just then Deans's own face came into a square of dim light projected from the farmhouse window, lit up all of a sudden, and he blinked, then fixed his gaze on Mantell's. The eyes showed a mixture of defiance and confusion, seeming to open wider and retreat backwards into his head, and flick gently, searchingly, from side to side. While Wills and the servant stood back, Deans stood opposite Mantell, put his hands on his hips, let them fall by his sides, then put them on his hips again. He said, I've heard a good many things about this country. The natives tell me of an animal the size of a small dog, with the body of a rat and the head of a bird. They told me it lives in a place inland to the south, past where the land is constantly ablaze. What do you think about that?

I don't know. Deans, I . . .

That's just an example.

I see.

A voice from somewhere—one of the other farmhouses—called, softly: Mary . . . ?

Mary said to Deans, Go inside, John.

Yes.

Once again Wills and Mantell were left alone. Mary walked across the small yard which separated the houses while John entered the house nearby: Good night.

Mantell heard Wills's breathing, then a small cough: None of it's true, of course, Mantell.

Mantell sighed. He felt a weight in his stomach as if having eaten the food from the farm he had been brought closer to it, committed to the place and its people, while Wills pushed and pulled him from where he stood at his elbow—though in fact Wills simply stood there, silent and unmoving.

When I returned to Diane's apartment finally after my walk in the park, clearing my head, there was no answer when I rang the bell. I didn't know what to do; I turned and looked out on the road and the road works, at the men shuffling from one side of a fenced-off area and watching a digger's claw strike against the edge of a hole in the road's surface with a shudder, then reach deeper in. From the vantage point at the top of the short flight of steps the road seemed like a landscape in its own right: the houses forming a brick sky against the harbour of asphalt, and above this sky another sky; then the drone of a car, the tap of footsteps. I shook my head and sat down.

The woman I had seen at the door of Diane's apartment, and whom I was sure I had seen sitting at some distance from me on a park bench, turned in from the road, pushing the gate shut behind her with a click like a thud. She said, Would you like me to let you in? You're staying with Diane.

I nodded and said, That would be nice . . . I said that I didn't know where Diane was; it surprised me that she should have gone out. The woman shook her head; she opened the door and started to speak, then stopped and entered the building, leaving me to catch the door and follow her before it swung shut. Once inside she stopped and faced me and spoke in a quiet voice, almost a whisper: She hasn't been herself. Listen, I think she got herself really quite worked up over your coming here. I don't think it's good for her.

I had no idea.

I think she was terrified of you coming. Have you been gentle with her?

What? How could I . . . ?

What have you been saying to her? She won't let on to me.

What have I been saying? Look, I haven't had a word in edgeways. She's done nothing but lecture me.

The woman paused. She said, She's upset, that's all.

I don't know what I can do about it. She said I could stay. I could always leave, find somewhere else . . .

The woman shrugged. She said, It was something about her daughter; she never talks about her daughter unless something is upsetting her.

I said, Listen, if Diane wants me to leave I'll leave. I don't need to be involved in her stories and dramas. I'll simply leave and she won't see me again. But I'm not going to be told what to do by you.

She stood for a second. I had been speaking quietly, much like her, but the sibilant sounds of the conversation had rung out up the four levels of the stairwell and seemed to drop back down about our ears in the silence. There was no other sign of life; the place, including Diane's apartment on the top floor—though even the door to it was out of sight from here—seemed to lack breath, to sit solid and sealed around us.

I said, Why was she talking about Meri?

I never know. But it's something that always upsets her

nearly to the point of breakdown. You know it's been years since they spoke to each other.

She told me.

Again she stood, then turned and walked towards the stairs. As I followed, she said, I'm sorry. But please be gentle with her . . . She was talking to the stairs and to her feet on them and, a pace or two behind her, I had to quicken my pace to hear. She said, You're the first person to visit her, from your country. I don't know that it's good for her.

I said, There's nothing I can do about that.

Yes, I know.

As we climbed the stairs I again remembered Meri at the funeral—it wasn't the last time I had seen her, but it was the time I remembered most vividly, even if my memory was somewhat confused, shocked by the feel of her lips one brief time and a hand on the back of her head, her hand on the back of mine, and, ashamedly, the feeling that I couldn't take my eyes off her, although her father had died; that I could hardly listen to her words, could hardly take them in, preferring to focus on her face and neck. At the top of the stairs, the woman opened the door to Diane's apartment with a key from her pocket. She said, I'll let you do the honours . . . She turned away again and let herself into another apartment directly across the landing.

Diane was in the lounge leaning back in the wooden chair with her arms back, her head also back and her neck forward in a position that seemed painful. She raised her head when I came in, said nothing, let her head drop back again, then raised it once more.

I said, Your neighbour let me in. I can leave you alone if you like. I can sit in the kitchen.

She shook her head; the movement was hardly perceptible. She began to cough, let her head fall, coughed into the air,

129

stopped, winced, appeared to swallow something (as if she had had something in her mouth the whole time, and had looked at me simply for permission to take it inside her). I sat opposite her where I had been earlier and immediately wanted to leave again, but stayed seated. She said, Can you help me to my bed?

Are you sick? Is that why you didn't answer the door?

She didn't reply. She looked at me and said, I don't know what I'd be doing if you weren't here. Do you know what I mean? I knew it was a risk letting you stay. I remember you only as a small child. You're different from how I remember—a stranger. You've only been here, what, two or three days? . . . She screwed up her face—against me? In pain? She said, I don't like feeling that I don't know what I would otherwise be doing, as though you'd changed everything, and you're not just a house guest. Help me to my bed and you can work on your notes in here. Just help me up, that's all.

I stood and put an arm around her back, pulled her up to her feet, let her drape her arm around my neck, rest the side of her body down the side of mine; I could smell her scalp. As we walked side by side with my arm around her back and under her armpit, buoying her up, her steps became firmer, her head dropped further to her chest, she coughed a few times then threw her head back and inhaled deeply. I let her lower herself off me into her bed, running a hand down my arm, gripping as she paused for a second.

I said, Your neighbour seemed worried that I was bad for you—that I was upsetting you in some way.

Judy! Did she say that?

She said that I was the first person from home to visit you here.

Diane laughed. She said, Yes! . . . She coughed. She said, Judy's worried you're going to take me away from her! Ha!

130

God forbid! That you'll make me so nostalgic for the place I'll have to return. Listen: I'm fine. There's nothing whatever the matter with me; I'm just having a bit of a, well—I just need a lie down.

Judy's your . . .

Almost too quickly she said, And? Oh, for God's sake. The look of revelation in your eyes . . . She said, So, here's your plot then: Diane marries someone she's hardly met, it all goes horribly wrong as anyone could have predicted, she's so traumatised she has to become a lesbian. Is that what you'll be writing now? That I couldn't handle another penis? Your family will love that—your family, my family. I should never have let you have this story; it was always going to be stupid interpretations, misinterpretations, misunderstandings if I let anyone else have my story. Why did I think I could trust you? Of all people, someone from back there, someone from my family—

No, I won't write that.

Yes, you will. It's too late anyway.

No.

You'll splash it about.

I said, 'Splash it about'? No one is interested. No one would read your story anyway. My family doesn't care about you; they don't think about you—hardly ever. I don't want your story. I don't want to have to think about your story and your research and your life, Diane. You can have it.

She said, That's right.

I said, What?

Have a go.

What?

It's good. Have a go.

No, I won't. Not . . . I remembered Meri, angry and crying at the funeral. Her father's death, Diane's husband Peter's

131

death had been a sudden, unexpected shock, finally revealed as a brain haemorrhage, alone, on the land, from which he hadn't returned one night but was found lying the next day, curled into himself with, I imagine, one of the large stretched skies of the area above him, the ground dry. I closed my eyes on Diane. I said, No . . . I turned and left her bedside, then turned again at the door to face her.

She said, I loved Peter. That's why I married him. I loved him until he died. And after that.

I said, Leave me alone. I don't need to hear any of your bullshit.

What?

You're really getting to me—I don't, I'm not sure I like it . . . I left the room now, remembering Meri again at the funeral and her face, once, reddened, teary, close to mine, closing her eyes. Out again in the lounge I breathed deeply; its light was a relief after the bedroom's close dark curtained space, its curtains drawn against the daylight and giving the impression of never being opened. My suitcase was in the room's corner, packed out of the way. There were still two days before I was due to leave for my conference; I was hardly thinking about my paper, which still needed a read-through, some last-minute revisions; I had hardly been thinking about my work, unable as I was to take my mind off Diane, her stories now complicated in my mind with an image of her daughter. I had been in love with her only in the most pained, adolescent manner, distant and intermittently obsessive and thrilled by the slightest company, nervous on our family visits to the farm. It had been nothing more serious than a crush, taking place mostly in fantasy, in the efforts to turn my body slightly towards hers at the dinner table and to be near her in small ways—but it seemed all at once complicated by a single kiss, a touch on the head at her own father's funeral, an event that seemed at once obscene and strangely out of my hands. It was, however, a long time ago, and now, if I was implicated somehow in Diane's family, even had once come close to her daughter, then those days were behind me and I had a family of my own that Diane knew, I realised, nothing about. I looked at my watch—it would be almost the right time to call; I tried to remember the effect of daylight saving on the time difference; I tried to locate the calling card I had organised before my departure.

The phone rested on the tiling at one end of the kitchen bench, the space cloying with kitchen smells of tea and cooking and a thin layer of grease or condensation, the feeling, suddenly, of other people's food. I stood by it for a few seconds before dialling.

My daughter's voice came on the line. I said, Hi sweetheart. I'm in London—do you remember I showed you pictures? . . . I said, Of course I'm coming home! Not for another week. Not for another few days, love . . . I said, What? Why did she say that? Of course I'm coming home. Janey, what have you been doing since I've been away?—At the Botanic Gardens?—Have fun?—Have you been going to school?—How is it?—Janey? Listen, Jane—Okay—Oh—Hi. Are things okay? I forgot to tell Jane I love her—I wanted to—You took the phone before I got a chance—Sorry; are things okay?—Normal? What do you mean by—Jane told me—why did you tell her I wasn't coming home?—We've already talked about this. Can't you see—Why do you have to—What's happening this morning?—God, yes. I forgot. I forget. I can't keep my mind on everything all the time. I can't constantly keep my, you know, mind on things—Listen, why do you have to go this early? Do you really have to go now? Aren't you starting at nine or something?—We've got to keep talking—Can I at least tell Jane I love her?—Can I at

133

least tell her—Yes—Come on, I—I couldn't not go, I couldn't not come. And this is the first time—I mean it was my first international conference. But I've said all this—We're going around in—Tell her I—Okay—Please?—Okay.

There had been a lengthy korero at each of the native settlements they had stopped at from Akaroa to the Deans's farm: at Pigeon Bay, Port Levy, then at Rapaki, and at each of the settlements their entourage had changed in composition, generally increasing in number as people decided to accompany the trip north to the ancient pa, though some of them also decided to leave at the settlements or disappear quickly, with brief words of farewell, while they were en route. The objections continued to the sale of land to the north of Kemp's block and Kaiapoi—the sale by Ngati Toa—and there were debates about who owned the land even within Kemp's block when many with title to the land hadn't signed the deed: if the owners didn't sell the land, would the Ngati Toa have the effrontery to sell even more of it? Thus they were split on whether to demand ownership of the land and refuse to sell altogether, or whether to sell it quickly to stop Ngati Toa from doing so—to stop them claiming not only the money but also the ownership of the land, sealing once and for all the conquest they had asserted years before when the raiders came down the coast, sacking the pa and coming secretly and murderously into Akaroa. If they sold the land, Ngai Tuahuriri would lose it to the government but gain it over Ngati Toa, and wasn't this a way to hold onto the land, even more strongly than if it wasn't sold?

In the morning the sound of discussion already rose from the native camp when Mantell, hardly after dawn, stood under the farmhouse veranda for a moment. Had they been debating all night? What could he do? While Wills stirred slightly inside—asleep? awake?—he thought, in fact Kemp had bought the land, pure and simple. If he was here to make that purchase good, then he had his instructions and couldn't afford to let the natives keep any claim apart from the reserves he was to set aside for them. And yes, he still remembered their cheers, 'his workers', as he rounded the bend, the tears almost finding their way to his cheeks, on the Porirua harbour, then turned with a feeling of sudden devastation. The Ngai Tahu had shaken their heads or hissed when he used the northern name for the pa, so that he had quickly changed his usage; and hadn't Te Rauparaha found occasion to claim that his rights ranged even further south than Kaiapoi, to take in the whole island? The land was owned, conquered, sold, reconquered, resold, owned collectively and divisively by one and all and Mantell shook his head and blinked against the light, and wasn't it good that, once and for all, the ownership should be established, the reserves laid aside, the conflict avoided through property plain and simple? This was reason enough—the establishment of lawful rights; the prevention of further encroachment by the northern tribe; the influx of the settlers who would come with a civilising influence, clear boundaries, capital, employment and development and new markets, new technologies and science to benefit Ngai Tuahuriri and Ngai Tahu as it was already starting to benefit Ngati Toa—reason enough for them to agree to the sale, as laid down by Kemp and completed by himself and Wills.

He set out across the field towards them with a strangely hot, damp wind in his eyes, sure he understood their position, sure he was able to follow his instructions to the letter and provide for the natives' needs, and open up this land to further development. And now the view, though in fact presenting nothing more than the fields and fences, the farmhouses and buildings, the wood, the curtain of haze out to the east, opened itself up to him as filled with life and potential: not the dead and desiccated bones of extinct species but the abundance of movement, of plenty, and his vision culminated in the imagination of these plains, despite the stench of swamp (which could, after all, be drained), as a cornucopia—which was then replaced in his imagination by the image of a slowly striding, impossible, upright, live moa.

Metehau shook his hand and said, Good morning, Mantell.

They stood at some distance from the tents and huts. A few natives lay in blankets on the ground at the entrance to one of the tents, and showed no signs of movement. Mantell, in the native language: I would like to get going.

Metehau said, You'll have to talk to one of the chiefs about that. I think we have to wait here.

Whatever for? I have work to do.

I think we have to wait while some more people from Waihora join us.

I can't just wait, Metehau. Can't you talk to someone? What's . . .

Metehau turned towards the small group of makeshift shelters, then turned back to Mantell. He said, I know you've got work to do, but you'll have to wait. We want to make sure you do the job properly. And anyway, you'll want to get as many signatures as you can on your document, won't you?

No, I won't have it. Can you talk to someone?

I couldn't approach the chiefs; you know us superstitious natives, Mantell . . . Now, whispering: If I came to him with a request like this I wouldn't live out the day. I couldn't set foot near his hut, it's against . . . He said, They are too great, these chiefs; their presence is too much for me. You'll have to talk to him . . . And, louder now: You're a Pakeha and a chief of sorts yourself and they will have to listen to you. But I think they won't tell you anything different.

Mantell walked quickly away from Metehau, to the centre of the space between the shelters where two women were preparing food. He asked for the chief who was, nominally at least, their guide. The women motioned to one of the two makeshift huts, little more than roofs; he leaned down and ducked his head inside to see the chief squatting in one corner eating from a flax basket. He stared at Mantell for a second before his eyes seemed to retreat into his face, and he smiled. Their conversation was quiet; Mantell in fact could hardly hear the chief's words, spoken in a high, soft voice, one that silenced Mantell further in the effort to follow them and their southern dialect. As he spoke, the chief passed across to Mantell the basket of food; then, when Mantell paid it no attention, he took it back and placed in front of him other items—artefacts of stone and wood—as if to illustrate the points he was making, perhaps to represent the players in the drama of meeting and discussion, of coming together of various hapu, of their journey to the pah site to the north. Mantell found the objects less than illuminating, seeming rather—as had the passing of the food and its retrieval—to be moves in a game. Each of Mantell's requests would be met at first with a silent shuffling of the objects, a presentation of them in a certain configuration, a meeting of their eyes over what seemed like a gaming surface, a presentation for Mantell to take in for a second or two before the chief spoke, his words increasingly seeming like an elaboration of the artefacts' message rather than the reverse. Was he expected to pick them up himself and shift them, or add pieces of his own? Mantell found himself struggling to keep up with the chief's long orations, his quietness, the elliptical nature of his words, and found himself asking at one point, in English, whether the chief could speak that language. This had been one of the chiefs on the boat when they had first arrived, with Mantell's refusal to translate Eyre's generous lapse; the chief didn't acknowledge the question.

After the meeting was over and Mantell had found his own demand complicated, silently rebutted, ignored, he passed Metehau standing close to the entrance to the hut, and, in fact, moving as if to enter it after Mantell had left. Mantell didn't think to speak to him, only a few steps later remembering Metehau's protest that he couldn't possibly be in the chief's company. Hadn't the chief himself mentioned Metehau? He had said, at one point, that Metahau had been a reliable advisor on the affairs of the Europeans thanks to his considerable dealings with them, in the north and on the whale-boats. If Metehau could be unreliable and impulsive, he was also experienced—they, the chiefs, listened to him with one ear, and kept the other to the ground. Metehau had told the chiefs that Mantell would, in any case, require more signatures to the deed than had been obtained by Kemp, so that it was in everyone's interest to ensure that more of the people from surrounding areas joined them and engaged in debate over the purchase. Surely this need for more signatures was inconsistent with Mantell's claim that the purchase was done, and that it only remained to set aside reserves? Surely he could see the need, therefore, to co-operate with them? Mantell had said that he never had any intention other than co-operation, but . . . And as he walked from the hut, wanting to find his notebook and quickly jot down the details of the conversation, he wondered how long Metehau had been standing there.

He passed a woman crouching, digging shallowly, and

beside her a small basket half-filled with the roots of ferns and other plants, who stopped and looked up at him; after a second transfixed by her sudden gaze he carried on past her, towards the farmhouses. The younger Deans brother was outside, crossing the bridge from the milking shed back towards the houses.

Mantell said to him, You know these people. Are they being deliberately disruptive? It's been argument all the way. In Akaroa, constant arguments, meetings, disputes, difficulties. I'm getting so impatient, Deans. I'm getting really impatient . . . He stopped at the near end of the bridge.

Deans nodded: I know . . . He looked around him—looking for prying ears? Simply surveying the settlement?—and Mantell also looked around, following his eyes and wondering, for a second, how he saw the place. He said, This is still theirs, in a way. Nothing's going to change.

Mantell said, What do you mean, nothing's . . . ?

Deans shrugged. He said, It's theirs and it's not theirs. We give them rent and they come here and have a feast on rent day. Did I tell you? They come here gathering food. I don't mind them. We've got a stable existence here and nothing about that needs to change. My brother is full of ideas of expansion and improvement and that's all a good idea but I wonder why we need to. Do you see what I mean? I think it's good to live with what you've got. Now, if you'll excuse me, there's work to do . . .

Mantell didn't know what to say; he wanted to say something to Deans's back as he walked towards the houses.

A few yards on, Deans turned again and said, If you put your ear to the ground in this place you can hear everything that happens for miles around. You can hear anyone coming. You can hear the animals moving. You can hear people's conversations from miles away as if they were happening right beside you. That's why I like it here. You should try it . . . He turned again.

Mantell crouched for a second, put a hand on the ground, and was that a vibration he felt running up his arm . . . ? then heard Wills, from the night before: None of it's true, of course . . . He stayed in position with his hand on the ground, and sure enough Wills emerged from the house, blinking around the yards before he spotted Mantell and came slowly over, picking his steps on uneven ground.

Mantell said, We have to wait, Wills. More natives are due to arrive some time, and we have to wait for them.

Wills shrugged. He said, What are you doing?

Mantell was still crouching, leaning to one side with his hand on the ground, and he looked up and felt as if he had been caught in the middle of something shameful. He felt his face give way into a tell-tale grin: John Deans told me . . .

That idiot!

He told me that if you put your ear to the ground you can hear everything for miles around this place.

Wills looked at him pityingly, kicked out a foot at him but only let it tap him gently on the shoulder, so that he lost his balance, almost fell backwards and, in the same movement, stood up straight. Wills said, Aren't you a man of science?

Perhaps a concentration of acoustic energies, Wills—in the manner of a whisper chamber? It doesn't sound impossible?

Try it then—go on. I won't stop you.

He watched Mantell closely, stood back, took a pace or two to either side and finally settled with his arms folded, leaning back and clicking with his tongue. Mantell was for a minute paralysed as if held fast by Wills's gaze. He said, This is absurd . . . He crouched again, looked around, looked up at Wills (whose expression was unchanged, or from below took on a still more mocking character), then looked to the ground. The dirt, still hard from the night's cold, was specked with moss, run through with the dying roots of grasses and ferns trampled by stock and human footprints, and crossed by miniature crevasses: here separating individual granules by their intricate tangles, there delimiting plains of perfect smoothness into geometrical patterns—in their depths, either long crystals of ice or a rich slime of muddy moisture, the one melting into the other and collapsing as he watched. The ground seemed to hold some of the night with it, a blackness that would never be fully erased from its pores and that, as he touched it, threatened to engulf his fingers with the same vibrating sensation he had felt earlier. He wanted to dive headlong into it, find himself underground, find himself pierced by the fingers of ice, and at the same time he thought he might lose consciousness—he looked up at Wills again and was momentarily blinded by the sky's light around him. He put his weight on his hands, leaned forward and, supporting himself on bent elbows, let his ear sink on his head bent sideways; even before it touched the ground was there a noise as of the footsteps of hundreds of people, shuffling on mossy ground and each heading in his or her own direction? The shock of freezing earth on the side of his head gave way to warmth; the moss quickly heated against his ear, even seemed to find its way inside as if by suction. The sounds: the beating of carpets? Whispered conversations about food, and the choking, coughing and retching of a child? People raking away the soil to find only skulls and other bones—perhaps ancient coins and entire ships interred for some ceremonial purpose; and a land inhabited only by the most ancient creatures: reptiles twisted around each other, with mouths at each other's necks, hundreds of feet or metres long and the shelled animals lying inert in the foreground, the whole

141

coloured (a sound-colour) by a deep emptiness, a silence at the centre of sound, the thin lines of engraved drawings creeping through the landscape and rendering it colourless, replacing it with words and signatures, making it deathly. Could that be the sound of someone approaching? Diane was awake, up from her bed where I had left her some hours before, and I heard her in the kitchen, small movements, while I took notes, sitting on the sofa as the darkness slowly completed itself outside. I felt reluctant to move and reluctant to speak to her, as if she were already standing over me, watching, expecting some report, expecting me to tell her my dream or daydream though in fact the door to the kitchen was still shut and she was only present through the small noises I could hear—or perhaps I could hear nothing, and my imagination was supplying the sounds, which I thought were someone approaching, which expanded into other sounds, which pressed into my ear, pressed firmly against the ground, my face contracted (as I realised) into a grimace, as of pain, or severe concentration—and slowly I got up, straightening, feeling slightly light-headed and shook my head at Wills.

He said, I knew it. He's an idiot. Come on, I think Mary has some breakfast for us.

A Departure

In a mostly bare room, west-facing and brightly lit from a low sun coming in through a set of windows that concertinaed open but were now ajar only at one end, letting in only a hint of air with no movement, he found me where I sat writing, my table against the wall, out of direct sunlight but caught in the walls' reflected glow. As he entered, instead of enlarged, broadened as his presence often was—in his gait, in his speech—he appeared narrow and quiet and, though I had been with him for years, I suddenly, once again, noticed that despite everything he was not large, that when standing still he shrank to his own size: slim, the slight barrelling out at the chest and waist hidden by a shirt that hung loosely on him. Outside our daughter passed in front of the window, and her shadow moved quickly across the ceiling.

I turned more fully to him.

He said, I'm going to have to let go of the workers . . .

I nodded.

He said, I mean I just can't afford to pay regular wages. I mean I'd like to keep them on but I just can't see my way through, I just can't. I don't feel good about it . . . Then: Or maybe we could get someone in, part-time, but I can't see them liking it, part-time work.

Okay.

What do you think, Di?

Yes, I guess you're right.

You know I can't afford to pay them any more. I like having people around but I don't know how else to—you know the new rates and things are—

It sounds like you're right.

Yes. They'll have to go . . . He screwed up his face for a second then smiled. He said, Sorry, I didn't mean to disturb you in here, darling. You don't need to worry about all this; you can't do anything about it.

No . . . I wasn't sure what to say. When he talked to me about the running of the farm, often standing over my desk or over me in some other part of the house, he never involved me in any real sense. I had no idea of the finances, the day-to-day spending, the work that took place on the farm, and in fact he seemed to keep it from me, or rather protect me from it, withdraw it from me as if sheltering me, telling me of his thoughts but, once they were spoken, once I had made some noise in response, he would shift his posture, sway and become apologetic and close his eyes in a smile that seemed to release me, then nod, his eyes still closed. Today his smile faded; his body seemed nervous.

He said, I was talking to Meri about it in the truck and she offered to help, you know, said she'd work more on the farm. It half broke my heart—she's such a good girl, Di.

Meri?

I was going on at her about all the money we'd borrowed for the new subdivision and the bank's about-turn and she's only fifteen! Poor girl, she doesn't need to hear all that— but I tell you she's good and strong and she can be a good helper.

As he talked the image struck me: Meri in the truck, on the land that stretched out flat, almost flat, its slight hill that gave a vista over the creek that ran in sweeps then into a straight line between paddocks, a mere trickle or nothing but a brown line, a grey line in late summer—for me the farm became landscape and view more than anything, more than the space to be subdivided and rationalised as it was for Peter, a place for walks during which I looked up at the mountains, down at the ground—and the image of Meri out with him gave me, as it always did to some degree, a shock in my stomach, a feeling of something slipping at the edge of my vision. Peter was standing looking at me and again I became aware of his look of narrowness, of something barely contained.

He said, What have I done wrong, Di?

What?

What have I done wrong?

What do you mean?

Oh—I don't know what to do. They put up the interest rate like that overnight, on top of everything else . . . He looked at me and sighed, then laughed shallowly. He said,

Maybe it was just some stupid idea thinking I could be on this farm.

No, Peter.

I just can't—it's one thing after another.

No, Peter. You're doing well—we're fine.

I don't know. You don't know how hard—

We're okay, aren't we?

Yes, of course we're okay, but—we've been fine until now . . . Again he smiled at me, and again his smile faded.

I said, But you can't use Meri too much. She's got her school work and—

Well, just during the holidays and after school. She loves it.

She's got other work—homework and—

She loves it. She did offer.

I said, I don't know if she knows what's best for her.

After a pause, he said, I don't see you offering to help, Di.

I wouldn't know what to—

If our daughter can see what I'm going through trying to keep us afloat and even—I mean I'm not going to take her out of school and make her a slave, Diane, I'm not going to use her. I'm just moved that she offered, it sort of surprised me and I don't see you doing the same. Why don't you think about what it's like for me—

I don't know, you never tell—

Why have you got no idea what I'm going through every time I try to get my head around the accounts? You could look at them, do you want to see the accounts?

I wouldn't—

Look, what do you do here all day?

I don't know.

He paused. His forehead was drawn inwards, and his head shaking slightly as if he were trying to work something out.

He said, I don't see you helping. You could do something to help.

I'm busy with the housework, and—

You're always in here, or off to some lecture or whatever it is.

I do the housework. Who do you think cleans the—

The least you could do is get a job—there'd be teaching for you in town.

No, Peter, I haven't got time.

You could work easily, find work at a school—time, you—

I can't, I can't work, Peter.

It was fine, working, teaching, before we moved here—wasn't it?

Yes—no.

You're always sitting in here writing your, what is it? . . . He stepped forwards and reached clumsily for the surface of the table, the papers and books spread about on it in a haphazard fashion, but pulled back before touching anything, letting his hand fall back, even stepping half a step away again, looking to one side with his mouth hanging open as I stood up to face him, then looked down.

I said, I don't know.

All your delving into the history of—what do you think you're finding out, some dark secret that means it's all wrong being here, isn't—

No.

Why do you hate the place? Every time the government or the bank takes another swipe at us you're laughing into your history book, let me— . . . He stepped forward again and this time took up roughly a handful of pages, crumpling them slightly in the process. He said, Mantell . . . And I stepped forward and swiped at his hand or the pages in it,

147

open handed, not knowing quite what I intended with the action except to interrupt his grasp in some way, and my hand hit his, or his wrist, and knocked it down and knocked the papers out, and while they fell in single long sweeps there was a pause, a single long beat before he lashed out, swung at me and caught me in the side of the face throwing my head to the side, my body staggering also and I felt my ear split—did it?—spilling blood and the pain down the side of my neck, before without a pause this time I saw him hit again with the same hand on the same side of my face, my head, turning me and knocking me down so that the same side of my head fell against the floor with a thud that was more audible than the pain, which only came after a second, two seconds, seeping up and down my neck and behind my eye, blinded now, damaged and the other open a slit, only a slit, and I rolled to see his foot not far away—moving? moving at me?—no, still, then walking away, or running, and I was already moving myself away from the pain easily enough, though it was growing, from its initial shock, only a shock, only pain that would, in time, I knew, fade. In the doorway, I saw, looking up with both eyes now, that he pushed past Meri, who stood looking in, on her face an expression of disgust directed in, at me. I groaned, rolled again away from her and closed my eyes; the look had struck me more deeply than his hit which, in truth, reached only the surface, couldn't penetrate far and dissipated quickly into the complications of its meaning.

The first time, we still lived together in his flat in the city at the southern tip of the northern island before coming south to the farm. The farm, however, had just become a possibility: his parents were thinking of retiring and Peter was to move there and work at first as a manager and, within two or three years, buy his father out. He told me with his arms about me, his mouth against the side of my head, where we stood in the small living room. The light faded and I half wanted to pull away and go about the room switching on the lights, brighten the room and give myself a view of him, as if to imagine him on the land. The image could only be appropriate: his dream, often talked about, of running the farm of his childhood, had begun to infect even me, though in his conversation he never used any but the most practical terms; it would be an antidote to the city and even to my own childhood—a new place. Then his grip on me tightened, his hug large as when enthusiasm made him grow affectionate and sometimes overbearing and I did pull out of it, at first to smile at him then to turn away; could I in fact see myself there now that it was becoming real? I had visited the farm several times with him; its land was laid bare, could have no secrets, unlike the hills of my childhood and of the city, but revealed every animal skull bleached and scoured by its winds. I had the sudden sense of myself there, unable to find anything to grasp, no feeling for it as anything but an abstract space of flat, of landscape straightened to the shape of paddocks or presented, distant, on the horizon, its mountains glowing faintly but hardly more than painted backdrops. I felt a quick shock of disorientation, turned to him again—his eyebrows were still raised at me.

He said, We'll have to share the place with my parents for a while. We can't keep living in this place, and frankly my job's driving me crazy. Mum wants to be in the city and Dad's finding it harder on the farm—but they want me to be there. I think it feels good to them to know that I'll be able to take it over from them. I mean I always knew it was coming, we've talked about it so much, but, and listen, you won't be stuck in this flat any more.

149

It's a nice flat.

He said, Well, yes, yes it's a nice flat—but aren't you excited?

Yes.

Good! Good—because I'm excited, Di. You know last time we were back there and we were off having a walk about, Dad said that he was feeling old. I thought he was just talking about his bones but he was talking about the farm. It's not the sort of thing the old man would say; he wouldn't normally complain about his age, or say that kind of thing at all, and I thought it was strange, that he must be feeling really bad, or sick. I got worried about him for a bit, though I didn't say anything. But that's what he meant! Nothing about being sick or bad or—just that he was almost ready to let the farm go. This is what I've dreamed of all my life! Every time I've seen them I've asked them for this, I told them over and over I wanted their farm, not like that but, they know, and they're getting old enough to retire. It'll be good for them.

Yes . . . Then: I'll miss Therese.

We'll find you new friends.

Okay.

We'll look after you.

Peter would have to drive me to the train or the boat at the nearby city if I was to visit Theresa. I could stay there for a few nights and feel the freedom of the city which had begun to open up here, mostly when the hills were not visible but instead hidden behind low rows of shops that, anyway, I seldom bothered entering, and why couldn't I quite make myself feel the freedom of the open spaces, the expanse of farmland which would surround me in my new life? Peter would come fully into himself as if finally obtaining that part of his body which had been (or so it occurred to me) missing—in his gait, in his facial expressions—but would I steadily lose myself, regress to something I had been before I left my own childhood farm? Theresa's company always enabled me to open my eyes, to have a certain amount of bodily confidence as if taking it directly from my friend, move sometimes as if dancing, take risks, such as that first risk standing over the ocean with the cliff's drop-off nearby, saying yes to him.

It was one of those rare evenings when he cooked dinner: simple, bachelor's survival fare silently prepared while I was in the bath. Theresa had stilled since the early, scarcely remembered days of our friendship, but moved, all the same, with an efficiency that I sometimes found I could copy in my thoughts; now, while I lay silently then dried myself as I imagined she might, I came up with an idea of my own. Facing him across the small table, later, I at first only looked at the plate in front of me with a feeling of looking down at myself, and said, Thank you for cooking.

Well, that's all right.

I said, If you go, I'm not coming with you.

A silence, a weight to the room; his face stretched at first up to mine then down. He said, What about our marriage?

Peter, Peter, we'll still be married . . . I reached out towards him across the table for half a second, regretting what I had said then pulled back, pulled back also at the regret.

We'll be separated—it'll be a separation.

No.

We'll be separated . . . He had put down his knife and fork, the latter still with a piece of meat skewered; his mouth was open as if still expecting the morsel of food, but at the same time his throat worked dryly, seeming to reject what food had already been eaten.

I said, We'll be separate but not separated . . .

Tell me the difference? Go on—what's the difference? You want to leave me?

No.

Then why? Tell me!

With his eyes open upwards against the weight of his brow, his mouth still open, it was hard to know where to begin, though I had rehearsed the conversation to some degree in the bathroom; and suddenly the reasons all seemed to float apart around a central one, inarticulable, a simple resistance that had no reason, or none that I could understand. I said, Your parents will still be there.

He breathed out, looked down at his plate, picked up the fork and popped the meat quickly in his mouth and, still chewing, said, Oh.

I didn't mean it like that. It will just be . . .

Be what?

It will just be difficult for us all to live there.

That's ridiculous.

No. Yes—I know. No, look, it's not just that: there's too much for me here, there's too much . . .

What do you mean?

I've got the relief teaching at Theresa's school. There's . . .

Relief teaching!

Someone's leaving, next month, to have a baby, and they need me to take over until they get someone permanent. I can't get out of . . .

Of course you can get out of it. If you hate them . . .

I don't!

Just say it.

I don't.

They're my parents.

I stood up and began to move around the table towards

him, wanting to touch him in some way, simply to stop him in his anger.

He said, Don't leave the table—I haven't finished eating.

I couldn't help a small laugh. I looked at him to meet his eye, nonetheless stopped in my tracks, and he was looking away.

He said, Sit down.

I moved back and sat, slowly, still trying to catch his eye while, still, he looked away. I said, I haven't finished eating either . . . Having in fact hardly touched the meal that now, with some effort, I cut into. I said, I couldn't easily leave; it's hard for me to leave the work . . .

You don't even like it.

It's fine, and it's good for me to—

You don't like it. And of course you could leave.

I feel bad—you know I said yes to them and—

I don't understand it . . . He had stopped eating again now and looked at his food with disgust, pushing the plate away from him. He said, You have to come with me; I need you to come with me. What will I say to them? They'll think it's very strange that you don't want to live with them.

It's not that—

How am I going to tell them you don't want to live there?

It's not—

I can't understand, and they won't understand either. They want you to come with me; they're looking forward to having you around and you go and say—

They said no such thing! I bet they didn't—

And you go and say you can't—

I bet they didn't even mention me—it was all about you taking over and I was just—

For God's sake! They want to retire in a year or two, and

they want to move out. They want to be in the city, Mum wants to be in the city where she can, I don't know, so it won't even be that long with them, just a couple of years.

He stood up with a crumpled look, and again I had the urge to touch him or reach him, make him see that I wanted to stay for a reason that wasn't the teaching, wasn't living with his parents but was another reason, simply something in me that couldn't move. I stood and tried again to come close to him and, as he lashed out at me, clumsily, what was the expression on his face? I understood that he had caught me under the chin, on my neck and again on the side of the face so that I staggered back—what happened to those seconds? There was only a picture of them, a missing few seconds covered by the memory playing and, really, what had happened? The sun had shone, burst out over a landscape like his farm, which, after his death, I sold—it was close enough to the city to be of interest to developers—and used the money to leave the country altogether, though how much longer can it last? But a picture of the missing seconds of his throat lunging, somehow his throat lunging before the rest of his body, though of course it was his hand, half open, thoughtlessly, not in a fist or open for a slap but relaxed and loose even as it struck? The places—the city, the farm, open and with wind driving across them or in harsh light. It was hard to believe this, and if the pain was real enough wasn't the distance that the picture allowed enough to let me look across at him—there was a sense now of looking not just at him, but across, though he stood no further off, even advanced half a step, threateningly?—to look across at him and make him understand that a deal had been struck? He hit me again, out of some stupidity, or was it because I already understood that he could hit me and said to him, Go on—hit me again . . . He hesitated and hit, and already the hesitation, the consideration, was louder than the strike.

Later—how much later?—I said, I'll wash up . . . I picked up the plates still half full with the dinner that neither of us could now touch.

With the sound of the water filling the sink, or filling the bath—the bath: didn't I have the bath after our meal, after he had lashed out at me, not before?—in any case with the sound of water running I knew or felt that now everything was different; my world was two worlds and I stood back looking at myself trying to breathe, trying to ignore the pain and the swelling, trying to gather myself, knowing that gathering myself was, for the time being, impossible, that I was presenting a front to him—why to him, as if he weren't involved?—but at the same time from here, from my position of watching, from a landscape run over with oblique light where there was a more genuine reality, where water ran on, and rocks, there was no question of needing to keep myself together, no question that I was whole and silently observing as the sound of water ran.

He said, Di?

I blinked, looked at the over-full bath, and turned off the tap. He was at the door, looking in, and when I turned to face him he seemed to shrink.

He said, I thought you might flood the place.

He had said, Don't come near me, Di, don't touch me . . . His hand, his throat had come out suddenly, surprisingly, cutting across my view of him, cutting him out and refiguring him, everything about him, the time on the beach, the times beside him in his car or here in this flat, leaving a shell and leaving me alone for the past five years.

In a voice which sounded like a croaking, which wavered, I said, I'll have to stay here for a while, when you go.

He said, Of course.

155

I said, I'll join you after a while.

He said, Okay . . . Then: What am I going to tell them?

I said, You agreed, Peter. Tell them I've got work. Tell them anything.

He said, Okay . . . For a second he gave me a look that seemed banal in its ordinariness—worried? confused?—then he left me alone.

I still remembered the conversations that Theresa and I had had when we first met. The city's history, the desire to strip away the buildings that somehow seemed to obscure its truth; its land, the forces shaping it, and the subsequent arrival of the first settlers giving it a naked past, a muddy and somewhat desperate one. Among other things, these conversations helped to keep me in the city—though I had, since I arrived, had few thoughts of leaving until hearing Peter's news. I missed the conversations, but still they stayed in the background of our friendship, and my own feeling for the city.

In truth, if her eye had been historical, mine was, increasingly as we had talked, geological; in the historical drawings she showed me it was less the development of the colony that interested me—though it did interest me to some degree, and I shared in her enthusiasm—than the simple shape of the hills, revealed by the rapid clearance of the bush. Even then I became fascinated by the processes that formed them, and that made the city merely a place, somewhere subject to the same geological logic, the expansion of time into dizzying pasts and futures, as anywhere in the world.

A few days later, she said to me, He did that to you?

I had, for the moments before I arrived at her bedsit, forgotten the bruising, and thought in any case that it was hardly noticeable on the side of my jaw. Her face came towards mine, she reached a hand towards my cheek, then, instead of touching it, she took some of my hair between her fingers.

I said, Therese, Peter's moving away.

He's what?

He's going to take over his father's farm.

She said, Did he do that to you?

Yes.

Bastard . . . Then: Come in, Diane.

While I sat, she filled the kettle, both of us in silence for a minute.

She said, He's been talking about going for a long time. He's always talked about that farm . . .

I'm not going with him.

Of course you're going, aren't you?

No—no, I wanted to stay here. Well, I had to stay here really, because of the work you found me. I wanted to stay in Wellington, and he's agreed to that. It's fine with him . . . I was conscious again of the bruising, and with each of her looks felt in some way as if my face were betraying me. I said, Therese, I wanted to stay here—and I'll be able to see you more.

She was looking at me closely now. She said, You've got to go. Don't you?

No. He said I should stay in the job, just for a while, until his parents move off the property.

She said, But the job? It's not really necessary, love. We'd find someone else for sure. How long till his parents leave?

Maybe two years.

Diane! . . . She looked at me, her face opened then fell into a frown; her head raised up on her neck and shook from side to side, then, slowly, she smiled, as if unable to stop herself. She said, You're leaving him!

No.

Yes, you are.

No, really, I'll visit.

How often? It's not close.

I shrugged.

She said, I can't say I blame you. Look at that . . . She came close again, and again reached towards my face but without touching. This time I shied away.

It might not be two years—it might be much less. I might move down there sooner. It really depends on his parents. I can't live there with them. I, it wouldn't suit them.

Or you.

Therese, it's just—

I know. You don't want to move with him.

I said, Therese, he hit me but it's okay—it doesn't hurt at all, and it was just once. It was just an accident. He didn't mean anything by it. He's not a—

She said, Diane, do you remember telling me, once, you were perfectly happy with Peter? I remember when you told me he had asked you to marry him and—you know even then you couldn't quite smile when you told me. I thought you were going to burst into—

That's not true.

You told me you'd stay with him forever.

And I will, Therese. I'm just trying something. I just decided, and, of course, I can't anyway, while his parents are there. There's not enough space in the house.

It's not as if you and Peter need separate bedrooms, is it?

Therese!

You've managed to fit all right in his flat, you've—

Therese, don't.

Why don't you leave him properly? It would be—

You don't—I can't. I don't want to. I love him. He's,

wasn't it you who wanted us together? Wasn't it you who introduced us in the first place?

But—

You seemed to think we were perfect and I agreed, I remember thinking right from the start that I agreed he was perfect for me. How could I? He doesn't mind at all, and you seem to mind more than he, you seem to be more upset about it than he is.

I'm not—

When this is just what I want, and shouldn't you be happy that I'm going to be here for longer? I mean it was because of you, or partly because of you anyway, that I wanted to be here. I wanted to stay with you in Wellington. Partly.

Theresa pushed herself back from me. After a minute, her face transformed into another broad smile; she laughed and said, All right, that's lovely, Di.

When I go I'll miss you.

I'll miss you too. But it's not going to be for a while, is it?

And we'll have the chance to see more of each other while I'm still here. I've hardly seen you really.

A pause, then: Actually, Diane, that would be nice. I've been, you expect things . . .

What do you mean?

I kind of envy you. You've got—

You kind of—?

You don't have the same—I'm still seeing Tom. You know? You met him once. But still. No, it's not about him. Or, that's the problem: I don't care if I leave him.

Did I meet him? I never know whether you've got someone.

It doesn't matter. I'm not ready to marry anyone anyway. Come on, let's talk about something—

159

Marriage isn't—

Yes, I don't want to marry anyone, really. I'm just alone so much, or, I'm sick of teaching. Sometimes I think of finding some other work . . .

I said, You're so good at what you do.

I know. No. I'll keep teaching. I don't know . . . She stood up abruptly, then, as if not quite sure which way to turn, or as if she would simply sit down again, she was still for a second, then looked at the clock on her kitchen wall. She said, Don't you have to go? No, I mean, won't Peter be expecting you?

I also looked across at the clock. She was right; in fact I would have to hurry to be home in time for him to return from work. I said, Of course, yes. Look at the time . . . I stood to leave; I looked again into her face, which was nodded towards me with eyes looking out from beneath raised brows as if I were one of her schoolchildren. I said, Therese, I'll see you soon?

Yes . . . She moved to kiss me on the cheek, hesitated, then kissed. Outside, as I was rounding the corner, she said from her doorway: Bye, Diane . . . She had followed me out and stood, uncharacteristically, a hand in a half-raised wave. I waved back at her and offered her a smile.

On the street, a blustery wind picked up newspapers and leaves, and already people were walking home from their places of work, heads down, or leaning back against the gusts as though against a wall. For a second, before I had stood abruptly to go, there was a sense once again of the distance of myself from myself that I had felt with Peter, that I always—did I?—felt with him now, or felt at all times even when not with him, a view of the world from some windswept bare land; perhaps a new feeling with Theresa now was the certainty that she understood this place, or this sense of the view across, of the bare land and the wind and the play of the elements on it, or that she could see it, or that I might in fact make it across the gap to her. Looking up now at a view over the city, it seemed as if the city was hardly there, was at most a collection of makeshift buildings, a simple, small outpost, whose roots hardly scraped the surface.

The apartment now that Peter was gone was silent in a way I hadn't experienced, and each night flocks of birds seemed to lift off its roof and swoop in front of the balcony, describing circles, letting me follow them with my eyes and then move away and stand and run a bath, which I would slowly lower myself into with a feeling of renewal. Peter's first letter came four days after I had seen him drive onto the ferry: Diane, I miss you so much here! Mum and Dad are fine, they are walking more slowly than ever . . . And in the same letter: I don't know if I can tell you how happy I am to be on the land. This is really what I was made for, this farming business! But I've still got a lot to learn, or rather Dad has a lot to teach me.

I wrote back: The work starts in a couple of weeks. It will be strange to be a full-time relief teacher but I'm sure I'll cope. Theresa has been a wonderful friend as always. I miss you too . . . But there was nothing more to write to him, and I found myself describing the small things I had begun to take pleasure in: The weather here has begun to be colder and I don't know what it will be like there. Does the nor'wester blow in the same way at this time of year as when I was down? I like the winds that come off the sea here—in the last few days I have been going to the shore and finding myself just walking. But the smell of salt has something I've never noticed before, and after walking in a mild northerly storm yesterday I came back wet and salty. The place is quiet without you and of course I miss you but there is also something nice about it. I hope you don't mind me saying that? It's quiet, like I've never experienced.

On that stormy walk on the beach, I was alone on the sand but with cars slowly moving past on the road beside me. When I looked up at them, men craned their necks from their steering wheels to look back at me, and I began to run, digging my toes into sand then stopping. The cars passing on their way from work, the buildings and, across the harbour, the wharves and more buildings growing dimmer behind the light, cooling drizzle, made me think of the development, the reclamations and the road around the coast, ringing in the entire city with itself. The city was lowering itself into a dusky evening where every noise was reflected into the low cloud, seemingly lowering further with each rumble of a truck's engine from somewhere unseen and, although it was cold I felt a sudden warmth from the feeling that I could keep walking, able to remember the time with Peter where the rain found its way inside my coat and he asked me to marry him, but no longer needing to return home to be with him and cook for him, but could walk back to Theresa's house again later, even after dark, and see if she was home. I took a delicious feeling from the decision not to eat: and, Peter, the house is strange with your things in it but without you. I thought I would be reminded of you all the time by your things, the things that were here even before I moved in with you but somehow they have become mine. It makes me think of you with your parents' furniture, all the dark wood and heavy patterns, and I prefer your own, well, our own threadbare existence and faded wallpaper . . . I screwed up that page, unable to finish it.

Theresa's bedsit was through the city. I walked on, enjoying a quiet community with the men who carried briefcases and looked up at me. Between the darkened shop windows were some lit by a lamp and the quiet view of someone—a man in shirtsleeves, a woman of my mother's age—writing carefully in a large book of accounts or mopping the floor, and I waved in, a feeling of exhilaration coming over me: Peter, this city! You can't understand how it is to be walking as if I could go anywhere, and Theresa always gave me that feeling! I'll miss her so much . . . But that page wasn't even started but only began to form its words in my mind before they were torn away by someone coming from a side street that seemed to be prematurely midnight: You okay, darling? A man in an overcoat barring the way as each of us stepped left and right and he caught my eye for a second.

Yes, I . . .

He looked at my hands, held up instinctively in front of me (the ring glinted in the light of a sodium lamp) and said, Where're you going this time of . . . ?

A friend, she lives in that building . . . Waving a hand in any direction.

In the fruiterer's there?

Over it, in the flat over it . . . I looked at the building's dark windows.

I'd say she's not at home.

She's asleep . . .

I pushed past him, quickly walked to the door set in an alcove by the shop and searched for somewhere to ring or knock, or appear to do so while he looked at me—there was nothing; a heavy door set at an angle, and the thought of what might be behind it kept my hand away from its surface. I looked quickly over my shoulder, but the man was already pacing slowly away, his head moving as if he were holding a conversation with himself.

After a further walk, hurried then again slowing, I reached

Theresa's house, or the well-lit home underneath which she lived. Around the side it was necessary to pass directly in front of a window, surprisingly uncurtained, and then down narrow concrete stairs to the lawn which was, to all intents and purposes, she had said, hers to use. With each step I hesitated and searched forward with a foot in shadows that gathered in the confined space, and with a hand on the weatherboard wall on one side and on a rough concrete surface on the other, topped above with a green painted wooden fence, I steadied my progress, and had I never come down here in the dark? Though overhead there was still a depth of blue that left me standing and wondering for a second before I heard, once again, in memory as if real, the voice of the man who had appeared in front of me like a wall; or the actual voice of someone in the house upstairs? Theresa's bedsit was dark and I pictured the man's face as I stood a few steps back from her door with its frosted glass panes reflecting only a faint city colour from a street light somewhere behind the garden, and, was that a corner of something glowing within? Therese? Are you . . . ? A faint clatter from somewhere and I turned around, facing into the lawn and its few isolated low trees that had become dark shapes. Therese? . . . I turned again and up at the door knocked a few times, then put my face close to the rough glass and felt its coolness: Are you at home? . . . There was surely a glimmer coming through the glass and a faint scrape, a whisper or a simple exhalation. Therese? . . . I turned again, and said it to the night, before turning once more and knocking again, and I whispered, Come on, be, be here . . . This was something, now, that I wouldn't write to my husband: Peter, how could you possibly understand this feeling of being stuck here on the threshold of her apartment? . . . And after another turn out to the night, darkening further above me I stood and whispered to myself,

I just have to walk home . . . But there was now another scrape, something dropped or a cupboard closing: Theresa, are you there? . . . Turned back now towards the flat.

The door pulled open enough for her head to come through: Diane, not . . .

Are you sick?

Her eyes seemed to blink, hardly open, even against the now deep black of the garden or the distant yellow light that cast its own strange colour over her face: No, look, love, now's not a good time, I . . . Her face withdrew as she looked back into the room for a second. Then: Sorry, love, can you go?

What's wrong? Can I . . . ?

No, please leave me alone! Diane . . . This was in a louder whisper. She said, Come back, come back tomorrow or something . . . From well inside there was the same hushed scrape I had heard earlier, though unmuffled by the door it was more clearly a sharp sniff and repeated itself immediately with a hint of mucus.

I half-turned and turned back, unsure on my feet, and her forehead was strained at me, her eyes waiting for an agreement as if I were a child, or was she pleading with me as if she were the child? I put my arms out to her and said, Please can I help, I want to help—what's happening, Therese? Is someone there, do you . . . ?

Go on! . . . The door closed further so that only one eye was visible: Go on! Come back tomorrow.

I, um . . . I stepped back and half-turned again, as if to walk away and up the concrete steps, but I still met her eye. She held it there, then in a sudden movement shut the door as if cutting me loose and I opened my mouth to take in air. Her footsteps receded and I stood as if now I couldn't possibly leave, despite the closed door and Theresa's sudden frown caught in my imagination as it closed; or was it because of the closed door that I felt somehow stuck in the dark space behind the house, behind which a hill sloped down on the other side of a corrugated-iron fence to a flat road lit with distant lamps and, further on, another dark hill? The top of the corrugated iron was caught by a light from upstairs that came on, and as suddenly went out. I could hear nothing from inside Theresa's flat, and could make out no signs of life, as if somehow she and her companion, her boyfriend, her lover or, as if they had managed to—I didn't want to call out again but softly said, Theresa . . . Almost to myself: I don't want to go—please? . . . But, no, now this was seeming ridiculous, and I started towards the steps. Before I had walked more than three or four paces the door opened behind me.

Diane? Take this, it's . . . She held out a bowl towards me: It's some biscuit dough, I mixed it but I got interrupted, didn't bake them.

What's going on, Therese? Why won't you tell me?

Go on, love, take this and I'll, you can just put it in the oven when you get home, you know, spoonfuls of it on a . . .

I took the bowl from her, or put my hands on it while she still held it herself; inside a loose ball of dough sat exposed. I looked into it and for a minute didn't look up from it at her face.

Love, I'm sorry you can't come in now, it's a bad time, you've just come at a bad, um, but you'll take this with you? Take it and you'll be, go on and I'll see you soon? . . . I stepped back and said nothing, now holding the bowl myself. She said, Gas mark three, about twenty minutes.

Okay.

Now I turned to go with the bowl. She said, Bye, love . . . Coming up the steps I held it in front of me with two hands, faintly afraid that without being able to steady myself I would trip in the darkness; and imagining that Theresa was peering up after me, watching me go. The faint click of the door shutting again, and slowly I made my way past the lit window where this time I looked in quickly to an empty room. I realised that I had no idea what time it was: Peter, I don't want to go home now . . . Would I write to him about this? But I couldn't possibly find the words for it; how could I? And forming in my mind the thought that even were he to be waiting for me at the apartment I would have to smile at him, for him, maybe turn away for a second quickly and turn back with, again, a smile. The empty flat, my only possible destination, had lost its quiet beauty. I held the bowl underneath its flat base with one hand and dipped the other in to feel the stiff dough, like feeling with my fingers the cold surface of the earth underneath the city. I took a piece of the dough, which came away stickily, coldly from the mass and rolled its rough texture, of oats and raisins and a fatty residue, between fingers that became buttery, and put the resulting smooth ball in my mouth where it dissolved slightly before I flattened it with my tongue.

What of the time when here, instead of the reclaimed land and the wharves and waterfront areas, there had been deserted beaches, blown with the same breeze but undeveloped, with the shadows of trees and a harbour that was still pristine, quietly lapping and breathing to itself in its tides but in all other respects, from where I could see its faintly moonlit form over the tops of houses, like a lake, set in the hills that ringed it with their forest? And how deep could the foundations of the city go when, from the top of the hill reached by walking up from behind the block of flats where we, where I lived, it was possible to see still-developing suburbs, tracts of bare hillside looking burnt or washed out to their layers of clay and exhaling dust into the gusts of wind? The hillsides, meaning nothing in themselves, from my own childhood, from the farm where, either lush or running off themselves in runnels of dust, they made me think of struggle, but more importantly struggle for what?—for the sight from the top, of further hills, of a land occupied only by animals that, I already knew then, were there for killing and shipping overseas—these hillsides depressed me and found their echo in the city suburbs and in my dreams of Peter's new life, where I would join him soon enough. Another handful of the dough and I heard Theresa's voice: Come on, love, eat up and you'll be, it's okay now . . . I was holding the bowl now under one arm and against my body where it warmed against me as I walked. Really, I wanted to be free to leave the city and follow Peter; I wanted to be happy on his land there with its different wind—not the city gusts but, I remembered, a relentless nor'wester that started sometimes and lasted for days, hot and lifting the tempers of everyone in the house, of everyone who returned home from dusty work or had stayed inside waiting.

At the flat I turned on the oven and, with the bowl whose blank grey in the darkness outside turned out, in the light, to be pink next to me on the benchtop, rubbed butter onto a tray. I laid out spoonfuls of the mixture and placed almost as many of them into my mouth. The apartment was overwhelming in its silence now and I thought, Peter, I do miss you—why can't I enjoy this? Should I come to be with you already? Peter, I don't hate your parents, I don't hate you do you understand?

In the morning the bowl was still on the benchtop, empty but for the crumbs and buttery residue on its sides; the kitchen and, through the arch that separated them, the dining room, seemed to be under the same residue and, not touching anything—the bowl, the baking tray still with its small circles of brown where the biscuits had baked—I went through the arch to sit down on one of the wooden chairs. I didn't go to see Theresa and, although I promised myself I would go the day after, when that morning came with a sun that seemed to pierce the layer of cloud to find its heat only once it struck at the surfaces of the flat I knew I would avoid her again; instead I wrote to Peter and placed the now-washed bowl on the dining room table to remind myself to take it back to her, as if otherwise I might forget to see her altogether.

When I left the flat, it was, as usual, to go to the city's library. I remembered the breathless conversations with her and the books she would show me from time to time. My night-time sleeps were disturbed, leaving my eyes heavy during the day, and each day I checked the mail to find nothing more from Peter until after around a week, already unused to speaking and having done little but sit in the library reading about the city and also about the wider land, its earliest years of occasional whalers and settlers and the native villages, the first ships of the Company. Reading it again, familiar material, and in more depth I tried to see the city for the first time and feel as if I could hold it in my hand, as if the place could become quite uninhabited for me, as if by knowing at what point I crossed the original shoreline when I walked along a city street, I could actually step into the original sea, I could dismantle the buildings around me and silence the cars and in this way capture my aloneness fully, as if I could sail to an empty land, caught by the romance of a sea voyage and the endless plains and mountains, empty, available for me to walk and claim my space and walk again and claim again, untroubled by anyone living there already;

untroubled. The pa site on the shore had been a miserable place, I read somewhere, drunken; but again, elsewhere, I read that the natives were co-operative, eager to help and gain from our knowledge.

I hardly read the books; instead, I skimmed through them, drawn to paragraphs and pictures here and there, and remembering nothing.

What I found more compelling was the city's landscape, its emptiness on a Saturday morning and the sense, from the top of the hill behind our apartment, when I closed my eyes, that it could be deserted, subject only to larger forces, to the earthquakes that it was notoriously prone to. Here the very land seemed mutable, and I had a sense of its changes: mountain ranges sinking and raising themselves up, valleys flooding, and perhaps there was some satisfaction in feeling as if, with this reading, I could negate the city, take some pleasure in overturning the land that it rested on. The city's faultline, the clash of the plates and the upthrust of mountains to the south, the precariousness of its surfaces, all movement—movement in a time that seemed to render everything with the impermanence of an eye-blink, that seemed to be the time-scale of my night thoughts, where nothing lasted of people's hopes and constructions; it seemed to interpret well the place from where I looked across, at the still jolting strike of Peter's hand on me; from here it was easy to forgive him, and in fact there seemed nothing to forgive. Instead, lithographs showed great lizards; extinctions came with the suddenness of cataclysm; I felt I could storm and walk with that same movement, with sweeps that wiped away everything—and, even in my moments of joy, moments that came mostly when I stood by a sea that seemed to share in my jostling sense, it allowed me to look at the daily commerce of the place with detachment, even a faint amusement. My thoughts were broken, one evening, and not for the first time, by a sharp rapping on the door.

Hello?

I opened the door slightly to our neighbour, a woman in her late forties: Just checking to make sure you're all right. I mean—

I said, Without Peter. Yes. Yes, I'm all right.

You're not—

No, I'm not lonely.

Well—that's good . . . She stood, her head angling slightly from side to side in order to get a glimpse past me. She said, Have you heard from him?

Of course.

Yes, of course.

Yes.

Her eyes maintained contact with mine only with difficulty, perhaps only because I tried to gaze fully into hers, not in a searching or connecting way but simply to pin down the movements of her pupils. She said, well, I'll leave you to your um, self.

Yes.

She frowned then smiled. She pushed close towards the door, causing me to open it further and admit her for a kiss, which lingered near my cheek for a half-second. Then she was gone, and, having waited for her own door to close, I swung ours shut. The bowl was still there, central, somehow dominating the room, at least to my eyes—what had she made of it? Nothing but a bowl, and not the evidence that, with each of her visits, this neighbour seemed to require, sharply nosing her way or edging her way in. Theresa would have slammed the door firmly in the woman's face? She would have kept the door open only a sliver so as to allow nothing, no view, and although I had tried that, tried to keep her out, she had somehow pushed past me anyway, though I had nothing to hide but a bowl perched, waiting, heavy, on the table, somehow in the centre of the room and immobile now; a mixing bowl that had taken on a grandeur and symbolism by being there untouched and becoming a heavy object, a rock. I had come face to face with the bowl with each meal I had eaten at the table alone. Hadn't Theresa in some way dug into the city, found a place here, while I still could not quite see the place, always saw it through the hills of my childhood, always woke not quite knowing where I was? She had read and talked and obsessed about the place until it seemed like she had always been here, and I wished that we could talk the way we once had about the city, so that she could show me how she had done it. However, I was due to be uprooted yet again, taken away before having quite arrived.

Could I try the same process, starting afresh with Peter's farm, and without Theresa's help? That flat country still seemed featureless, a faint smudge, hardly habitable, though of course I knew that people lived and worked there. Could I dig in there, could I find something the way that maybe I had found a vague, incomplete sense of this city? Is that what I needed to help me to move there? Now, when I sat and tried to pen a letter to Peter, it quickly became evident that what I was writing was not meant for him. For Theresa? Was I writing to her, to try to convince her of something, of my sight? Or was it for another purpose altogether?

A light breeze and the gulls and pigeons fought for space on the stretched ground of the few grassy open spaces, erupting in the shrug and recrossing of wings in light that fell obliquely from over the hills to the west and cast their fluttering shadows over each other. I walked with the bowl to Theresa's bedsit and shook my head at how strange the object had become, and how here in the daylight it was nothing but a bowl whose rim cast its own dipping line opposite itself, delineating a quarter-moon of silvery pink at its edge.

Something had struck me, on the previous day: a picture in a book on the fossil hunters, of a landscape, empty and hardly sketched out—a landscape that I recognised, as I had, on each of my visits to Peter's family farm, climbed to the one high point and looked out on it myself. The chapter was on Gideon Mantell, but the picture was one of a small set intended to illustrate the travels of his son and his role in Mantell's science. I had been about to put the book aside, but flicked through its plates—I had found the stories on Gideon Mantell interesting, but was not intending to get caught up overly in his own history. Now, however, this flat land, one that I had found dull and windswept, with its distant mountains only adding to the featurelessness of the foreground, came into view as if for the first time. The eyes that saw mutability and extinction, that saw vast changes, that saw plains not static but slowly growing out into the sea, had been cast on my husband's home; the imagination that saw great lizards—in truth hugely overestimating their size, as I later found out—turned around one another amidst a romantic vision of prehistory and its flora, this imagination had been present, through his son and through that son's role in his science, at Peter's farm. Couldn't I now dig my way in there, force it open the way that no other land had opened up for me? It wasn't in the details of its history, but in this view that threatened to wash it away, with its inhabitants, the dull daily life of tractors and crops and livestock. Suddenly the moa, which had never interested me quite as much as the even more fantastic creatures of more distant prehistory, seemed to step out onto the plains, and take on a new life.

Now, with the image in my mind of Theresa's face rubbed pale by the hint of streetlight over darkness, appearing cautiously around the edge of a door pulled open as if against her will, I was relieved—Therese . . .!—to be met with her door already open. The bedsit was shady, catching sun only in the mornings, and inside no lights were on. I couldn't see her from outside, and, coming forward, leaning on the door jamb with the elbow under which her bowl was held against my side, I drummed my fingers on the frosted glass of the door, which swung loosely under my touch: Are you here . . . ?

Who—Diane? . . . From the toilet: Just wait, I'll be out.

I was held for a second, with my fingers stopped in the middle of their action and my whole body also stopped, before I let my arm fall to my side; still, I stayed leaning in the doorway, not wishing to go any further in. The toilet flushed soon enough in any case and she emerged, looking as always from side to side and around her on the floor as she walked, and with her hands moving busily as if gathering something—a bulky item of clothing—to herself.

Come in, come on, you don't have to hang around there . . . She took the bowl from me with a continuation of the same gathering motion, partly pulling me over the threshold as she took it and left it on her dulled metal bench then, turning to me again, she reached up, put her arms around me and gave me a kiss on the cheek: Hi, love. What have you been doing?

I, nothing really. I'm sorry I didn't bring the bowl back earlier.

She nodded at me, now standing opposite me, as still as she was active a minute before. She said, Come on . . . She sat on the edge of her bed and indicated the one chair for me.

I said, What about you? How, what has been happening?

Oh, nothing unusual.

But—

Well, I've been at school as always. Listen—

Theresa, the other night? When I came around?

That! It's nothing, love. I'm sorry—I'm so sorry I—

Were you okay?

Of course.

But what was—

Really it was nothing. It was just an awkward time, nothing more. Listen, Diane, about the teaching . . .

What?

They've found someone else.

Oh, I . . . I looked down. I said, I thought it was settled that I would—

They found someone permanent, and it just works out better. Sorry—we, no one really knew if you wanted to—

But I've been there before, I've taught classes.

Yes, but they needed someone permanent anyway.

I could be permanent.

You never said that though, did you? You never told me, actually, you told me you couldn't, or you didn't want permanent teaching work.

I don't. I don't know . . .

Sorry. I'm really sorry—I would offer it to you but, well, it's not entirely up to me anyway. And it does make sense just to make an appointment if there's someone who can—that is, you know, I'd like to do you a favour but—

Okay.

We can't—

Was it just a favour?

No! No, it's good, you're a reliable reliever. It's great to have you when we need you. But, the truth is, I'm not sure whether you're going to go south or not.

I ... I looked at her and smiled, maybe to give the impression that I also didn't know whether I would go south; or rather, didn't know when I would go south. Was it so difficult to talk to her about the imagination of the land that had been forming or re-forming in the time since Peter had departed, that I felt the need to write about in letters that soon became something other than letters and were never—or seldom—sent? And now about the sketch that had rendered it possible for me to at least think about the farm. When we talked in recent years it was about nothing; the excitement Theresa had felt when I first met her, her own excitement in her subject, or in the history of the land, now seemed to have faded, and I could hardly imagine the face opposite me lit up with it. Now she was all efficiency with, yes, the same energy and the same quick laugh, but with none of the drive that she had once had. I didn't know what to say, and felt a sudden sadness that maybe there was little left for us to say to each other; if I felt a need to write these letters was it only because talking had become impossible? The realisation, however, allowed me all of a sudden to talk.

Theresa, I don't know either. It doesn't matter about the teaching—it's not what I want to do anyway. I've been thinking ...

Yes?

Is it stupid to think I could write a book?

Diane!

What do you think? I think I want to write a book.

What about?

I began to laugh. I said, I've no idea!

She looked at me, then softened, then sat back and smiled and joined in my laughter.

I said, Anything! About land.

176

About land? Diane, you know what I think?

What?

That is the most ridiculous idea I've heard in my life . . .
She laughed, then stood up and moved to the stove to fill the
kettle.

Yes, it is, isn't it?

It'll be a best-seller, that's for sure.

I'll be an author.

Will you still talk to me?

If you're lucky . . . Then: God, I don't know. I guess I'll
move south then . . . Our laughter, rising suddenly, a reminder
of the times when we had first met, now dissipated, leaving
the room silent. I said, Actually I'm sort of serious.

I know.

Do you think I could?

I've no idea, Diane. Probably. Why?

I don't know.

A novel?

No. No, something else.

A history book?

History, geology, I don't know. I don't really know
anything about anything, so . . .

Theresa said nothing now, looking at me while leaning
back against the benchtop and, next to her, the flame from
the stove fanned brightly under the kettle, the brightest object
in the room. I said, No, you're right.

Oh look, look, you've always been the one who's good at,
somehow Diane you've done well with Peter, you've stayed
with him all this time. So why don't you go and be with him?
Diane? I just think, you're so—I can't do that, well, I haven't
been able to do that, to stick with someone and—

It's not . . .

But I think it's marvellous, love . . . A pause during which

177

we both looked at the floor. She said, It's good, and you should just follow him. I mean I understand, it's so, I find it so—but you're with him and you've been with him for five years . . . ?

I love him and I'm going to go there, I'm just waiting for his parents to move out of the house.

Why don't you just go?

Because I won't have any time to breathe there. Well, maybe I should. Maybe you're right; I'll be fine there. Maybe I'll just go . . . I stood now, feeling inspected in my seated position with her standing, still, her arms crossed in front of her body, her head bowed slightly. Then I said, But I don't want to talk about this. It's always this—these are my options, either go and be with Peter or stay and teach, either Peter or teaching. I'm tired of this question—

It's just that—

I'm tired of those being the only options. Don't you—

It's just that you're so good with him, Diane. You never even wanted to teach, you never liked it. You might as well go with him.

I'm going anyway.

Yes, I know . . . Then: You're still as strange as ever.

Now I turned to look out the door at the various contours of clouds that hung and shifted over the tops of the hills. I said, Do you think I can't do anything? Do you think I'm hopeless and can't do anything, can't think for myself? . . . Then: Why don't you tell me what was going on the other night, Therese? . . . I turned around and she was standing and looking away, her face twisted into a half-frown. I said, You're so, you've been so good to me, I want to help.

Tom asked me to marry him. But it's okay. I'm okay.

I stepped away from the door, then turned and sat down again. I said, You told him no?

178

Yes.

And what are you going to do?

Oh, it isn't the first time! . . . She laughed quickly.

You mean with—

I mean with him. I'm just not sure. I don't think I could ever be sure enough to—

Are you okay? I mean—

Diane, it's nothing.

Really?

It's nothing. It's nothing, it's—sometimes I feel so involved in people. Sometimes I get so involved, it's good, and the rest of the world can just go to hell, and then all of a sudden I look at myself and I can't stand it, I've got to get away from them—from him. The thought of marrying him!

Is that why you couldn't see me . . . ?

Everyone seems to want to marry me, eventually.

But that's nice, Therese.

Is it? . . . Then: Thanks for bringing back my bowl . . . She laughed again and turned a tense, hard-eyed remainder of smile towards me once her mouth was closed. She said, Come on, love, you'll have a cup of tea?

As if involuntarily I nodded. She was silent as she poured the cups and, carrying them back towards me, her legs brushed close to mine as she passed and sat, leaning in, reaching out to me.

I walked to her flat heavily, quickly one evening, later than I would normally have visited but with a still bright sky, frowning against the familiarity of the streets and my own habitual turnings. She seemed to keep me company even before I arrived, a feeling of her body leaning over me, its warmth, its breath, even the brushes of loose ends of hair, and the widening of her eyes as she read what I wrote. And she was here not only as a quite deliberately imagined presence, but in my own movements, my too-quick, too-heavy steps that seemed to clatter amongst the buildings and the tall, narrow wooden houses lined up, passed on my left on the long, gently sloping road. This amounted to a solid, contented, feeling of companionship from her, the suddenly comforting feeling of the familiar street, the step speeding in time with hers then slowing to coincide with my own feelings, so that all at once I was in my element simply walking. How could I leave this buoyancy, this feeling of her in my stride and then outside of me looking on as I slowed? I stopped and turned, looking down the length of the road from what was once the crest of a hill but was now simply the point at which the street flattened slightly, the geography annulled by the network of streets arbitrarily planned on too-steep slopes, but also the very mountain once here flattened to a slight rise early in the city's short history, and the pleasure of clear sight thrilled me, gave the view an even more tangible weight and a luminosity over and above the sun's weak shine, as if the past, the barren truth were lighting it up from below.

I turned and kept walking. In front of me a figure had appeared as I came over the top of the rise, walking in a shambling way, looking to the left and right, and was it to be a repeat of the same darkened encounter I had had in the centre of town on my night-time visit, the man who had nearly embraced me in his suddenness? This man wasn't wearing the same overcoat, but seemed to have something of the same air; in any case, he was familiar, in his step, in his sway, and all of a sudden he turned in from the street apparently without having noticed me and before I had come close. It was Theresa's gate; I stopped for a second, then ran forward and looked to see his heel disappear around the edge of the house at the base of the concrete steps, then stood again watching the space where, for a split second, his shoe had—hadn't it?—been framed against a background of heavily shadowed grass that seemed to release into the open square of step, wall and fence a haze of itself or its own dust or simply a blur over my eyes.

Under my breath, caught and expelled in deflating bursts from the brief, unexpected run: Therese?

What's that, darling? . . . A voice from inside the gate and off to one side of the path, and at once I thought Theresa was waiting there, had been unnoticed by Tom—Tom?—and now was ready to emerge. But the woman was older, had been bent and now straightened with, in one hand, a posy of weeds, and drew the other across beside her nose: Are you . . . ?

I've come to see Theresa.

Oh, she should be in. Her boyfriend just went down. Go on . . .

Instead I stood for a moment, meeting the woman's eye then looking back down the path. I was inclined instead to say no and back away. After a moment I forced a smile at her, shook my head under her look, which I was somehow unwilling to meet, and, as if finding my way in the dark once more, felt my way down the steps to the door where I again knocked, sending the shuddering of the door's own rattle against its jamb through the small space, a sound that both broke and intensified what seemed to be a complete silence. This time I didn't want to call out; I felt suddenly small, no longer buoyed up by the feeling of being accompanied, being with Theresa or having her in my movements, but I knocked again and, resting my hand on the glass, stared for a minute at the back of it. There was no response from inside. I tried once more, then turned away and, unhesitating this time, walked up the stairs at the top of which the woman still stood, as if waiting for me to come past, with raised eyebrows.

I'm sure she's there. You should—

No, I'll come back.

All right . . . As if speaking to a small child who has been in trouble or is stubbornly refusing to move. Past her and out the gate again, I turned back the way I had come, retracing the steps I had earlier walked with increasing weight and at the same time lightness, and now both were gone. A tension grew over my face as I looked around, unable to conjure the easy world I had seen from the same vantage point a few minutes earlier, where the land in all its form, the sculpting of water over mossy surfaces and rock, had shown through briefly and where I could smell, or feel at my fingertips, something to make me—I don't know—and I knelt for a minute to feel at the ground, maybe looking for a piece of it to take with me; my fingers felt while I looked ahead and down over the city, which seemed to be darkening too quickly, under the shadow of clouds to the west, and I scratched at cracks in the footpath where weeds had taken hold, half-heartedly, easily removed and pulling with them a faint patina around their thready roots as if of an under-surface of soil below a thin crust. I stood up again, fighting a faint dizziness and, looking over my shoulder for a second—was the woman from the garden looking back at me, her hand on one of the gateposts and the hem of her dress moving faintly about her shins?—I walked on, and wanted to write, Theresa, aren't you supposed to at least—you knew it was me? Facing down the slope of the street I let myself break into a run, awkward in my flat shoes that sent their clapping loudly around me and, Damn, damn it, you can't understand where I am now, if only you'd let me talk to you about—if only you'd let me show you what it is that, what—and you'd see the buildings gone, the sky suddenly naked over the city with nothing but the creaking of trees, no, not even that, nothing to hide amongst, nothing to hide behind, Theresa, nothing, the future laid out and the past empty. But maybe this can be some comfort, wanting to get rid of this past, this time now with Peter as if he'd never happened to me, and as if you'd never, as if you'd never introduced us in the first place there and left us alone on the beach to—the same beach still grown over, or the hills covered in salty scrub and not burnt back to pasture, with the fencelines pinning it back over its bones, and out there, on waves pushing themselves up and over each other then flattening for the retreat, webbed with a thin coat of white froth, the first-comers in a ship utterly silent except for the creakings of itself . . .

I screwed up my face against something like a wind, though today's breeze blew, now that I was walking again, from the south, faintly against my back, and gusted each time I came to the edge of something: a building, a kerb. The city felt like an accumulation of closing doors, like a shanty town made of paper, but one that had been there for so long I couldn't imagine, and here, a place before Peter, even before you, Therese, see? Even before, when all I did was sit, and walk.

From faint lines drawn over each other—at first flat, then seeming to recede into the page and against the one vertical, a fold flattened by the photocopy into a thin divide—a sky separated itself, then become the foreground for yet another faint jagged horizon above it, a horizon that—behind the dark patch of closely drawn strokes that resolved itself into a rock in the stream, hastily sketched only by its banks and the scumble of a rapid—I couldn't shake from my vision;

until, as the drawing resolved itself into its depth, into its missing colour, into the breezes, and then the relentless wind bringing clouds of dust, or, from the south, sheets of rain, alternating from left to right and rendering the mountains as blank and as featureless as the drawing itself, but in shades of grey rather than the thin penned lines, I recognised with an intake of breath, a capture of space as if I could breathe in the whole scene, the view from the one small hill on the property: Sketch of an unknown location, W B D Mantell [1848?].

Out, to the front of the house, past poplars which lined the drive from the out-of-the-way dirt road, approaching cars would raise a pillow of dust behind them as they crossed the base of the hills opposite, turning towards the house sometimes. Each time a car turned in I would stand and put a hand on the window, see the driveway's dust, not thrown up like that of the road but slowly filtering through the poplar leaves, changing the light that shone through the curving line of trees, then settling on their leaves, giving them a colour which progressively greyed until the next rainfall, when milky grey droplets would run from them. Still, after some months, then some years, the flat valley—hardly a valley at all but simply the space through which the stream sluggishly ran—with its single road, single farm, remained a mystery, though I walked out onto the land and tried to see its shape. The farm, in many ways so familiar to me from my own upbringing—from the farm I thought I had left forever when I moved to the city—was constantly forcing itself on me, as if I were repeatedly waking up to a new, strange environment; it was as if I was constantly arriving at it, always in motion and never fully at home. Once, early in my time on the farm, I wrote, Dear Theresa . . . Then I crossed out the greeting and carried on writing: Here is a place where the land is bare and I can see its bones, and the houses and the stands of trees do nothing to disguise the feeling of it, unchanged from the beginnings of—or no, an utterly tamed country but, as if things like this can be tamed or untamed, as if there could ever be a wilderness here.

Peter was transformed, his step lightened, and he became someone I had forgotten: the man who had taken steps ahead of me on the hill above the beach; the man who had asked me to marry him. He would talk about the farm and his happiness there, about this place where no one could tell him what to do: Diane? I'm my own boss here—this whole place, this whole land is mine!

I took no interest in the workings of the farm, in the work that he had to do which sometimes kept him, with the workers, out late at night, after which they would come in dusty and walk heavily and talk in the kitchen while I lay, not in bed, but on a sofa in the lounge while the darkness grew around me and I listened to their voices but not their words, imagining the men seated around the formica table, leaning themselves back on the kitchen chairs away from it or tilting bodies forward onto their folded arms, until the workers, two men he employed and who lived in quarters out the back, behind the vehicle shed and an old oak, left, and the house was silent for a second, before he found me on the sofa as he came through: Diane? You're—are you asleep? Come on, let's go to bed . . . As if something had been amiss, and, looking at me with his head cocked to one side, his face rigid with his chin pushed up to pout his lips slightly and ruffled in something like concern while his body made sudden movements, as if to wave me into action, and to wave me into a cheerful jollity so that I could follow him, light-footed.

I said, Nothing's wrong. I just thought I'd leave you to it.

On Sunday afternoons his parents would visit, or we would drive to their new suburban house set amongst other new houses in a neighbourhood where the buildings still stood taller than the trees, and new development meant that every third property was occupied by a frame, a house with no glass in the windows or concrete-mixers parked by a garage, still with no door, with building materials scattered around and, during the week, or so I imagined, the sounds of hammer blows ringing loudly and the birds—magpies and blackbirds—that had once pecked at the fields or walked across the quiet roads now found themselves circling, landing and circling again.

Their visits to our home were different, worse, and reminded me of the time when I first arrived on the farm, sharing the small spare double bedroom that had once been Peter's childhood room with him, and had retained its wallpaper so that I found myself staring at it and imagining his boyhood; wasn't there something about the way he looked at his feet, almost bowing with his eyes to his father, as if ducking under a hand suddenly swiped in his direction? In bed, didn't he then shrink slightly away from me, where in Wellington when we had shared the apartment, though he had walked more heavily and frowned, he had still shuffled my body into position to fit with his as if I were unable to move of my own accord, placing my legs and arms carefully where he wanted them (and I had let him, with pleasure)? During the first few months I made myself keep a routine of walking about the farm and seeing the landscape, again and again from the same spots: the low hill; the shallow dam near the inland boundary of the property. Here windbreaks and the occasional farmhouse provided the only features that interrupted the almost fluid sweep of land out in all directions towards the mountains or the sea, a sweep sometimes mirrored above by the clouds in mottled punctuation or their own dovetailed smoothness.

On a cloudy day Peter said, This is why I had to come back! Look at the sky—look at what you can look at! . . . Still, while in bed he seemed only reluctantly to put his arms around me.

I wrote, in those first months, Can you understand the change in him? The way he is all energy now, and the two of them—him and the old man—seem only to go about on the farm together while I negotiate the house with Beth and have endless cups of tea . . . When Peter returned to the house I had sometimes been talking or reading or walking, either avoiding or spending time with his mother, and wanted to talk with him and also wanted to turn away from him and have nothing to do with him.

They moved out, earlier than I had feared, less than a year after I moved in. Their new suburb seemed empty, still rural but at the same time paved with attempts to deny the smells and the wind that still whipped up dust—silent, slow, at once affluent and destitute. We stood, four of us, watching men move furniture in from two trucks; then Peter said, Look, Dad, we'll go, and leave you to it?

Yes, of course, go on . . . They shook hands, and while they looked on Beth gave me a kiss.

In the car, after some time, I said, What a place to move to.

He said, What do you . . . ? I looked across to him and saw him grip the steering wheel hard, holding it steady on the straight road and pulling his body upwards towards it, straightening and shuffling himself backwards at the same time on his seat then throwing me a quick look.

Would you want to live there? There's something sterile . . .

187

No, it's good. It's a good house, and the neighbourhood will attract good people.

You—I just think . . .

Mmm? I'm glad they've found somewhere nice. And, now we've got their house to ourselves, Diane.

Yes . . . There was a minute or so of silence. We both looked forwards at the road dividing fields on either side, before the car passed under trees that seemed to form a tunnel—as we drove through, they unleashed into the narrow gap of sky between them the darting of birds. I said, Yes, it's wonderful, it's good, I think it will be so good with us there and only each other . . . His head stayed watching the road; his face remained unmoving for a second, before a smile lit his cheek and closed his eyes briefly. I said, And it's not their house any more—it's our house!

He didn't reply, so that the words stayed with me, with us, for the minutes to follow, which stretched into a longer time inhabited by the car's whistle and the vibration of the mirrors that started, stopped, started again, and I was tempted to repeat myself. I said nothing, except for perhaps a faint mouthing under my breath, about the house, the land surrounding it that had also passed into our joint possession and then came into view as we turned off the main road and crossed its seaward boundary, with in front of us the setting sun illuminating the fissures of a streaked cloud that lowered to obscure the mountains. Peter maintained his speed on the sideroad, and sped again up the rutted drive past the poplars, then skidded slightly before he brought the car to a halt in the dark, cluttered garage dominated by the shape of the farm truck beside his door. He silenced all mention of the uncharacteristic skid with his face, screwed about the lips into an expression of effort as he opened the door and lifted himself out, leaving me in an empty, dark car and the dark space between my door and the deep brown of the garage wall, boards and a heavy beam that gave off a tar smell or the smell of old oil, perhaps from the floor, a temporarily alone space. He was already walking away in the day's brightness, his back a solid mass against something, as if against a wind; and the brightness resolved itself back into a sort of gloom once I was out in it. At the door to the house he paused, took a step back and waited for me and, as I approached, smiled softly: Come on, then . . .

I filled the kettle and stood while he clattered somewhere, expecting him to join me in the kitchen the way he had always, the way his whole family had always done after we, they arrived somewhere, but the kettle's whistle and my own clattering, with a pot, cups, a jug of milk on the table, was met now with silence. I sat, poured cups and put my hand on the handle of the milk jug before withdrawing it, aware of the same sense of emptiness, a motionless quiet of being alone, that I had felt as Peter emerged from the car and I also pushed my door open and stepped into the dark gap under the heavy structure of the garage. I pushed the kitchen chair backwards, straightened my arms from the edge of the table, stayed still a moment, and was I alone again? Now, the feeling that I could exhale at the kitchen table, breathe out something held inside me for the entire chaotic time I had been here with Peter and his parents, where the rooms were charged with a feeling of walking on tiptoe, became the feeling of once again being in Wellington for those months until the silence had become too much and the land under the land had ceased to be a comfort, though I still held onto it as if it were a book that contained all the answers. Here in the kitchen, the walls were unpapered, painted white so that the vertical grooves were visible as shadowed stripes or even cracks, as if the wood concealed something that it would allow to be glimpsed behind, in movement or, worse, in stagnation. I stood and, in the hallway, I also looked at the walls, papered here, with an embossed pattern of yellow flowers that, for a second, I again thought might conceal something, and overhead at the brass light fitting with its frosted glass shade, also floral.

Peter, how could anyone stand this paper, this . . . Spoken to his back, where he leaned on a door jamb, in the door to what had been his parents' bedroom and was now empty, revealing indentations on the carpet from the bed, the chest of drawers, a tall wooden wardrobe. I said, We'll have to do something with it?

He responded with a sharp intake of breath as if woken from sleep, shoved himself from the door's edge and shook his head so that, though I couldn't see his face, I could imagine his pained expression, his closed eyes, and the subsequent smile, forced and beginning to relax but which would always make me want to back away. He said, What, honey? . . . He turned to me now. His face brought shadow with it, and I had trouble making out his features against the glaring evening light from the windows in the empty room behind him; the windows formed the upper half of an entire wall and would concertina out and away to make the room into a sun room, but I only remembered them, when the room had been occupied, with a blind drawn over them.

This is beautiful! . . . I pushed past him now into the room, aware of it, maybe for the first time, filled with a light that, when it hit the opposite wall's striped wallpaper, was a red, in contrast to its apparent brilliant white outside, where it lit the smudges and insect spots on the glass. I said, Peter, this will make us a wonderful bedroom! . . . His face was towards me again and he seemed to be calculating something, shaking slightly from side to side.

We don't have to—we don't have to change anything, Diane. It'll be just like it was . . .

What do you mean?

No, I didn't mean that, I just—and what about the wallpaper? What's wrong with . . .

Not in here, in the hallway.

He turned away from the room, stepped out. He said, Come on out . . .

It's—Peter? See it's so . . . Following him and looking at him from where he had stood earlier, I said, Don't you just find it, busy or . . .

He had paused beside me for a second, but now he kept moving, through into the kitchen, as if sealing me off into silence once again with the square of his back, and with his shoulders and the forward hunch of his neck, and his voice seemed to come from a distance, as if from over some horizon: Come on, Diane . . . He was standing at the table, with his back to the windows which, on this side of the house, opened only onto a dusky lawn and the roses I had promised to look after, dark shapes now in shadow. He was holding a cup by its saucer, and brought it to his lip with the other hand, as much perhaps to stop the rattle as to drink. From the saucer in his neglected hand, held close in to himself, a dribble of spilt tea ran over the edge and down the front of his shirt then, as he caught sight of it and straightened the saucer, clung in a few drops to its lower surface, slowly wetting his fingers before hitting the tablecloth in two or three spots. He said, Damn, Diane . . . He interrupted the slow motion of hanging, falling liquid with the clash of his cup back on the saucer and the saucer back on the table: Why don't you sit down?

I'm—

Come in and sit down with me—you, you're already rearranging things as soon as they're out the door, and you can't sit down for a minute, now you've got your way, and can't we just sit and have a cup of tea, before you start tearing down the bloody wallpaper or moving in on, come and . . . ? He didn't sit down himself, but stayed with a hand on his cup and with the other brushing at his shirt where a brown stain blurred and reached itself outwards, and he was looking down at it after the brief angry raising of his eyes as he spoke, a raising that came again: Diane? . . .

I felt as if I couldn't move. This is where everything seemed to turn around, and I backed out again into the hallway.

Diane, I'm sorry, listen, come on and have a cup . . . He followed and, then, we stood face to face in the hallway, silent for a second before I noticed in his hand, the cup and saucer—his, which he had picked up again without thinking? Or another, to offer me? He seemed to notice it at the same time, looked down at it as its rattle began, and he steadied the cup by holding it down, his two hands seemingly involved in forcing together the two pieces of crockery, held in front of him as if to keep them under control, stared at as if to fathom the strangest of appearances and here in his own hands who could, who could—bringing the whole thing clumsily, stupidly up to his face where he drained it in a single swallow, both hands still on it as if cupped on liquid scooped from a pool in them, then his head shook, his throat moved with the same nervous quiver, his eyebrows forced themselves down over the tops of his fingers and in a movement he took the empty cup in one hand, the saucer in the other and threw them hard at my feet, my legs, where they hit with a shock: I'm not a, I'm not unreasonable, I . . . The word 'unreasonable' slowly, thoughtfully pronounced and strange in the middle of his outburst.

I said, Peter, don't? . . . I held out a hand to him, knowing already that it was the wrong thing to do, but unable to stop myself, seeing his face, the small movements of his eyes, the look almost of confusion creasing his face into a widened, thinned version of itself.

He said, Keep away.

I flinched before his hand raised to the side and he swung at me, hardly noticed beside the still greedy upset look on his face, until his hand caught strangely on the side of my head, and I was on the floor.

He said, I'm sorry, God, I wanted to—can't we talk, and . . . ?

The only thing I could think of was to lie, thoughtful.

He stood over me for a second, then, keeping his feet where they were, his knees buckled, slowly, then a foot crossed and his torso heaved down into my field of view; his legs unfolded beneath him as he leaned back against the wall by the door to the kitchen, and for some time, with me lying on my side and him leaning there, we said nothing, and a further dusk found its way from corners to the air over us. He reached out and found the saucer, taking it from where it lay near my head, still intact, and placed it on his lap, then picked it up and turned it over in his hands, reading the mark on the base and looking abstractedly at the pattern around its rim and flipping it again, taking a newer interest in its surfaces at each turn and also from time to time looking up and away, but not at my face, and not at my eyes. He looked out instead into the hallway, up over his head, at the brass light fitting, studying it as if he were a child and with, was it, a tear running down his cheek? I closed my eyes and opened them, and closed them again, and put out a hand in his direction but left it trailing along the carpet while I rolled back so that I also looked upwards and the space came into a new, darkened perspective, so that I felt, to fill it, a need to stretch out my other arm, over my head. I said, Peter . . . ?

I'm sorry, I'm sorry I'm sorry—can we . . . ?

Yes, we can talk, Peter.

I mean God, God, what a way to—I was just so, I can't say, I . . . He shook the saucer now, in both hands as if it were heavy, as if to dislodge something from its surface. He said, I didn't mean it . . . ?

It's all right. It doesn't hurt too much . . .

But I couldn't, I didn't, like the sort of, the way you walked in there like that and threw yourself about.

Threw myself about . . . ?

No, I'm sorry. I didn't mean . . .

What did I do?

Nothing.

He put the saucer on the floor next to him and reached out again, not for me but to find the cup, lying somewhere near my feet, so that he rocked over and stretched his body out and, bringing it back upright with the cup in his hand and picking up the saucer to put them together in front of him, with the concentration of a craftsman and the curiosity of someone experimenting with the workings of a machine, he frowned, and closed his eyes, before opening them again to study the base of the cup and the mark there which matched that on the saucer, and to tap it with a fingernail. He said, I mean you have to change things? You have to criticise, don't you? You have to walk in and, you have to say that their house is terrible, and their wallpaper is shite, you have to claim everything for yourself and change it all around, and you won't be satisfied with it, you'll set yourself up here, park yourself here and, and not move you'll—why do you have to just, I mean, you know, Diane, you're . . .

I'm what?

You . . . He tapped the cup on the saucer, looking at me for the first time since he had sat, repeating the movement so that the clinks sounded like a geological hammer tapping out at rock, growing louder. He said, I'm . . . Until with a wider gesture he swung the two together once and for all and with a shock of noise that sent my eyes closed they shattered into I don't know how many pieces, and he stood up again, or so I felt with my eyes closed, heard his feet on the carpet up and down the hallway, heard also his breathing that seemed to want to suck up all the air in the house, to be sawing at the air or grasping at it.

Peter? Come and sit down.

He continued pacing for a minute and started speaking a few times, in small plosives, before his feet came to rest close, it seemed, still with my eyes closed, to my head. He said, No, I didn't mean to say . . .

I don't want to change everything.

I know Diane.

I just—I've come here because of you.

I know.

I like your parents and . . .

I know.

It's also good to have this place to ourselves. I, do you think we shouldn't make it how we want?

Of course. Yes, I know, I didn't mean it . . . Then, after a minute, after he had once again sat down with the deflating sound of a sigh, he said, That bedroom. It's strange to see it empty, with everything gone and—it's so emptied out. It hasn't changed since, well, since I've been alive. I never knew it had walls and windows. I've never seen its carpet. Where the wardrobe stood, where the chest of drawers was, also the bed, they're all—there's an imprint of them. Where the colours have faded and the carpet's worn down around them, and for some reason that's very strange. Diane, I'm sorry I hit you.

195

You couldn't help yourself.

Yes—no, I couldn't.

It's all right. It didn't hurt so much . . . I laughed for a second and opened my eyes. Peter's face was pinched inwards towards an upper lip itself twisted to one side, his eyes narrowed into downward curves, swollen, focused as if on the inside surface of his face and I moved now, pushed myself up on an arm and swung myself about so that I sat opposite him against the wall, looking at him amongst shadows that gathered and darkened still against the reflected glow, now deep red, that shone from the bedroom door and the pale one, fainter, coming from the kitchen. I willed him to look up at me and match my smile. I stared, still trying an eye-laugh, hoping to break through into the thought that gave his eyes a rapid sideways movement every now and then. I wanted to lean to him and touch him, even hug him, if only to feel the tension in his body. I said, Peter talk to me? Peter? Don't worry about, you know it was only this, um . . .

Instead he stood up, his movements jerky and containing something of his eye movements, and pulled closed the door to what had been his parents' bedroom, closing off at the same time most of the light coming into the hallway so that it was reduced to a half-blue-dark play of surfaces and edges and, once he had walked into the kitchen, I stood and looked in at him from the doorway, where I had a hand on either side of the jamb, and watched him empty, first, a teacup, then the pot, leaves and all, into the sink.

When finally Theresa wrote back it was to say, Don't write like that to me, Diane. You can't let him do that to you, but there is nothing I can do. I can't do anything, and it doesn't do either of us any good for you to write to me about it

. . . It was a short letter, with no information about her, her teaching, the struggles she had with finding someone she could imagine sharing a life with, and in response I tried to write to her asking about these things, imagining already as I was writing that she would again respond, late, angrily.

I pictured her in her bedsit. Although she had moved out since I had left the city, I could picture no other life for her, with the combination of her movement and her energy with her enclosure in a space too small, and I felt the contrast with my own situation here on the farm, where there was only too much space, and I felt inclined to turn away from it, or at best stand still and look. We continued to sleep in what had been the spare bedroom; for a long time the room with its concertina window remained empty until, once, I moved one of the kitchen chairs into its bright space and pushed the window out onto a bright still day; and, after that, finally I bought a table from the nearby town to serve as my desk. In this room, I would read or write while, in the afternoons the sun, on days when there was sun, lit the whole room, until it set and suddenly gave its silhouette of the mountains a precise outline, a haze that burned and abruptly stopped where the distant jagged line cut its premonition of night-time darkness into it briefly, before that same darkness rose, suddenly, to cover the whole sky.

Once, he found me there after his return to the house, writing on blue unlined letter paper a letter to no one, and as usual looked in only briefly, tapped a hand on the door frame to signal hello and smiled in and shook his head, as I knew from times when he came in and I looked up to meet his eye, although this time I didn't, and simply voiced a wordless greeting to him, what felt like a comfortable, negotiated and agreed syllable like his own hand tap. When I didn't after a minute come out to join him at the kitchen table he returned, entering the room as if crossing ice, afraid both of slipping and of falling through, as I saw, looking up at him now, his face tentative, his feet curled claw-like inside his shoes and his legs kept at a stilted vertical, making it seem as if he were hoping to surprise me, as if any surprise he could spring would move me more than the surprise I was wondering how best to break to him. He stood for a minute, and I felt the frustration of him standing there, a frustration all mine at his own patience as I looked again at my paper and wrote nothing further but re-read a sentence then hid it from his view. The room, in any case, was just becoming too dark for writing. He said, Hi, love. What's . . . ?

He was standing over me and I looked down, not wanting to have to talk yet. However, I said, You can't hit me now.

He stepped back as if I had hit him. His face seemed to reflect the blow, as if from the side, twisted against impact running through to his whole body, while I watched, partly dispassionate, partly aware of my own cruelty and at the same time wanting to stand and go to him.

I said, Peter? I'm sorry . . .

His falter, his beginnings at protest (Diane, I wasn't going to . . . I'm not . . .) were stopped short, as if he were already in my embrace, and he looked more fully into my face, eyes wide both against the room's darkness but also against what I had almost said.

Do you . . .

I nodded. I said, At least I'm almost certain.

Had you stopped using, um, taking . . . ?

Yes . . . I stood at a slight remove. I wanted to go to him; I wanted to touch his face but, all the same, I wasn't quite able to step across some boundary, as if something had grown up in the times we were too silent together, in the times when talking was too easy or between us it had been easier to agree—to agree that he would knock me to the ground, frustrated, nervous, clumsy, and somehow had I agreed to his violence, let him and encouraged him to swing wildly and give me bruises, which, a cliché, I hid from the friends we had? Therese, I know I shouldn't have let him but there seemed to be nothing else for it. When we tried to settle into a routine, of his own work and my work, my writing if that can be called work, just filling pages with my writing, when we tried this something would emerge that frustrated me: I would move something, I suddenly couldn't stand something how it was, or the neighbours would visit, an old couple whom Peter had known for years and afterwards I would gasp so much, can you understand that? That I would, by the time they left, or his parents left or we left his parents, I would be so desperate I couldn't help but pick a fight. The people here are so polite, so talkative, so able to converse and it makes me feel, well, like the people anywhere but I only get a sense of trying to lift something too heavy for me, of labouring through sentences with them, always an outsider. Is it simply the nature of the land? That, while I am used to the convoluted hills—denuded and bringing with them shadows and darkened damp gullies that at once threaten and yet seem to conceal nothing, leave open their dampness and expose the brutality against animals that break through fences and fall or get bogged down in the swampy streams— here everything seems open, picked up and deposited by wind, natural as if the tilled, top-dressed soil were in its original state, a state of grace, and the polite syllables skip across the surface of it. How can I not want to take the people here, take *him* and show him that things here, things anywhere are—but no, of course it's him, it's his stupid violence and nothing to do with me. I know, and yes of course I had to stop him somehow.

He said, Diane, I, why didn't you . . . ? But he straightened, looked about the room we were in, once his parents' bedroom, and out the windows the land was dark under what had become a deep blue sky with a brilliant fan of red, streaks that ran over a slight red mottle giving the sky its sheen that seemed to extend it, as so often, to broaden it even beyond the horizon and emphasise the land's dimensions, its stretch, away on all sides; and at its centre, it seemed for a second, was Peter, standing upright in front of me in the way I imagined him standing upright when on the farm with his workers or alone, in the way I hadn't myself seen for—how long?

He said, Maybe it was a good idea.

I said, A good idea! . . . I couldn't help a laugh, and another at the sight of his body and his face now thrown into a slight, easy confusion.

I mean . . . He also laughed: I think it's fantastic.

You do?

Fantastic.

I moved towards him now, standing close then, after allowing him to put his arms loosely over my shoulders, I put mine around his waist and pulled him in closer, until my head was sideways against his collar bone and I could feel his trachea working against the top of my skull as he swallowed, hugged tighter, let me go, before he pushed me gently away. For a few minutes neither of us could say anything.

Lines Drawn with a Blade

The sky was light with streaks of blue and cloud, and suggestions of red still from the east. I looked out over the native encampment to see the tents and huts now being dismantled, and a crowd of around twenty walking with their heads down or leaning back against the gusts as if against a cushion. Breaking through the silence, a few shouted words from them, and the sounds of Wills stirring inside the house. Then, from the elder Deans: Good morning! . . . To which I raised a hand.

Wills emerged behind me. I took some steps in the direction of the encampment, and said over my shoulder to him: Come on; we've lost a day already. I'm beginning to think the problem won't be covering ground but dealing with these people; getting them to understand the notion of a deadline.

To the north the plains were drier, if still shallowly swampy in places, and we pushed through scrub and across the shingled fans of streams, grown over with a low sparse covering of trees. After two or three hours, a steep bank gave way down to a wider river, flowing in several channels—the Waimakariri—and, following it downstream, accompanied by its rushing and choking, we met a group of natives carrying with them the bodies of two lean, black pigs still dripping faintly steaming blood from their wounds, and were led on, still further downstream, to their village, a small assemblage of grass huts gathered around a stony yard and here and there a carved pole or raised food platform. A man sitting outside one of the huts raised himself, welcomed his friends from the hunting party, and welcomed us; his face was impassive, partly tattooed, and under his shirt he had a scrawny but tightly muscled neck and arms. He said that we would have to wait, that more natives, his relatives and others from around the area, would be joining us here.

To Wills, in English, and quietly: I don't believe this! Are they out to make things difficult? . . . And to the chief: There's so much left of the day, we should go on . . .

He replied that there was no hurry, and that the night would be spent here.

Metehau appeared from behind me. In English, as if translating for me: Again we'll have to wait—I'm sorry about that. The people here are very concerned that we do things right, and that we discuss your visit to our land with everyone who has a claim to it.

That'll take—

Trust me, it will be fine. We don't want issues with you like we had with Kemp; be careful not to push things. I know a bit about the world, Mantell. Now, come on, I think you can set up your tents back over there . . .

I said, You see, Metehau— . . . He walked ahead of us, holding an arm out to a piece of silty ground on the edge of the village's yard. I followed, caught up, and said, I only have a certain amount of time to get this done—to get reserves set aside for your use from the land we've purchased from you—and it is important that I get them surveyed before the next instalment . . .

Listen, I know. You've said all this before, at Akaroa, and at Rapaki and all the kaika around there; you've explained yourself very clearly. The thing you haven't understood, though I think we've explained ourselves very clearly too, is that you've only bought land from a few of the chiefs. There's other land that you haven't bought, such as the land I belong to around here—and I'm not sure it's for sale. Now this should be a good place for your tents, do you think?

Metehau, frankly I feel stifled at every turn. Can't you say something to—I don't know. They seem to have your trust. What can I do?

He raised his hands in front, in a gesture that could have been a shrug or could have been to push me away from across the small cleared area. He said, Mantell, you don't listen to anything. I mean, you seem as stubborn as the rest, and when I thought you might be different? I'd like you to be welcome here . . . He stepped forward. He said, Really, I'm frustrated too. I want this to be settled too. And, okay, you do seem very—well, you seem to understand things well, and I'm confident that things will be arranged well, and that all this difficulty with Ngati Toa will be worked out. It's obvious that Europeans bring a different way of working things out, and I've seen it in the courts at New Plymouth, I've even seen it on the whaling boats, and it could work out very well. But who am I talking to, but the representative of the Queen! . . . He laughed, looked down, shook his head, shrugged. He said, You know all this. You know all this and nothing I can say will change anything. My position is really very humble, Mantell. You know I don't have any influence over anything here. I can't do anything that—I couldn't even presume to petition the chiefs, couldn't even present myself to them . . .

But you . . .

But I what?

Our guide says he respects your experience of the world.

No doubt. No doubt my experience is respected, but that's, it's complicated, and I thought you knew enough to—well, Mantell, didn't you get this job because of your experience in dealing with the natives, with us? You've come from Wellington, from Porirua—from Ngati Toa country and representing a Governor who has only ever bestowed favours on Ngati Toa.

Grey? He—

And it's hard not to think that you've already taken sides yourself. But you haven't, have you?

Of course not.

So we have to do things properly.

I sighed and took a step back to look again at the ground where we were to set up tents. The loosely silted rocky ground seemed to mirror a granular grey sky above; a breeze lifted the corners of dry flakes of silt and blew dust onto the leaves of the shrubs that grew around the clearing that housed the entire village.

I said, Where's Wills? . . . The surveyor was nowhere in

sight, and in fact the village seemed to all intents and purposes deserted, but for the chief who had welcomed us, lying by the entrance to the hut where we had found him, looking up at us and down again to either side, and raising his eyes again.

I thought I saw him going down to the river with some of our party.

What are they—what is this place, Hau?

This place? This is just somewhere for fishing. Or sometimes hunting . . . Then: I know, it's not much, is it? It's only a place to stop on the way, or to stay for a while and get food. It's only a dusty little clearing but it's—here, come with me.

He signalled me to drop my swag and follow him, between the low shrubs on a path that was practically non-existent, a few yards from the clearing and up against an old fence, or rather row of thin vertical posts around an area that was bare except for a thick carved post standing at a slight lean. I said, A sacred area?

One of our ancestors died on the water here.

And . . .

And we keep it as a fishing village. Not permanently, but . . .

You keep it as a fishing village because of . . .

No. I'll show you why we keep it as a fishing village . . . He led me back to the circle of huts, keeping his eyes on the ground as we passed the chief, who, when I cast a quick glance at him again, to see him older, weak and supporting himself on an elbow, caught my eye as if it were a challenge and held it long enough for me to look down, only to raise my eyes to see what had stopped Metehau in his tracks, with an arm across my body: a woman shuffling up the slope from the river, and in front of her body a flax basket fully laden with fish and swinging awkwardly into her knees as she carried it. Metehau pointed towards her, his other arm still in front of me.

The woman's eyes also raised towards mine, and also as if in challenge, but, flicking to one side, to Metehau, to the chief, she dropped them again. Behind her, three of the native men from our party followed and, looking over their shoulders at each other, smiled briefly, said a few words that I didn't understand or hear, and finally, at the end of this short procession, Wills, also bestowed with an over-the-shoulder grin from the men, and silently returning it before himself catching my eye with a suddenly straight face, another grin, and a shrug. At that moment, from behind me and to the left, the sound of voices and footfalls heralded the arrival of more natives in a party of about a dozen, some from the group that had been accompanying us thus far and some whom I didn't recognise. The old man was up to welcome them, starting a casual chaos of ceremony, of welcome and greeting and talking, in the midst of which I found myself to one side with Wills, then pressed in and spoken to in short bursts of oration, pressed to speak myself, an offer I declined with a short shake of the head and an aside.

I said, Wills, this is a travesty of efficiency . . . And throwing my hands up at his steady lack of response, his eyes fixed on no one and unmoving, his body squared against notice and against involvement in the spectacle of faces and voices, I sank finally into the same folded resistance myself, refused the names and genealogies offered to me, and, bewildered by the uncertainty of my own place in all the movement and hierarchy, chose to look at the ground, even to squat and put my hand on it and the other across my eyes, looking up now and then to see that I was now included only by sidelong looks, by gestures in my direction, and by the occasional, accidental meeting of eyes.

Later, by our tents, now set up to one side of the village in the place that Metehau had indicated, and while the natives now sat in the village's open circle and carried on the speeches, each longer now and rising to a louder peak, in terms that came to me vaguely through the sometimes unfamiliar dialect and my distracted attention, I tried to compose a letter to my father on a page torn from my memoir book: My dear Father, let my begin with a few lines to explain my present situation and the reason, no doubt, that this letter will be so long in reaching you. I am further from civilisation now than I have been since first setting foot on the shore at Pito-one, and now not surrounded by my compatriots and able to bargain in good faith with the natives but only accompanied by a sullen surveyor, my co-worker Wills whom I will have mentioned previously and who is now, as far as I can tell, asleep in his tent; this in mid-afternoon. I am anxious, as I write, that the box I packed and sent to you from New Plymouth should arrive in safety as it had fragile eggshells. Grey was most impressed by these and it seems if they should be broken it would be a great loss to—Father? If I have not had time for science it is because my time has been full, with worry, with attempting to deal with the natives and if I, if everything seems set up to, by the natives to block my progress, to stop me in everything that seems important, while the bones that I have sent are now out of my control and if they do not arrive safely I . . . The page was becoming confused with deletions and new starts, and I took one freshly from the book in my chest of drawers to copy it, recompose it, but my pen stayed over the inkpot and I was somehow unable to begin the letter again. At the approach of footsteps I covered the old page with the new.

What are you writing? . . . It was Metehau, approaching

slowly, his head to one side and a hand out in front of him.

A letter.

A letter? Who are you writing to?

I looked up at him, silhouetted against the glare of clouds. I said, To my father.

Yes, your father. He's the scientist.

What, you . . .

Yes, I know about your father. Well, people talked about him. He knows the Governor . . . ?

Well, distantly, he . . .

And you were digging about up north for him.

Look, Metehau, I want to . . .

He said, in Maori, You seemed to be absenting yourself from things here, you and Wills both? Don't you want to hear . . . ?

In English, I said, Right now, I want to . . .

Now we each spoke our own language. He said, Isn't it important—

Just for now, can you let me—

Because there are things you should hear, things—

Write this letter to—

Now in English, he said, Letter! That's just a blank page! Doesn't your father want to get more than a—

Well, right now I would love to write him more . . .

He paused, still standing over me.

I said, See, Metehau, I think I have heard a great deal already from you, from your people. You've done nothing but damned—ah, there's been plenty of talk . . . In Maori, in what I was aware was still somewhat close to the northern dialect, I said, The land has been bought as far as—well, as far as I'm concerned I can only do what I was sent here to do, to . . .

Yes . . . In English: To set aside reserves and nothing else—

how often have we heard that? You say the same things time and time again and you think that you've heard all we have to say, all the different korero from the, from different—damn you, Mantell . . . He picked up a stone from near my foot and stood, hefting it gently in one hand; he scuffed a foot at me and then, with an energetic movement that seemed to come too suddenly, threw the stone hard into the scrub nearby. He said, You won't even come and listen? Some of the chiefs who have just arrived were saying they want you to listen.

Now, stopping, he looked down for a minute, then sat heavily beside me. He closed his eyes, heaved a breath inwards, raising his torso and shrugging his shoulders before screwing up his face and putting a hand across the bridge of his nose, pinching in at his still closed eyes and letting a stream of air out from between his teeth. After a minute, he said, I don't expect anything to really change here. Every time I come back it's the same. We can keep our land, like the Whanganui iwi. We'll see that this sale, it's not—

I don't want to talk about this, now. I don't know anything about this. I'm not qualified, I'm not here to talk about this and I simply don't know, Metehau. For all I know, you— listen, leave me alone now, will you?

There was the sudden impression of a silence that had settled over our conversation. Metehau's voice had dropped since he had been seated; he had directed his words at the ground, whereas before he had seemed to speak into the air, even to speak as if to an audience, and, yes, the sound of discussion from the village clearing had dropped almost completely. A few faint words came across, and blended into the sound of the breeze in the bush that issued in a chattering hiss from all directions, overlaying yet another sound, from Wills's tent, close by: his breath, coming at regular intervals that suggested, too strongly, sleep, or someone trying to suggest sleep while carefully aware, and I wanted to simply say to Metehau that I was growing tired, that all the debate, the endless koreros, were exhausting me. I longed for the simplicity of the rocks, and in fact I wanted to be alone and nothing more. I said, now in Maori, at Metehau, and at the bush surrounding us, though I hated saying it: The reserves have to be set, and that is all. Nothing more will be done, not by me . . . Now there was a sound, as of a sudden gust disturbing the leaves and letting them clatter against one another, or the hiss and clatter of the crowd as they shuffled their feet and turned back to one another, and Wills turned in his sleep, or false-sleep, shuffling his blankets and the mattress under him. I stood.

Won't you even talk to me? . . . Quietly, and in English.

I'm going for a walk.

You won't sit down for more minutes? I want to tell you . . .

I'm going for a . . .

Mantell? . . . I walked around the side of the tents, in the direction of the sacred site he had shown me earlier, and away from the village. He said, Do you hate me so much?

I stopped, still facing away. I said, What? I . . .

Why? What have I done?

Metehau, I'm going for a walk. Nothing more.

The shadows were long now, and came from the direction of mountains visible as a distant suggestion of themselves, loosely cast by a sun sinking there, itself invisible but present as a fiery haze. I pushed through scrubby trees that seemed to resist now, as they hadn't done when Metehau had been with me, perhaps guiding me on a path not visible to my unaccustomed eyes. But, no, within a few steps I emerged at the same point before the fenced area and its standing figure, lit now against the west, reddened over its pale wood, cracked in a few places down its length, splitting one of the figure's eyes that were open right through to the sky behind. I skirted the fence and pushed through the scrub again, taking care to keep the sunset at my back, the vague hints of my shadow pointing ahead that appeared, now and then, between those of the trees or, now, on a rock that stood in my path. I stopped and leaned on it, forwards and with my head sideways against my arm: the dusty, loose texture of a diluvial sandstone. This plain, once a silty seabed? Or, rather, had deposits washed from the mountains, carrying ground-up rock from there out to sea, extending the land outwards and away from their shrinking presence?

In my free hand I still held, absentmindedly, the two pieces of paper: the blank one, and the one with starts, crossings-out: you can't imagine this place, its distance from civilisation, the miserable dry winds that come across it, even now in winter, and dry the mud into pale bland surfaces . . . I took matches from my waistcoat pocket and set the pages on fire, from their corners, allowing them to drop at first then flutter upwards with the flame into loose, flat ashes that fell apart as they were caught on the wind and scattered out over the trees. The Deans's farm, only half a day's walk away, seemed to be in another world, inaccessible now and missed in its comfort, and itself surrounded by the confusion of swamp and wasteland that I stood in the middle of, leaning back now on the crumbling sandstone to face into the west, into the sun that streaked outwards to either side in a glowing cloud horizon above the actual horizon, then, as I watched, came down against a jagged line of mountains visible suddenly in their precise form against it, as if it were forming in a fiery teardrop off the base of the horizontal cloud, to detach itself slowly and become, all too quickly,

211

obscured behind the dark array of peaks.

Now I walked, even hurried, towards it, to the shots of red that seemed to be its last protest, retracing the few steps I had taken, then, stumbling in a darkness that gathered around my feet and seemed to come too soon, broke into a few running steps before stopping again. If everything was far off now—the Deans's house representing all the houses of settlers and civilisation, and as I looked around all I could see was the fading scrubby crowding of trees and the dust and darkness that seemed to rise from the ground as if they were parts of the same breath—then my only connection back to a civilised world, my only connection back was through the miserable grass houses, the yard in between them, and through Wills and Metehau and the whole crowd waiting for me and watching me to tell me, time and again, the same complaints. The small page, closely written and heavily edited with deletions and insertions, and then burnt: Father? . . . And letting itself be taken up, with the other, blank page, over which my pen had hovered briefly but made no mark, taken up that is into the wind and blown to invisible ash and deposited into the silt and onto the leaves of the trees as a thin layer, over everything, against everything. The South Downs, the Tilgate Forest, the quarry there and the view down over the weald, all had their beauty, and this, in comparison, could you imagine it in its great dramatic sunset, distant over a scrubby, dusty and unfinished land? In need of soft grasses to spread it out to its horizon, to do justice to the mountains? Even the single line of a stone wall to cut it, a road to follow back . . .

Now I stumbled again on the sacred site, at first a mere dark clearing glimpsed from through resistant brush-like foliage, then, as I pushed through, resolving itself into vertical stripes of its fence against which I pressed my forehead, at first unknowingly as against a branch or tree that might bend

212

or break out of my path, then intentionally, gently, as I put my hands also around the posts and let the standing figure slowly come out against a sky slightly less dark than itself. I followed around its edge, and stood at the gap there where their priest would go in, looking at the figure without the interruptions of the fence and seeing nothing but its rough silhouette, and standing so that if I took one step I would be inside the circle of posts. In its outline I imagined, briefly, the face of the woman carting the fish from the river, walking heavily with her burden, glancing at me for a second as if her eyes were charged with light shining through holes carved straight from the back of her head like the carved figure; the similar gleam in the eyes of the woman I still knew only as Mary Ann, held fixed on mine, held at arm's length away from me with her grip on my shoulders: Leave me alone . . . Although at that time she had agreed to come out of the tent with me and walk for a few steps, out of earshot? She said, I don't want to be at your command. If we passed each other in broad daylight I would pretend I didn't know you and I would avert my eyes as to a rangatira.

I had stepped back from her, aware that her words were getting louder, their whispered sibilance ringing over the waves' repeated lapping. I said, What? I'm sorry, please . . . I stepped quickly through the hands on my shoulders, shrugging them off me so that I was close enough to smell something like her hair or skin. I said, Please be quiet?

Listen, you're not a rangatira and I'm not at your command, and you—you can't tell me what . . .

Please be quiet . . . ?

No one is listening or watching. And that's exactly why nothing is happening, Matara. Jack. That's why you and I aren't here now. So now I can make the rules just the same. Now I can be 'European' too.

213

What do you mean? . . . However, now she pushed past me, ducking under the level of an arm held out to hold her, and was there another pair of eyes on me as I flinched but otherwise remained standing, looking straight ahead?

From behind me, a voice: Did you deliver your letter?

Why . . . ?

Come back to the village, postmaster. Come and have some food with us.

Metehau . . .

Why are you standing around out here anyway?

I turned to him. He was about as far from me as the carved figure was, and I didn't answer his question but let him lead me, easily now, as if the trees had shifted to make the path that he led me on, back to the village and the still excitable crowd seated and squatting outside the houses.

In darkness, as the wind shifted to the south, lifting the edges of the tents, carrying the sound of rustling foliage from the bush, I lifted myself onto my elbow with my pen in hand and a notebook leaning on the small chest of drawers. The page remained blank, but for the few names I had been told by the natives as we walked today, and which would partly serve to peg out, through the pointed fingers and the features themselves named as we sighted them—mountains, rivers, even stones and the scarcely visible but regularly used paths we followed—the claim, the reserves, the maps that Wills was charged with producing. The sound of the surveyor's sleep, through the walls of the tents, came in short rushes of breath, as if he were being chased in his dreams, then a half-mouthed syllable, faintly voiced, as if roaming for a word to apply itself to, like the half-articulate noises I imagined my father had made when I sent word to him that I had decided to leave for the colony—as always in his office where, behind the closed or slightly ajar door, but never thrown open and left that way—he would work on his bills, notices, notebooks, correspondence with other scientists and with his clients, and now opening my letter: after these years of training how . . . ? This, another loss to him, along with the house and the museum. At hours past midnight he would still be there, and then up again at dawn as if he had slept a full night; on his horse to Whiteman's Green to stand by the pool and talk to the quarrymen. He was so pleased when I talked at the *conversazione*. But it was only some fossils I had scraped out of the chalk, lying visible for any enthusiast to take them and run to the local expert, in fact to him, someone who can be both surgeon and scientist, allowing time late into the night and always great, Father, always finding favour amongst the nobility that, in any case, you—didn't you despise them? Looking over the museum and making their pronouncements? Father, the collection is on its way. If it doesn't arrive, then just know that I sent it. Here, in the middle of—what was I doing here, with a page only faintly marked with a few names of rivers and other localities? The name of this village was not amongst them. Had I been told it?

The sound of the conversation from the village clearing continued unabated, with laughter and voices raised in excitement. I listened for Metehau's voice, but it was difficult to recognise. Then, listening more carefully, I understood that they were also discussing names: the Korotuaheka . . . Ruataniwha . . . the Kawari, Waitueri . . . the names were called out in a litany, then a pause and more words I didn't catch. Someone raised his voice with a new name and there came a clamour as of agreement.

Mantell, what are they—don't they ever sleep? . . . Wills's voice from his own tent: What are . . .

215

Quiet, Wills!

Me, quiet! I'm hardly—

Be quiet, will you? I'm trying to—

Oh, I—listening, are we?

Please, Wills.

For each name, a pause, then another, briefly discussed and then, sometimes, laughter and more discussion.

What are they talking about?

Shhh! . . . Then: I don't know, but I'm getting an idea.

Well, I'll just lie here then.

For God's sake, will you . . . ? By now, however, I was becoming certain; I looked at the brief list of place-names I had made earlier; I tore it from my notebook, screwed it up, and threw it at the wall of the tent. I said, This is a waste of my time.

What was that, Mantell?

They're busy making up false names for places.

Well, of all the . . .

If I could only hear better I could hear what they're saying and . . . I dipped the pen again and tapped off a drop of ink, ready to take down the list that I could almost overhear, but each time I became uncertain, started to note something down but quickly lost the syllables in the noise of the wind and the flapping of the tents, the general confusion of conversation. Then: No, it's no good, Wills. This whole thing is . . .

Ah, what do the names matter, Mantell?

You—you've got to produce a map of the reserves, and without . . .

There are always new names. There are always other ways of fixing something to a position on the land. I don't need their names to make a map.

I tapped the ink from the pen back into the pot and replaced its lid . . . What, Wills? Are you suggesting . . .

I'm not suggesting anything. I'm just trying to get a good night's sleep. Listen to them, will you . . . ?

We can't just . . .

We can do what's necessary. Or, rather, you can do what's necessary. Who am I to say? I am just here to survey and make maps, and you're here to deal with them.

I sighed, pulled from my chest of drawers my bottle of brandy and put it to my lips. I said, Wills? A drink?

Gladly.

I stood crouching with the bottle, pulled my blanket around my shoulders and ducked outside. Overhead one or two stars tried to force themselves through the cloud layer and the tips of the trees flicked against them, seemingly driven not by the wind but a gust of laughter from the natives; I looked over at the group, lying and seated around a fire that illuminated a single figure standing over them, and who seemed, at first, in a position of authority, except that he was back slightly, not taking part in the conversation, only catching the fire's illumination because of his height above the rest, and, I realised, looking directly at me: Metehau. He raised a hand at me. I shook my head and squatted in the entrance to Wills's tent, pushing through the flap and extending the bottle out before me. Wills was lying on his back, fully clothed in his trousers and waistcoat, and with his hands folded behind his head and his blanket folded neatly beneath him. He raised his head suddenly, as if disturbed from sleep, and reached out to take the bottle from me.

Arh, that's . . .

He passed it back and I took a substantial swig, feeling the liquor's burn on the back of my throat; I took another immediately and passed the bottle back to him. Finally I said, I don't care overly for this.

Really, Mantell? . . . He laughed into the bottle before

raising it again, letting the contents drain liberally for a second. Then: God, what can I say? Oh, for heaven's sake, come in will you? Don't stay crouching there like, here . . . He handed the bottle back while I settled, sitting down, in the space beside him, next to his chest of drawers and neatly folded coat. He said, Well, for a start, Mantell, I'd do anything for some decent brandy.

You ungrateful . . .

Oh no, not ungrateful. You miss my point entirely. I'm very, very grateful . . . Taking the bottle back again, he said, You see, good brandy, a decent bed, a fireplace, for God's sake. We've hardly left the Deans brothers and already I can't wait to . . .

Decent food! And this is only the beginning of a long, long trip. But it's not the time or the food or comfort or, not the few days we've been out here, it's . . .

Here, have more.

It's that suddenly there's nothing to hold onto.

Have more, Mantell . . .

Not even the damned names of things any more. Well, what do you think we're getting ourselves into, with . . .

Well, if you won't . . . Upending the bottle over his face.

No, no, give me some . . . I took it from him and took a sip. Then: No, on second thoughts, you . . . I passed it back to him and moved so that I was once again crouching in the entrance to the tent, looking out this time. I spun around to face him again, and he looked up at me, half-raised on an elbow and twisted around with his face close to the bottle's neck.

Mantell, for—what are you doing? Why don't you come and . . . ?

You're right.

Good. Then come on and have a drink. This bottle isn't going to last you long anyway, so we . . .

No, no, you're right about their false names.

Oh, that. Well, nice of you to say so, but—where are you
. . . ?

I was already out of the tent, and took some tentative
steps away from it as if I might trip on the rough ground. I
heard Wills's voice in an obscure mutter from behind me, and
in front the ongoing discussion, now evolved into a general
and excited chatter, still merging with the sounds of the land
and the bush around: rustling, crackling and the whistle of
a wind that was picking up more from the south, flicking
the blanket that was still wrapped around my shoulders and
hanging there like a cape, and giving to the surroundings
a movement and confusion that played on the edges of my
vision, as if something might emerge from beside me, behind
me, unexpectedly. Metehau was still the only one standing,
as if supervising the crowd, providing a single still point
amongst the hubbub and movement, and with his eyes, once
again, focused on me. He called out, in English, over the top
of the crowd: Have you come to join us?

Yes—no. Not quite, Metehau . . . At my words the
discussion quietened and attention turned to me. I was also
standing, facing Metehau; I looked over my shoulder briefly
to see Wills's face in the entrance to his tent, a pale shape
turned up slightly and watching. Would he see me swaying
slightly—and would Metehau see the same thing? The
brandied hurriedness of my thoughts swung me back around,
and I cleared my throat: No, I'm not here to—Metehau, I
want to say something . . .

Yes, by all means.

In Maori now, I started: Your place-names aren't important
to me, to us. If you want to arrange false ones, if you want
to change the names, that doesn't concern me at all . . . I
was still speaking as if directly to Metehau, over the tops

of the assembled heads, holding his eyes and I felt his gaze and looked down, then cast my eye about the other faces meeting mine; in my mind still, however, was Metehau's, grinning tolerantly as if for that moment he was supervising, not only the crowd, but myself. I felt myself sway towards him now, felt a brief surge of anger, though I was still looking down from his eyes, and all at once I felt more thoroughly isolated than before, held at a distance from everything by the expectancy of the crowd, the chiefs and their companions gathered, whose lives consisted of nothing more than places like this, the dusty wind-blown existence far from anything and bordered only by the darkness of mountains and the equally gloomy ocean, somehow finding food from rivers and swamps and their sparse crops.

I said, As far as I'm concerned all the features here will have to be given English names anyway, so whatever you decide to call things it won't make any difference.

At that I turned quickly, imagining despite myself that the capelike blanket might give me a dramatic appearance, but stumbled and half-ran, then slowed, back to Wills's tent, where he was still crouching half emerged from the entrance.

He said, What were you saying to them?

Is there any more . . . ?

I'm not that partial to your liquor to have finished it off. Here.

Holding the bottle to my mouth I turned to the side, looking out past Wills and over his head and with, on my left side, the open space where the natives were assembled, still talking amongst themselves in much the same way as they had been, perhaps with a hush now as if the energy of their speech was waning, and sending a quick sideways glance in that direction, I caught sight of Metehau, who raised a hand to me in a thoroughly ambiguous salute.

I said, Well, hopefully that cut that discussion short . . . I looked quickly down from Metehau to Wills.

What did you do?

I told them—I told them we'd be assigning new names to the localities hereabouts. English ones.

Ha! You're a cunning one, Mantell!

I don't know if I like the repercussions.

Repercussions? For God's sake, come in and sit down for a minute. You're standing around here like, I don't know. Come on.

Inside the tent, seated once again opposite Wills, it seemed as if the noise of discussion had fallen off almost completely, replaced by a whispered rise and fall that could again have been simply the unaccompanied noise of the wind and the trees. I said, At least you might be able to get some sleep now?

I dare say.

But Wills, I don't like this. We're here without anything but them to take us back to—we're on our own in this . . .

You're worried about them? What they'll do?

Tell me what you think . . . After he looked at me, silent, his eyes dark in the tent lit only by a single candle, dim and flickering and giving half his face highlights and leaving the other to retreat in the vague sketches of shadow, I said, I feel as if I've just made enemies of them—finally now. If they were belligerent before, then they're certain now to be more so. They'll be resistant to everything; they'll hinder us at every move; they'll—give me that . . . Taking the bottle from Wills, who was now cradling it against himself and gripping its neck. I said, What are we doing out here? If Eyre knew these people and the impossibility of this he wouldn't have sent us out . . .

We're not here to make friends with them.

221

No. We're just here to—

Yes, yes, for the reserves. Actually, maybe it's time you stopped . . . He reached out to me, signalling the brandy as I took another swig. Then: Maybe it's time you tried to get some sleep yourself? We'll have to be moving on tomorrow.

But, Wills, do you . . . ?

Listen, get some sleep. Go on, you'll feel all the better for it. They won't do a thing to you, they wouldn't dare—you, the representative of the Governor, and of the Queen? They know they'd have the army down on them in no time. Of course Grey is more than happy to deal with Ngati Toa, and they won't want that. Now, isn't it time for bed?

Why are you—do you really think . . . ?

Goodnight, Mantell.

But our job? It's . . .

Sleep well.

It seems more and more impossible . . . He turned away from me on the blanket, still dressed in his waistcoat, and folded his hands under his head. I said, Damn it, Wills, I don't understand you. Aren't you worried about them? If we don't do this right, that's our last chance of work for the government . . .

I don't work for the government. Now, would you kindly —

You, what? Yes, you're employed by the Company, but —

Quite.

I, um . . .

Would you put out the candle when you leave?

Wills? What do you . . . I stopped and let the tent stay silent, the warmed glass of the bottle, now almost empty, against my hand, and Wills's form dissolving into the textures of the tent and the blanket, the back of his head an oily dark

222

mass glinting in streaks against the varying light. I shifted on my knees towards the tent's entrance, then turned to blow out the candle. By the entrance, still kneeling inside the door, I said, Wills?

What is it, Mantell?

I'm concerned about the bones I sent to my father. If something happens to them en route? If they don't arrive . . . ?

They will. I wouldn't worry about that.

Yes. I'm sure you're right. Goodnight then.

Goodnight.

The following morning, the natives demanded payment before ferrying us across the river. Metehau said to me, That sounds fair?

No. Repitch the tents then. We'll stay here until some other way is found for us to be ferried across. Perhaps someone amongst you people will see fit to take us without requiring payment . . . Two men, standing by the rolled tents where they had just deposited them, ready to carry onwards, both sought out my eye, and bent down, shrugging at each other, recovering the poles from where they had been discarded and preparing to set up the tents where they had been. Then, standing, they hesitated, looked at each other and me once again and stopped the work, letting themselves lean on the poles. I waved a hand at them, but they remained watching while Metehau looked over his shoulder at the three further men standing behind him, and for a few seconds a silence seemed to hold everyone in position. I said, in English, Listen, I don't want this to be more difficult than it has to be. Maybe last night I . . .

No one wants it to be difficult. I would like nothing better than for this all to be over right this minute.

You and I both.

All right, come on . . . He said, in Maori: Let's go, then. Mantell will pay us as and when he sees fit . . . His words were spoken as if with the understanding that they would be obeyed; and indeed the men behind him turned away immediately, those to one side lifted the tents again and began to carry them down towards the river, following me, following Metehau, to where Wills was already standing, at a short remove from a group of natives and two canoes, and looking alternately down at his feet and up at the clouds. The river's channels moved in and through each other, separated by banks of shingle, trees dotted here and there on islands and collared with stiff low bushes, and seemingly moving, falling and disappearing into the flow as we watched. Downstream the river formed an alternative sky, taking on the sun's dissipated light and flickering it with its own movements into a smouldering airy expanse suggestive of the estuary and the haze of ocean waves that must have been somewhere in that direction.

Wills said, You go in the first, Mantell.

I dare say we'll both fit in the same boat? Come . . .

No. No, you go on . . . He turned away, tapping his foot and kicking at the stones . . . He said, I just need to sit down for, ah . . .

In the same boat instead, then, with Metehau and a number of other natives, we slipped into the stream then shifted in sideways movements, shuffling across onto the side of each small standing wave while drifting downstream, then were thrown back as the bow forced itself upwards, paused there and fell, all the while surrounded by, and confronted by, the water's sky and its noise of ticking and birdsong, and Metehau stood up in the boat while the others' paddles dug sideways then pulled back against the surface. He put out his hands and stood there as if commanding an army, then laughed, let his arms drop and, in a movement that made my stomach turn for fear that he would fall into the river, though at that moment we were gliding smoothly over a section, between channels, of shallow water over red-brown shingle whitened in moving undulations by morning light, he turned to me as if standing on solid ground and squatted in front of me. His eyes seemed to catch something of the burning water's surface to the east, which, now that we were shifting with its own motion, washed from side to side, its light washing over us like the water, surrounding the boat and shocking us with its contact, like the pool about our feet that soaked into my boots.

Metehau said, The whalers would throw themselves up on the sea like this, but so much more. Not like the big ships, just rolling and crashing, but—I can't describe it. The small boats we would go after the whales in, you've seen them. I suppose you've even been on them, on the coast around here, but in the open sea—the European boats are magnificent! And riding a big swell, not a small chop. And we all stank of whale after no time. And come back with salt crusted on us like some seafaring story, you know. I was never told those stories but I lived them. Look at your surveyor there! He's . . . Wills, as I saw over my shoulder, was stepping gingerly into the second canoe, still unlaunched upstream from us, with a hand covering his eyes and supported by a native on either side. Metehau went on: He would rather take the long way around?

The long way . . . ?

There is no long way around . . . Metehau laughed: You have to cross the river at this point. The noise of this, of the water under the boats, for example, that noise you don't hear anywhere else but in a boat. I've seen so much out there on

225

the water, even if most of the time we had our eyes trained on the horizon and there was nothing but ocean everywhere. Look! Hooray! They've got him launched!

Metehau? What are you talking about . . . ?

Your surveyor, they . . .

No, what are you going on about like that?

What? Mantell, I was simply—you know you're a difficult person. Maybe they should have sent us someone less difficult. But you've got this reputation of being good with the natives, haven't you? Of knowing so much how to deal with us. I think maybe you're worse than Kemp, who just stayed on his boat and let us come to him—at least we could ignore him, as, quite frankly, Mantell, I did . . . Abruptly he stood up again and turned to face the other way. Then he turned back: You know I'm never quite sure I trust you. I never quite know what you're saying, and I just want to be straight with you . . .

I've been nothing but—

I just want to know exactly what—

I've been nothing but straight. But who are you, anyway, to ask so much of me, to want to know so much? You told me yourself, you're insignificant, you have no authority or significance or . . .

I told you my position is humble. I think those were the words I used.

Well then.

He shifted his weight in the boat, which was by now coming up alongside the far bank, slowing into the still waters by the river's edge and rocking as it made the transition, the back end swinging in slightly so that a native there could reach and grab at a tree to finally bring it to a halt. Metehau said, Now, Mantell, once you have set foot on this side of the river you are well and truly our guest. You and your surveyor are our guests . . . He stepped out of the boat, swinging down into the knee-deep water. He said, So, can I help you out of the boat?

I declined the hand offered to me and lowered myself, much as he had, over the side of the canoe and into the water. The other canoe was approaching, with Wills holding onto his hat with one hand and the other across the bridge of his nose pinching and forcing his eyes shut, and it passed just downstream then came in also to the still water, a muddy brown now from our feet that seemed to make the water into a new kind of surface, dull, dimly reflecting the outlines of the figures around me as I walked through it for some yards to the shore, forging past Metehau, who followed close behind me so that I could feel the heat of his body, his breath. As he followed he began talking again: Mantell, I have spent so much time at sea, and I learned to love the waves and colours of the water and different ports. You know, I'm practically European. That's why they respect me. I'm Ngai Tuahuriri and I'm practically European and that's also why I can ask you so many questions. I know what it is to be European and how to handle things the way you do. I've seen courts and lawyers, and the thing about us Europeans is that whatever we touch also becomes European, it also becomes like you and Wills and myself, and all these other people don't know it yet but they're slowly becoming European.

That's ridiculous . . .

It's true.

Leave me alone, Metehau, with your . . . I climbed up a short bank layered with shingle and mud, where, somehow, away to the right, Wills was already standing, with mud streaked down his trousers, as if he'd been there all along and was waiting for us to arrive. He threw up an arm towards me, in welcome.

Small birds darted upwards from the islands of fern and scrub, stabbing at clouds that seemed just overhead, pushed by a steady wind from the mountains and becoming ragged and disappearing into a strip of blue out to the east. Cool air came off the clear layer of water that sat—disturbed by wind-fans and occasional expanding circles from something flicking up from under it, or from the edges of the plants sending up rushes from a scarcely submerged mud—over the obscurer depths, resisting the diffuse light, seeming to flow in this direction or that, generally out towards the sea but almost imperceptibly, as a hint, a dragging sideways of the foundations of things; after I had stood a few minutes at the edge, near the remains of the structure—palisades now fallen into burnt stumps and logs rotten through, becoming part of the damp ground that once supported their upright stature; earth mounds still surviving but retaining none of the sharp utility of defensive structures, being instead rounded off into overgrown vagueness—this sideways flow gave me a brief spell of dizziness.

Wills and I were welcomed onto the site by the natives, now around fifty in number, who were silent at first, staring blinking into the north, the light from there signalling a sun behind the cloud layer that served only to hide its position, if anything increasing its glare and transposing it also to the water's surface. I was led up a mound that, higher than the rest, gave a rare view over the flat landscape, towards mountains and to the north to the faintly visible slopes of lower hills that hadn't previously been in view through the scrubby forest that had surrounded us on the way here. The breeze seemed, from this small hill, to contain the distilled essence of the landscape itself; the curled and dampened smell of swamp, like paper, and edged with snow. It was also, from this small hill, on the northern edge of the pa site, that the chiefs, one by one, stood up for their speeches. The pa had finally fallen to Ngati Toa seventeen years before, and the defeat was part of the northern tribe's claim to the land, a claim that sometimes extended even further south, as far as Akaroa. Now, the Ngai Tahu chiefs conceded the loss of the battle, but not the land, to a tribe that had simply conquered and then left again. Did it seem now that the battles would be on paper? With the five hundred pounds they had already received, they were prepared to cede the land north of this point to Kaikoura; they insisted on retaining the land as far as the mountains between here and the Waimakariri River.

I said to Wills, Again they're trying to sell land that has already been sold to the Government. How many times can I tell them it's impossible? What can I do about this . . . ?

Reserves, Mantell. Nothing more.

The speeches continued and became a kind of background in their familiarity. It was the sense that the trip was only beginning, that this, the northernmost point of the block, marking one end of the ground I would have to walk with Wills and whichever natives would accompany us, was in a way the starting point of a walk that led back to Akaroa and then much further south, along beaches that, so it was said, stretched for miles, featureless and relentlessly blown and eroded by sea and weather from the east and south, an ocean that felt unending. This sense took over from the words directed at me and at the other natives assembled, dulled not only my ears to the words but my other senses, so that the swamp smell, the cold damp of the breeze, even the view that glared from all the surfaces—of water, of ground, of fallen and rotting wooden structures (here, a food platform that had tilted and fallen, the buried end having prised up a disc of earth at its base some time past)—all were easily ignored, in favour of a 'view' of the landscape of our trip in a single line, south to Otakou, behind a mist of spray from the ocean, behind the shimmer that made the land itself seem as unstable as the sea abutting it. This imagining, and, suddenly, a clear view of the ground at my feet, the only surface worth studying carefully: trodden clay, the remains of tussocks, and an irregularly shaped stone.

Again, speeches that this land had not been sold, and that they had made their own peace with Te Rauparaha when he returned his captives taken at the fall of the pa. One chief said that it seemed only now that the battles were starting again, wars of money that they understood only too well. Was it that they were now to understand ownership not by who cultivated there and who lived there—who lived there for long enough—but who could simply, at just *one* point in time, say, I will sell this land to you, and for how much? Weren't we here to say that this land belongs to them, now, and so forever, giving them the right to sell? He wondered, therefore, whether our paper didn't have the strange power of right now and forever, of making everything permanent. He said that the money we offered could preserve things like salt? In that case, he would sell himself and become immortal. He began to call for offers: how much would we pay for such a fine specimen?

The speech ended with the same stirrings, the same laughter that had kept us awake in the camp by the Waimakariri, and I shook my head, both to signal that I would not answer the native's absurd question—hand him some bills and take possession—but also a broader refusal to respond to the belligerence it represented. Their hilarity at once seemed to express an anger, a sort of pummelling threat, but also to turn attention away, to render me and Wills irrelevant, a sort of bad joke. This irrelevance, the anger, the resistance of the natives, now laid itself in turn over the picture I had been developing in my mind of our line from here to the south, of the ground along that line varying in its geology and in what fossils it concealed, so that as we walked along it, southwards, we became less and less visible, blown as vapour into the vapour rising off the surf or disintegrating into the land itself, our bones resting, preserved, immortal, under its surface. The new speaker said that things—words, questions—would slide off me; that I was always the wrong person to talk to; that I was only employed here for one thing and not the other, not the real thing. That I couldn't talk about the extent of the block because I was only here for the reserves. That I couldn't use their names, but would rather make up my own—he said that everything slid off me, and was there anyone whose job it was to actually answer their questions, who wouldn't just shrug like myself, like Wills? Was there anyone who understood what they had sold—in many cases, in the speaker's own case, nothing, since he had put his signature on no deed? Increasingly, the speeches were addressed directly to me, as if they wished to force a response from me, to involve me in the jokes and the anger. Finally I climbed up the small hill myself.

I said, I know you don't want to hear that I am only here for one purpose, and that I can't talk to you about the boundaries of the block, or what the first instalment can be taken as payment for, or who has sold what to whom. But I don't know about any of that, and what can I do? All I can do is report your case to the Lieutenant Governor, and I am willing to do that if you let me get on with my job, if you stop delaying and resisting at every turn ... Looking at the assembly, I searched the faces meeting mine for something: a recognition, an acceptance, or alternatively a denial, but I found no obvious sign of a response to my words. The faces seemed to contain, in their refusal to listen, a sort of turning-away even as they remained focused on me and, clenching my teeth for a minute then opening my mouth to speak again, closing it, half turning to one side, then back, I threw my hands up. I said, I will undertake to report your case to Lieutenant Governor Eyre if you conduct yourselves better.

Still searching, I understood that I was searching for a single face amongst the crowd. Metehau was nowhere to be seen. His voice echoed in my memory, kept up amongst others throughout the previous night at our camp some way to the south. He had said, I know the value of the land around here. I have been north and seen the exchanges, talked to the settlers, talked to the government agents, and I know what should be sold for how much! Listen to me, I know this better than Mantell does!

Had I seen him since? Hadn't he walked with me some of the way here? In fact, though I had been thinking of his words, the open bragging about his knowledge, even as he approached me to point something out—an eel darting away quickly as we crossed a small creek—his presence had come as a strange comfort, as someone I could, though with difficulty, consult. Wills was silent ahead of me, walking heavily then slipping awkwardly to one side as he crossed the stream.

I had said, Do you fish them from here?

He said, Most of the eels are from the larger rivers to the south, where we can let them build up a lagoon from sand pushed up by the waves and then cut a channel. Then you put a net across and you've got a feast! You can eat so well from those catches. You should see it, Mantell . . .

Now, missing his face in the crowd, I felt a sense of dismay. I wanted to step back, away from them, at once all unfamiliar, even those I had shared some words with as we walked, but I felt the presence of the swamp nearby, behind the ruined palisade. How could I say anything to reassure, even pacify, the crowd? Had they become, all of a sudden, such a mystery to me? Hadn't I joked with some of them, talked with some of them as if they were friends? I paused, uncomfortable, looking around into the landscape. I started speaking again: Of course, we will be able to come to some arrangement even if it means my taking a case back to Eyre, to Grey even, to negotiate once and for all—for all time?—the ownership, the sale of the land, something that will prove comfortably acceptable . . . Again I faltered and they continued, it seemed, to stare, unrecognisable—was Metehau amongst them after all?—expecting my next statement, and I became unsure whether I could open my mouth without uttering a plea to them, or without simply resigning my post there and then, and partly because, amongst them, to one side, was Wills, I turned partly away. With the crowd to one side of me, and looking out, I felt the swamp's pull, the ruffle of its surface into fans of darkened water. The sun, hidden behind its layer of cloud cover, cast vague shadows of the scrubby islands onto the water's surface, with both the fans and the shadows standing out against a sometimes brilliance of reflection that quivered and broke and, in the middle of this, an island with a considerable growth of ti stood out, the trunks grown densely enough that all light seemed banished from between them, and their leaves bending and flicking lightly in the wind overhead.

I said, still facing away: There—that island shall be at the northern boundary of the reserve. And it will include this pa site as you would wish . . . I turned back towards the assembly, still indicating with an arm behind me the island which, in any case, was unmissable, and repeated my announcement, before stepping down from the hill.

*

On the walk back to our camp at Tuahiwi, I looked over my shoulder at one point to see Metehau behind me. He looked down quickly and stepped to one side, halting, allowing another native to pass him, and only once he was some distance behind did I look again to see him, this time meeting my eye and not looking down before he disappeared from view behind a tree—no doubt pausing to relieve himself. The natives were for the most part silent, walking single file through wooded country; perhaps the initial sense of humility, perhaps, or awe, on entering the site of the battle, now already legendary as something of a last battle, had returned to them. Wills seemed infected by the same reluctance to speak, turning at once from me and walking ahead as we set off. On the other hand, I—turning my head again to look towards Metehau, and finding him now nowhere in sight—felt a chattering energy, shook my head, tripped and half-fell (no one seemed ready to help me), and only wanted Metehau to point something out again: some edible plant or the beginning of a trail which led to some other destination, and which would be visible to me only as a continuation of the same forest. When we broke into the open briefly, coming across the shingle of a creek, in the half-light before dusk, and not far from our camp, the sandhills to the east became visible for a second, caught in a brief red from the setting sun, and I took some quick steps to walk beside Wills.

What is it, Mantell?

I don't know, I, nothing . . .

Good, then . . . He quickened his pace slightly.

But, Wills, tell me what your impression of this situation is. I told them that I would take their case to Wellington, as seems only proper since I'm not the person to . . .

234

Metehau translated for me.

Metehau? He . . .

Translated for me. What's my impression of the situation got to do with anything, Mantell? How many times must you ask me this? Careful of the rocks here . . . We crossed the stream whose shallowly submerged bed was covered with a red, slippery layer. He said, I mean, my impression is the same as it was. What could I say, as mere surveyor? Well, of course I would rather be elsewhere . . .

Rather be where?

Elsewhere. It's not your business where I would rather be, Mantell.

Sometimes you're as belligerent as they.

Look, I just want to get through this with my job and my life and my sanity. Right now you're not helping with the latter.

Well, should we be feeling safe? You've been on trips like this.

You'll get used to it. You'll learn.

Now don't—well, all right, what will I learn?

You'll learn how to survive.

Wills . . .

If you'll excuse me . . . We were entering the forest again, low and scrubby still but high enough that the branches met above our heads, and with trees growing densely enough that walking two abreast was impossible. He ducked under the trees first, leaving me to follow, speaking to his back.

Wills, what do you mean—will you tell me . . .

Over his shoulder, his head in profile and nodding forwards again repeatedly as he watched his step, he said, You learn to know exactly what you're doing. You learn what is your job and what isn't, and for the time being you become nothing but your job. That's how you survive. You're getting there, but it isn't your job to take anyone's case to the Lieutenant Governor.

Do you think—I wanted to pacify them a little . . .

Of course, it's not my place to say anything about that . . . His cheek, turned towards me for a second, showed a half-smile.

Wills?

Mantell, if you don't mind?

His pace quickened still further, leading him to stumble and reach for a tree, turning partly as he did so, but only looking briefly to the side into the scrub, and, steadying himself, he again walked on, not casting so much as a glance towards me.

Towards the middle of the following day Wills began his survey. After more debates with the natives concerning the extent of the reserves, more demands that they keep the land from the Waimakariri to Kaiapoi and now extending from one coast to the other, I had walked with them to the sandhills, and from there north to show them the extent of the reserve I was prepared to grant. Finally they acquiesced, though, despite the signatures, a doubt remained in my mind as to how final their agreement was. Metehau walked with me from time to time over the next days while, setting out to the north from our camp and following a broad loop, we followed Wills, watching him take bearings from one pole to the next at the boundary locations I set down.

Metehau said, This is only the beginning, Mantell. I'm setting great store by the Lieutenant Governor to have the purchase looked over in its entirety, and this reserve in particular. I hope you will speak to him?

Yes, Metehau, I will see what I can do.

And he understands you? You have his ear?

I hope so.

You hope so? How else can we get his attention?

Listen, I will do what I can.

What you can? It seems as if you're slipping away from me, Mantell; only ever able to do what you can. I mean, this land—I don't even know if I care about it but I don't want it to just be lost without, I don't know. So if you don't speak to him I will speak to him myself.

You . . . ?

No, you're right. You're right. I should just let you do your job, and do what you think is possible. Just between you and me, the land doesn't mean very much to me. I could leave it and go back to working on the whale-boats, and I'd be free of the place, with nothing to worry about but my health . . .

You won't have to do that. The reserves will work out well for everyone. You can stay on your land.

I've hardly stayed on my land up until now.

Well, there'll be a place set aside, Metehau? And the benefits of the new colonies to add to that: hospitals, schools . . .

Yes, the benefits that Ngati Toa are currently getting?

If you like.

Right now, I'm not feeling unhealthy or uneducated, Mantell, though you might think otherwise.

That's not what I meant—

I know. Yes, I know, all those benefits from European science. But actually I think there's almost nowhere I'd rather be than on the water. That's starting to seem like a good option.

But, listen, I will take your case to the Governor, and there will be a correct procedure.

He said, All right, Mantell.

I'm sure I will be able to have some sway.

I caught his sidelong look at me as we walked, with the surveyor some way behind us. He said nothing for a minute, and in his eye a studied gaze and a certain distance, as if he were already deciding to leave, or already feeling the rise and fall of a ship's motion. Then he said, And the Governor, he will also do what he can?

Yes. It will be out of my hands, but, yes, I'm sure.

He nodded.

On one of the following days, as Wills took the bearings to a pole erected at Waitueri, two men emerged from one of the huts there, inspected the pole, took it from the ground and discarded it. Our man didn't protest, and even allowed the extra poles he was carrying to be taken from him and thrown also in a loose pile under a bush at the edge of the village.

Wills said, For God's sake tell them to let the poles alone! They can't just throw them—how can I do my work if they throw the poles away? Tell them to keep out of my way. Tell them the poles aren't to be touched. Mantell?

It's all right, Wills. They just didn't understand the use of them.

I explained the poles and stayed with the men, while Wills, already walking quickly back to the theodolite, clenched his fists and relaxed them, looking at the ground as he walked. I looked up to the crowd, only a small gathering that had followed us today from the camp, again looking for Metehau's face amongst them. The previous night, in fact, he had been arguing again, as the speeches were kept up, for a greater payment for the land, or for only a small portion of land to be ceded for the money already given to them. He had said, once again, that the northern tribes showed greater resistance, and that this was an example to follow; in the northern case it was successful, and they didn't have to give anything more than they wished to. He seemed a different person from the man who came up beside me with his questions, and while I felt the same strange desire as at Kaiapoi for his company— now, as I stood with the old men who had thrown down the poles, facing Wills and the natives at some distance—I also wondered what northern tribes he had been talking about, wondered what payment he was advocating for the land that, in any case, he didn't overly care for. When I saw him, at last, in fact amongst the group but at its back, he raised a hand to me, in a gesture that seemed at first genuine, but then also half-hearted, automatic, as if no thought had gone into it. Then, as they followed Wills—who had noted the bearings in his book, taken down the theodolite and, with an arm around it holding it against his body, set off towards me— Metehau seemed to trail behind by a few steps, shrugging his shoulders to himself and kicking out his feet at rocks and exposed tree roots.

I said, Metehau, last night—

Don't talk to me, Mantell.

Metehau, come here, I—

Don't talk to me now. I've ceased caring.

What?

Leave me alone ... He turned his body from me and continued towards the group which, with Wills, was standing to one side now and looking towards me, waiting for me to join them.

Wills said, Come on, Mantell, don't worry about him.

Listen to your surveyor. Don't worry about me, Mantell.

Metehau? I want to ask you about your—

He continued on past me, silently, and, joining the group, found his way to its middle or far side, hiding his face from me. After I had joined Wills I said under my breath, You heard Metehau last night, giving speeches? It was all about getting more payment, about resisting us.

Haven't they all been saying that from the start? . . . He set up the theodolite again at the point where the pole had been.

I'm sure you're right. But I want to question him about it once and for all, and now he won't say a word to me. You know, sometimes he's the epitome of reason, and you'd think his mind was miles from any thought of resistance.

Maybe it is? . . . He jotted a bearing in his book and turned to me. He said, Let it rest for now? . . . He indicated the group watching from only a few yards distant, Metehau amongst them.

As night fell I stood at the edge of the camp, looking out into a darkening wood; the remaining surveying would take no more than a day, and we would then be retracing our steps to Akaroa before the southern, and much longer, leg of the journey. Wills was amongst the natives, unaware of the meanings of their words, which continued in an excited fashion about the Ngati Toa sale and native successes in the Hutt and Horokiri, but I found it impossible now to join them, much as I had in the kaika at the Waimakariri, and simply stood, wishing to let their words become mere sound as they were to Wills or as, sometimes, they were also to myself. Instead they broke into my thoughts in an unwelcome manner: was I listening for Metehau's voice? In any case I couldn't hear it. I wished for silence, or better to simply enjoy solitude for a time, but I felt fixed to the spot, unable to step away from the camp and enter the space beyond, which grew heavy, tangible, and seemed to congeal with a cold that grew upwards from the ground and wrapped itself about the trunks of trees, the undergrowth and over the damp surface of the ground. The wind that had accompanied us for days, animating the landscape with small movements, pulling at our coats and sometimes gusting at the survey poles, causing one to lean, another to fall just as Wills was taking its bearing, was now gone. In the brief silences, pauses for emphasis or between speakers, there seemed to be an overall downward movement, a settling into the ground, as of dew falling, though without moisture, or of a blanket spread over the landscape and dropped all at once, interrupted only by the rise of the smoke from the fire behind me and its accompanying crackle. With each such silence, I waited, tensed, to see whether this time it would last, if not for hours, then just for minutes, for time enough for me to compose, under my breath, a letter to my father—or even its opening lines—or a note to the Lieutenant Governor. Each time, of course, before I could follow the thought through to its conclusion, I was interrupted by another burst of speech.

Then later, from the darkness of my tent, the speeches seemed to have quietened, the air settled once and for all, interrupted only by whisperings and the hiss and pop of the fire, or an occasional movement that seemed, once or twice, to be directly outside the tent's canvas: the upsetting of the leaf litter or fallen twigs by a footfall, or perhaps just the scratching of a weka? I let myself dream of Metehau's life on the ships—did the smell of the oil pervade everything? I imagined his face against the wind of the ocean, open mouthed and catching a mist blown off the tops of the waves and the small whale-boat bearing down into swirling water, the ship itself out of view, and was it turning away, moving under the weight of its furnace? Had his world opened up at sea, the way mine had aboard the *Oriental*—stretches of ocean previously unimaginable to me? Then the sighting of new land, hinted at initially by its clouds that, as we learned, sat over land differently from over water, seemed solid as if mirroring what was beneath them, until, finally, it became visible, a dark smudged line waveringly present over the waves, sometimes waves that threw the ship up—the small boats, even more so—sending those on board grasping for rails and whatever didn't move, even as they went about their business, hanging for a second over the edge of something, a chasm opened up in a darkened landscape of water frozen for an instant into craggy terrain before the rush and righting of the ship, the replacing of the trough by its opposite, an equally impressive wave-crest. Would the collection find its way through all this? The eggshells, thrown about in their packing, remain unharmed? It seemed impossible.

With the surveying we had entered a sort of limbo, where the land became a set of points, and where we moved slowly about it, looking at it but not taking it in, and it seemed, as I thought of our progress, to mean that we floated somewhat free of it, as if looking from above. Its obstacles were no longer something to be passed, but something that might appear on a map—one that represented only the surface. Was there more to be found beneath? The diluvial silt, glacial in origin and washed down to an ocean that was in fact always retreating, so that even here, some walk from the sand dunes, had there been an ocean once separating the peninsula to the south into its own magnificent island? The land's slow wash eastwards, its swamps and, in between, fertile soil; the swamps would be drained, as could the lagoons at the river mouths. I needed sleep, and, finally, the natives had quietened almost completely—I suddenly became aware of it—allowing my thoughts to drift uninterrupted back to the collection: Father, I have carefully packed and sent boxes of your New Zealand bones, or what was left over after the natives helping with the excavation had trampled them into dust in their excitement. Grey was particularly pleased and would recommend me for further positions should they reach you safely . . .

A noise outside, and close by, brought me fully into consciousness again: my name being called; the crack of twigs and undergrowth; and the sound came with a new flood of speech and excitement, the sound of the fire bursting upwards again as if (was this in fact the case?) it had never died down.

Metehau was standing some yards from the tent with, in one hand, a flaming brand pulled from the fire and in the other a tomahawk. A nearby hut was in flames, casting a light from the side on his face.

He said, Mantell, I'm very, very reluctant to do this . . . He held the burning log out towards me, shook it at me for a second before throwing it down.

Wills! Wills, where . . . ? His tent was collapsed in a heap beside mine and I cast about for him in the unsteady light of the burning hut, its roof in a single shallow slope towards the rear forming a cavern beneath the flames, then coming down with a noise like a sudden voiceless cough, as if from someone hit hard in the stomach. Metehau turned towards it for a second, away from me, and I ducked back into the tent, pushing against the canvas heavily in my haste.

I shouted again, Wills!

Metehau said, I'm not sure the Governor will understand any other language, Mantell. It's the only way that seems to work with him.

Wills!

I'm sorry it has to be you.

Taking up the shotgun, powder and shot I put my head

outside the tent again; Metehau was still standing where he had been, his face broken into a mask of concentration, his eyes screwing shut once then opening. He said, Come out, Mantell . . . I saw behind him, at the edge of the circle of light cast by the campfire and still by the smouldering remains of the hut, the figure of the surveyor, dim and hazy in outline, his hands stiffly by his sides, his eyes focused blankly on mine, his face in an uncertain expression, wavering from side to side, caught in a shrug or in the act of backing away, perhaps his chin chattering, and I felt my own grip on the shotgun begin to shake, its surface become slippery with sweat, and I looked at it, able only to look down at it now, unable to look up at Metehau or Wills, though still I shouted, Wills, help me! . . . Shouted in fact down towards the gun, or half-shouted, as if I were shouting to myself, cursing over a stumble, shutting my eyes against the pain of something, trying to remember back to something, seeing something involuntarily, the distance, the distance of this situation presenting itself to me now with a shock of my own irrelevance. What would my death justify? It would take nothing for Metehau to run at me and put the tomahawk through my head, and hadn't this been my understanding from the start? My hand stopped fumbling with the powder, somehow now letting it fall into the barrel easily, flowing as if liquid, and, slowly, I stood up while still focusing on the shotgun, unable to look around me but breathing a calm breath, in and out, looking at the metal of the gun, which, as I looked at it, I loaded with shot and, finally, standing and looking up at Metehau, I saw him standing as if suspended in front of me, and Wills over his shoulder—this picture seemed to stay with me, unchanging, a long meeting of eyes though I was uncertain whether our eyes met, whether as I stood we were there for longer than a second, whether Wills was in fact behind Metehau and visible, inactive. Later I tried again to picture all of this and the instants afterwards as he ran at me brandishing the axe; remembering this in the almost complete darkness in front of me where, now, walking or running away from a glow that came from behind, flared and died out, sent itself between young trees growing close together then faded out altogether as I kept stumbling with my hands out, wondering what direction I could be walking in—along the path? Now all directions were identical in their blackness.

I had simply wrapped the blanket around me over my shirt and was not wearing the waistcoat that had the matches in its pocket. I stopped my advance, stood perfectly silent, and could the darkness become as much a comfort as a threat? Shouts reached me still from the camp; shufflings as of people walking in every direction, struggling against each other, and overhead there was no sign of a sky, either in the form of a faint glow of cloud, a star here and there or the moon. My own breath was loud, then quiet, and a thumping in my ears of my own heartbeat, and that, and the sounds of the camp muffled by distance, and a closer rustle and snap as of footfall, all seemed to raise themselves into the air and come from above, or to surround me and be coming simply from the darkness itself. I was exhausted and felt my eyes searching out, making out vague forms after all, the vertical shapes of the trees only as hints, the occasional faint white streak that could have been nothing or the product of my own wishful imagination. I would write a letter to the Private Secretary in the tent, even if my hand would be still unsteady over the paper, leaving dark drops of ink here and there. And carry it with me—I was still dependent on these people, even in order to find a ship to take my letter, to survive the strange, dark, empty surroundings. Now, putting out my hand to walk a few more steps, to feel for the vague images of trees I thought

I could see, to steady myself, I heard someone nearby behind me.

A woman's voice, in Maori: What are you doing here?

I turned and stepped back away from her, crashed into a stiffly wooded bush and turned, half leaning back against it, to face her; at first little but an imagined outline, without even sparks reflected from an unknown source, for her eyes. Without thinking I put out a hand, but drew it back before I touched her. In English I said, Sorry . . . Then in Maori: I was sent here by . . .

That's not what I meant. I followed you away from the camp.

You followed me?

Don't worry.

I couldn't sleep there.

No one will be asleep tonight. But you're not going to get any sleep out here either.

No . . . A silence for a minute, and I began to think she had vanished, though there was no sound of movement. I almost put out my hand again, but held it firm by my side. Then she said, Are you scared?

I don't know. No. Yes. Someone tried to kill me . . . Metehau had run at me, his head down, a simple run as if he were in an athletic event, a fast dash towards me, though he had simply come forward three or four yards to stand, within striking distance, and he raised the tomahawk as others, other Ngai Tahu, came up behind him to restrain him and at once I was struck through by the vision of him struggling against them, tomahawk over his head, trying to force his way out of their grip, concentrating on bringing the weapon down on my skull, finally, visibly intent, not on me, but on his task. I stood with the shotgun pointed at him. After only a few seconds he was pulled back, broke his efforts, and dropped the tomahawk, and the commotion of noise that had grown up around me became, all at once, audible. I dropped to my knees, felt around on the ground at my feet with one hand while, with the other, I let the gun's barrel rest against the ground while still gripping its handle, then dropped it. Finding a small, irregularly shaped stone, I picked it up, still squatting, held it in the palm of my hand, let it warm in my grip for some time, then put it in the pocket of my trousers.

Now, in the darkness, I felt the stone still there. I said, Why did you follow me?

She said, I don't know. To stop you getting too far away. There's nowhere you can go.

They might still kill me.

She said, Tell me about Te Rauparaha.

I should be quiet—we should be quiet. They might . . .

They think you're in your tent. No one else saw you leave.

Wills. Where is Wills? You know, the other . . .

I didn't see him leave. I don't know where he is. Will you tell me about . . .

What?

What is he like?

How old are you?

Young.

I don't know Te Rauparaha. I . . .

But you were sent by him.

I . . . ?

Did they think that? In the silence that followed I again wondered whether the woman, the girl, had suddenly gone. I could still, or so I thought, make out her outline, more as an absence than anything, as the absence of clues or hints to the presence of the forest, even as the absence of herself, of clues to herself, as if this was why she might disappear, as if she had never in fact been anything, a voice, my imagination, my disorientation in this wide, flat, sometimes swampy country that needed to be drained, stripped of its forest, given its shape and expanse, a place for houses and fields.

I sighed. I started to say, I was not sent by . . . I stopped; I couldn't think where to start. I said, Te Rauparaha is an old man. By all accounts.

She said, But when he was young?

Listen, I can't talk to you now. Please go back and leave me here.

You won't escape from the camp. You should be back there.

Shouldn't you also be back there?

Yes . . . There was a pause for a minute, after which some audible breaths, and, in English, faintly, whispered, perhaps: Can you take me away, can you?

When after a brief pause she said nothing more, I said, What? What can I—listen, what do you need?

I was interrupted by a noise coming from the direction of the camp, but closer, a crashing rustle and, in the same instant, a noise as of the woman or girl moving, quickly, and without thinking I lunged forward with my arms wide to grasp at her and hold her but found nothing but empty space, the same darkness as of her outline but filled in with nothing. She had—hadn't she?—ducked away too quickly for my grasp, for even the quick movement I had made to gently restrain her, just to hold her and keep her here for some minutes, for a short time while the danger, while the crashing, rustling passed, and now, footsteps seemed closer, several sets, a confusion of noise layered over that from the camp. Holding out a hand to one side, I found a young tree and leaned, grasping around its trunk as around an arm and falling in closer to it as around an arm, a body that I grasped in the darkness to keep me up after a stumble. There was the sound of conversation at some distance, a rapid whispered interchange, a movement of shifting undergrowth, coming in my direction? I stood still, holding onto the tree and feeling in my pocket to roll the stone between two fingers, to feel the texture of its surface, to test its hardness with a fingernail, to try to visualise its colour. I let it sit in the palm of my hand as I had when I had first found it, growing warmer still against my skin.

I wondered at the woman's quick escape, imagined myself following her, moving back towards the camp. But why was she moving in that direction if there was something there she needed rescue from? Another movement was audible ahead of me and to one side and almost involuntarily I called out, then stifled the call, letting out only a quick syllable never in fact intended for any articulate word and, taking some steps in that direction, I hit against someone, entangling briefly and inevitably before pushing away . . .

Good God . . .!

Wills?

Is that you, Mantell? I wondered what had become of you. What are you doing here . . . ?

I might ask the same—look, Wills, keep your voice down. Did you . . . ?

I came to find you. And I couldn't sleep. I can't imagine sleeping, with what happened.

I said, Keep quiet, would you? Yes. Yes, I feel the same way . . . After a brief pause I said, Did someone pass you here? A young woman.

Oh, yes, I bumped into a woman. She surprised me nearly to death, as you yourself did . . . Then: What was she doing? Mantell?

Please, Wills, keep quiet. Where did she go? Did she say anything to you?

Well, we had a few words . . .

What? What did she say?

Nothing of consequence. I was surprised at her English.

What did she say . . . ?

Mantell, what have you been doing?

Nothing. Nothing, she just seemed upset.

Upset? I didn't take that impression. For all I noticed she could have simply been going for a midnight stroll.

Isn't that in itself strange?

Well I don't suppose anyone is sleeping tonight, do you? Tell me what is going on Mantell. Or perhaps I don't want to know?

Quiet! For God's sake, keep quiet . . . Even the sound of my whisper seemed to echo unnaturally in the forest, where, under foot, I noticed what was the first sign of an oblique light, casting its contrasting shadow in thick stripes, from the now closer camp fire. Wills was visible in the larger shadow he cast, but still only as a suggestion against the forest floor, and when I blinked it seemed as if the whole play of light and dark vanished, only to reappear seconds later as the uncertain hint of itself. Was that her, hanging around the edge of the small circle that seemed to be defined by Wills and myself? I said, It's nothing, it's nothing. Just, if she . . .

She didn't say anything.

But, Wills . . .

You should just be careful, Mantell. You don't want anyone else trying to put an axe through your skull.

I beg your pardon? . . . But Wills had, with that, turned away.

Listen, Mantell, I think I will go to my tent. I'm no safer out here, and nor are you.

For a minute or two longer, I stayed while he moved his way back towards the camp, not taking any care to be silent in his movements. Shrugging in a manner that I thought I had taken from him, I also started to walk, deliberately, in the same direction; and, looking overhead, was there a hint of light, not only from the still-lit fire, but now from the sky itself—a steady gradation of colour from almost-black down to the eastern horizon's deep blue? Then, arriving at the collection of tents and makeshift huts in their small clearing, I was met with a fire and some of the natives, seated around it in a circle, staring silently at its flames.

It was a contrast to the scene as I had left it earlier. Then, Wills had come to me, after Metehau had been pulled to one side by his companions, in a step-by-step approach. He had said, Well, Mantell, I . . .

I had looked up at him, and he had squatted beside me.

He said, I should get my tent back up . . . He made no effort to move but remained squatting, beside me and at an angle. He said, Mantell?

I'm okay, Wills. I didn't think it would actually come to this.

I imagine a few drops of that brandy would help. But it's finished, isn't it?

I nodded.

Now there's a shame.

I nodded. Wills stayed there, silent, his gaze focused on the ground, occasionally flicking up to my face where I met it, raising my own only for a brief instant. From the fire there was the familiar noise of discussion, heightened into whispers and raised voices, and Wills and I seemed to form a separate world in our slight remove, in our silence.

He said, Why don't you—um, what will we do . . . ?

Carry on as before? I don't see any other way.

No. Nor do I. Why don't you retreat to your tent now? There's nothing more for it.

251

I nodded. Still, however, we stayed in the same position except that I rocked backwards to sit, folding my arms over my knees, and, a minute later, Wills also sat, resting his chin on folded arms and with a look as if he were staring, not at the surface of the earth, but through it, at something far distant.

I said, This is hopeless. This is hopeless, Wills. How much further have we got to go now, and already this is hopeless . . . I was speaking in a low voice, looking at his face that stayed, unmoving, in the same posture. I said, They've got no qualms about killing us. They meant it. He meant it in earnest.

They pulled him back, Walter. They won't do anything more. And, listen, this is in the north, at the farthest point north on our block, right up against the Ngati Toa purchase, so of course here there will be more conflict . . . He shook his head and winced. He said, Down south there will be much less for them to be concerned about.

He was interrupted by a native who approached from behind him, hands out in front in a suggestion of offering or reconciliation.

I said, What do you want?

The native gave a brief speech.

I said, Good . . . I nodded at him and, when he had retreated again, I said to Wills, It doesn't make any difference. It doesn't make any difference what they say, Metehau can still kill us both in the middle of the night. My God.

What did the native say, Mantell?

He was apologising for Metehau. But we're nothing to them, just—none of them would mind if we died, I'm sure of that . . . I stood up quickly, picking up the shotgun, noticing glances in my direction from the natives, and up at me from Wills, and turned and ducked towards my tent. Two of the natives were already re-pitching Wills's tent, stepping carefully around its outside so as not to disturb any of his possessions.

Wills said, Mantell . . . ?

I stopped for a second. Yes?

I'm sorry.

I opened my mouth to speak, then shut it, and nodded to him. Then, looking past him, to where the natives were seated, Metehau now unrestrained amongst them, I started to back away—he was talking fast at them, and occasionally they glanced back at me where I stood, still holding the shotgun. I dropped it. Wills also turned to look at them, and, when I was certain no one was looking, I ducked quickly behind my tent and out, away from the camp.

The following morning the silence from the natives persisted. My sleep had been intermittently heavy, disturbed by dreams, such as the now half-remembered image of my father looking up at me while he bent over a crate and prised off its top, to reveal, not the bones and shell fragments I had hoped for but an impenetrable black, and, horribly, he dipped his hand into it, still looking up at me though seeming already to know what was inside; starting towards him to keep his hand from the dark inside of the box, I instead lurched awake and raised myself to my elbow, throwing the blanket half to one side before I realised fully where I was.

Outside, the natives who had slept around the fire were gone. Wills's tent was standing, and the huts, but there was no sign of anyone else in the camp. I slapped an open hand on the canvas of Wills's tent to awaken him, and for a moment, when there was no response, I imagined it to be empty.

Wills! We'll finish the survey today.

Then, reluctantly, a voice: God, Mantell—is it early?

Not overly.

Where have they . . . ? With an elbow and an eye looking out from the tent's entrance.

I said, I don't know.

Are we alone now?

I don't know, Wills. I doubt it, but . . . Then, in the shadows under the side of one of the huts was a movement, and a woman's face appeared from beneath a blanket, blinking at me before looking away. I opened my mouth to call to her, but before I could utter a word another native emerged from the hut, signalled to me and approached to tell me that most of the Port Levy natives had left, that a boat had been arranged from Port Levy to Wellington in order to seek an audience with the Lieutenant Governor, and that they had gone early. The native handed me a piece of paper, then, retreating, said that he and the others remaining would stay with us, would help us back to the Deans's farm, and to Akaroa.

After reading the paper, I said, I've been left a demand, Wills. A threat of sorts . . .

Yes?

To extend the boundaries of the reserve, to an absurd degree, or he'll come and throw down the poles.

He's welcome to.

Come, we've been superseded in their attentions by Eyre. We might just as well get to work.

Wills, with his back to me, held onto both sides of the canoe, looked to either side and hunched himself downwards, screwed up his face, or so I imagined, let go of the canoe with one hand to hold onto his hat, then let the hat go again to hold the canoe. I was beginning to feel the play of its movements on the river as a sidelong dance, perhaps to feel some joy in the movement that Metehau had described. We had crossed yesterday, and been ferried to and from a deserted pa on the river that one of the natives had requested for the reserve, before, today, fulfilling another duty: measuring the depth at the mouth, Wills having estimated that the best location for a town on the north plains was on the Waimakariri, some way inland of the Deans's farm. The two natives with us made quick comments to each other as they navigated the river's currents, stood up in the canoe to sight further downstream or sat again to ply forwards or to one side with the paddles, keeping the boat's movement faster than that of the water so that the land to the right, a crumbling bank of some feet in height, and close by, unlike the distant left-hand shore, swept past quickly, retreated as the channel curved away from it, then approached again. Birds came off the water's surface, or a thin strip of silty beach; large clumsy gulls that rose, dived at us, rose again and circled behind, seemingly to dive at us once more but then hovered into a dusty haze so that they appeared to dissolve in it, becoming first unmoving sketches of themselves, then a collection of specks amongst countless others: blemishes on the cloud surface or on the surface of my vision as I craned my head to look back. The channels met, widened, slowed until we were on water that was scuffed with a wind from behind us but otherwise calm, and bright to the east with a still low sun and the disappearance of the horizon into a shimmering white. The sound of the ocean increased, a steady low roar and the cries of seabirds. On the river hadn't Metehau still been friendly?

Wills said, I don't like this.

There shouldn't be too heavy a swell, with the wind behind us, should there, Wills?

The bank flattened away to the right, revealing the dim

silhouette of the peninsula rising from over its flat sweep, the tension of a bay curving from the approaching river mouth and, ahead and to the left, the low shapes of dunes stretching themselves down onto the horizon, into the bar that protruded out as the thin line now beginning to separate the river's surface from the sky, disappearing at a point directly ahead of us. Another horizon, higher and brilliant with the reflection of glare, was the waves, appearing as we came nearer and steered away from the bar, and moving down and up and superseding themselves in height as each crest broke onto the strip of sand, now submerged and closer still, throwing up its confusion of spray. Wills said, No. No, it's too rough.

I could already feel the force of the swell on my face and neck, though it was too far off still to reach us. The natives slowed the boat, also looking concerned, then stopped, digging the paddles back and forth to keep us steady. They spoke to each other in terms I found it difficult to hear or understand.

I said to them, Go ahead, carry on to the mouth . . .

With the boat still stationary, I could imagine the sense of it moving under me, its bow awash and then the whole length of it skipping from side to side, buffeted by the pull of waves colliding and pushing back, throwing up the stern. They moved the canoe on, closer to the mouth, running parallel now to the bar, which finally sank out of sight under a tracing of foam and the opaque water moving back and forth over it, but which was indicated still by the yard's width of flat over stirred-up sand and, at its other edge, an ocean throwing itself up then down before running towards us in a dissipating chaotic motion. The noise was becoming overwhelming and, looking at the waves, I shouted again over it to the natives to keep going. I thought of Metehau and his raised tomahawk, his face concentrated but the spark of light it caught from the fire coming, not from the fire, but from these waves that were raised up and held back by the bar, and in their almost deliberate motion was the motion of his arm and the weapon, and I shouted—did I?—to keep going, around the end of the bar and into their full force, to keep the canoe going into the dangerous surf, to be overturned, and had his face been concentrating as if to keep his balance at sea? As if the ground might be thrown out from under him? His feet had been planted at some distance apart when he came to a halt within striking distance; the other natives, close behind him the whole time, mouthing at him to stop and finally taking an arm each and pulling him back long before he had time to let the encounter come to its full, to its final conclusion. His eyes had met mine only at the end of this, after he was being pulled away and was already giving up against the struggle of two others; before this they had been focused determinedly away, even on some other part of my face, on my neck or upper arms, as if his face, though intent, directed at me, were in fact turned fully away. And didn't I recognise this same turning away from an image of my father at the door to his office, looking at me for a second after a walk together on the streets then turning into the room, shutting the door to go about his business? Even here I reached a hand into my pocket again to find the irregularly shaped stone that I had picked up after Metehau's attack, its surface smooth with the oil from my fingers.

Wills was now leaning to one side, slowly letting out the plumb line as the boat was held steady again, still inside the bar. His hands moved close together, one over the other as if he were counting money or shuffling cards, the line unravelling from its spool on his lap, paying into the water with a soft liquid fall. If I wanted to stand up in the boat and once again

257

urge the natives on towards the surf, the heavy swell that was washing around the edge of the bar and turning over itself as it flattened out into the narrow lagoon, I checked this urge, somehow seeing the ocean's size for the first time and the ease with which it could, yes, overturn the boat.

On the return journey, Wills said, What were you thinking, Mantell? Even the natives had more sense than you . . .

I'm sorry, Wills, I wasn't—

That swell would have had us all drowned.

I know, Wills . . .

And this measurement should be good in any case, no need to . . .

Yes, yes. I can't quite explain it—I just wasn't quite myself.

The natives laboured against the current, choosing slower channels and keeping close to the edges. Wills had resumed his former position, his back rounded in front of me, his hands to either side or periodically holding onto his hat, and when he spoke I had to concentrate to catch the words spoken downwards.

We stayed some nights at the Deans's farm while Wills worked on mapping the reserves—a total of 2640 acres of which 1540 were good, open land, the remainder being swamp or bush; this in addition to the old pa at Kaiapoi, a separate reserve not yet surveyed, and around five acres surveyed for a small kaika on the Waimakariri. Wills worked from his notebook and Kemp's map, shutting himself for a day inside a room of the old farmhouse and asking not to be disturbed, while outside the wind brought gusty showers that rattled against the walls and windows. In between these showers I stepped out, pushed from side to side by the gusts, and walked around the farm with my sketchbook, looking closely at the soil, cut suddenly here and there with streams that ran a good two feet or more below the land in shallow chasms and had been utilised as natural trenches to divide the paddocks.

Late in the day, the younger Deans sat with me outside the old farmhouse.

I hear you had some trouble with the natives?

I said, Metehau tried to kill me.

Metehau comes and goes. I don't really know him. I'm sure he doesn't represent anything more than himself . . .

One of them told me afterwards that he was just hot-headed.

I'm sure that's true. I wouldn't give it any more thought.

The dusk was approaching, giving the land a grey uniformity, as swamp mingled into pasture and the forest lost its individual trees for an overall shadow. Showers that came across from the south from time to time darkened the view still further, then gave the ground's surface a quick gleam of reflection from the west as the water settled, but missed us, under the north-facing veranda—instead they caused the older brother, visible making his way across the fields with one of the natives, to throw up his arm across his face.

It's not so easy for me just to forget, though of course I've tried.

You can forget anything, Mantell, believe me. It was, what, three or four days ago?

Yes. Four, five.

My brother there—look at him. He has forgotten everything. He forgets everything except what's in front of him. Well, maybe I'm like you, not so good at forgetting—but I do well enough.

Deans . . . ?

Well—my fiancée promised me she'd come to be with me here. Just once, and I'm not sure she meant it. I'm still waiting.

I'm sure she'll—

Yes, very kind of you, Mantell. I don't know whether I've given up hope or not, so I keep my head down and I try to catch my brother's—look at him . . . The older Deans was walking quickly, his arms swinging and the native with him lagging some distance behind. He said, I don't know if this is the place for a woman, Mantell. I mean, Mary survives here, but her husband will hardly talk to her—nor she to him. And she's busy with her duties; she's a servant. What kind of life is this for someone in love?

Deans, I'm sorry . . .

It's really not a civilised place, is it, Mantell? You're a man of science; you can see what I mean. You think I'm naïve, but don't you agree? I mean they outnumber us a hundred to one, more, and who'd want to live here, really?

That will change . . . As I said it, I couldn't imagine anything changing; I couldn't imagine anything but the swamp, the pasture and these buildings, and I felt at once almost invisible, irrelevant, as if I were still hiding in the pitch-black forest after Metehau's attack, waiting, silent, at some remove from the camp and the tent, as if I could, despite the darkness and the forest, in fact look back at that tent to see myself, or see only the surface of my skin, my face strangely impenetrable even to myself.

They just need to say the word—we're here under their sufferance, of course. You found that out, Mantell. If they hadn't stopped him? He was held back by other natives . . . ?

They did stop him.

But what if they hadn't? Did you think about that? What if . . .

Of course I thought about that, Deans, but they—listen, you're not here under their sufferance any more. As far as this part of Kemp's block is concerned, the deed is settled. The natives were satisfied with the decisions on their reserves. Deans, why don't you go back . . . ?

Why? Why would I go back?

For your . . .

Well, if she doesn't want me? If I should arrive back and find her cold to me? I should wish I'd stayed here.

Deans stood up now as his brother approached, wiping his hands down the front of his coat, the native who had been with him no longer in sight. The skin of his face was reddened against the rain, water gathering in the spaces under his eyes and slicking his cheeks. He said, You're outside in this? Come in, Mantell, by the stove . . . He stepped up and strode past us into the room where Wills was busy with the maps, saying, Wills? Stop your work now . . .

To the younger brother, still out under the veranda, I said, Deans, listen, you don't need to pay them rent now. The land you're on is no longer theirs, so you won't have to give them anything. Once a title is arranged for you, they will be here on *your* sufferance.

The Geological Eye

Out of Port Cooper on the way to Heaphy's house once again, through a rift in an almost vertical cliff, whose face was dark and cast its dark shadow over the water, over the flooded swamp at the head of the port and the settlers' few houses, we climbed over steps of rock, one after the other, up to our armpits in height until, at the top of the ridge separating Ports Cooper and Levy, there was a view to the north: the land we were leaving unchanged in its flat expanse, in the diluvial shingle and silt, its pasture and swamp, and the same also to the south with the stretch of the mountains falling gradually into the distance.

Having left the plan of the Kaiapoi reserve with the Port Levy natives, and having spent several nights in Akaroa and one in Goashore on the way further south, we again caught sight of the southern view from a long grassy slope. The remainder of our journey spread before us until no longer visible: the long, dreary 'Ninety-mile beach', a continuation of the same sediments, and, at the foot of our hill, the lake hemmed in by it, an enormous copy of the smaller lagoons that formed where the rivers broke out into the sea, repeatedly filling and breaking or filtering out through the beach piled high by the energy of the waves. The small stone was still in my pocket—as it turned out, a pebble of green quartz. On this hill, in contrast, were rocks of the same volcanic formations that characterised the whole peninsula, broken here and there with metamorphic outcroppings.

The natives here were apathetic about our task; at a small, miserable kaika at the foot of the hill, we could persuade only one to accompany us, and had to leave behind some provisions with the men who had brought us from Akaroa and no further. The long spit at the edge of the lake, at first grown with various grasses and covered with a layer of rich loam, then finally running out into bare sandhills as we approached its furthest point, became exhausting underfoot, shifting its shingle surface into sliding craters—finally, we were walking on a sodden, incoherent stretch of gravel, thrown over with the sea's smell and the cold haze that built over our faces a layer of salt, which we would rub off and roll between our fingers. A canoe took us across the mouth from the end of the spit to another village, where we sheltered in a decrepit grass hut.

Over the next days we assigned and surveyed a reserve in

two sections, containing the kaika and cultivations and the gardens at some distance. Swamp encroached closely against the shingle beach and lake-front, covering the substratum of loosely coherent shingle; green quartz such as the small rock I kept with me—this type of rock was represented with other quartzes, with jasper and schist under the soil layer. Wills worked in the hut on producing an initial map of the reserve before, finally, leaving the village, we followed a path to the south, skirting around lagoons and swamp at their inland edge.

The same formations—the range of rock types, the layer of rich soil laid down by repeated flooding—continued further down the length of coast, uninterrupted by significant outcroppings or headlands, drained by meandering rivers that sometimes broke out into multiple gushing channels in a triangular delta-like area as they approached the sea, the whole area bounded by crumbling cliffs that we would slide down, holding onto what significant rocks or roots cohered in the dirt, knocking them down the few yards of the drop and letting them roll through the stands of toitoi while behind us the layers of the cliff seemed like multiple horizons, stacked one on the other. These sunken delta areas had the feeling of damp shallow bowls cut off from the noise of wind felt above, instead inhabited by the water's sounds—chattering and a hiss—that would come on suddenly as we broke from a thick outgrowth of grasses and let our feet slide, without warning, into a foot or two depth of stream. Clearly the bowls had been formed in the same way as the lagoons that repeatedly broke and refilled, these having broken to sea-level once and for all, leaving a wide or narrow gap between the ragged remaining outlines of the sandbars, through which the sea was visible, its swell breaking with the same violence as ever on a narrow beach but its noise, too, somehow banished from this shallow valley. At one of these valleys, the first cliff was only a mild downward slope, the valley itself nearly imperceptible until, almost down into it, I looked up to see, over the tops of the grasses, that the horizon had disappeared, that a corresponding low slope at a considerable distance had obscured the run of the land behind a definite line, above which nothing until another suggestion of land: the mountain range always visible faintly in the distance. Coming into this much wider valley signalled the beginning of a series of channels that slowed us even more, running close together between dense toitoi and tutu which we had to scramble through and over. The far edge, like a true horizon, seemed to come no closer but instead simply grew more solid in its shape, as if a low wall were blocking our path. Once, I looked up to wonder briefly whether the slope I could see was to the south or the north, as if, caught in what seemed a maze of channels and grasses, we might now be heading in entirely the wrong direction. Then, seeing the water's flow from right to left, the mountains in their place, I regained my senses, looked down and, wedged amongst the rocks at the edge of the stream, saw what looked like a fragment of bone.

As we passed southwards the land drained increasingly through narrow chasms and gullies that would lead us on detours one or two miles inland. The land rose gradually as we proceeded, though there was no obvious slope, until at one point, after two days' walk, the drop to the beach was around seventy-five feet, and the ocean's horizon, when we came to the crest of the bank, set itself out before us with a clarity we had not seen since the view, taking in the land as well as the ocean directly to the south, from the hills of the peninsula. Then, dropping to the beach itself and continuing along the shingle, we became used to the laboured footsteps, the approach and wash of the sea, wearing away at the landscape and at the same time washing its sand up over the beach, pushing the hills back and undermining them at once. Then, towards the end of this enormous, continuous beach, where we camped near a number of native villages for the purpose of setting aside and surveying reserves, I looked back along its length, with a sense of the intervening days, of the looseness of its earth, constantly worn away from within and from the ocean, with a sense of our own footsteps already worn away, the river banks crumbling on themselves and washing as silt out to sea, then to be thrown back, retaken, thrown back, exposing rocks here and there on the banks, the river beds, on the beach itself, and amongst them the ends of bones and sodden preserved branches—only then to have the entire view obliterated by a veil of rain apparently thrown up by the sea itself. The rain whipped at my hat and coat, pushed me to one side, filled me with the melancholy of this place and the desolation of the natives' existence, their attempts to grow wheat in miserable plots, their tiny populations, increasingly failing in villages whose ground drained reluctantly, whose huts were damp. Here, a native in an attempt at resistance threw down the survey poles; another, arriving from the north in a whale-boat, brought the news of the death of Colonel Wakefield and of the Port Levy natives' meeting with Grey and Eyre—he went around the inhabitants, having brief conversations, nodding his head and handing them letters that had come from Akaroa and Wellington. Finally, the boat took him and his companions further south.

Then, after the narrow spits of two further lagoons, we came to the end of the beach. Here the country raised up into hills, with long low rises and cliffs of up to fifty feet in height at the sea, revealing here and there a volcanic substratum beneath the same superficial deposits we had been used to from the plains. As part of a long letter, carried and added to over the course of our journey, I wrote: I have collected samples for you . . . The vesicular volcanic rock underlying the country dipped gradually to the south, disappearing once again but leaving the country not as one extensive plain, as it had been to the north, but as narrow areas cut across by rolling downs and finally broken by a river that ran in a wide flood channel, whose bed was scattered with basaltic and porphyritic pebbles washed down from the interior. Abutting it to the south some way inland, where we had been forced in our attempts to cross—which we did with difficulty one morning on rapidly improvised, unstable rafts—a high spur rose up suddenly, darkening the way ahead, sparkling faintly with a mineral dryness, rough under our feet as we made our way up its gullies, and the grass that grew in them giving way to a conglomerate of quartz pebbles in a ferruginous base at the tops of the slopes, and, breaking out of them and standing at an angle to the sky, highly inclined, jumbled strata of slate. In the next valley the slate, interrupted with veins of quartz, dipped steeply to the south; we crossed the plain at its base diagonally, towards the coast again, in search of food and stumbling somewhat with fatigue and now seeing, now able to see the land for all its distinct features, spotted here and there with villages of one or two huts, scarcely populated, the sweep of beach and the punctuation of the rivers and hills, and tentative European settlement: a whaling base now abandoned, a sheep station which we made our home for some days, at first waiting out a south-westerly gale that swept bitterly cold rain across the land, under eaves and the gap under the door, wetting the rough floorboards for the time it took to sink between them.

From this farm we set out on trips to gather the local

natives together, to arrange for meetings and for the assigning of reserves.

Here, south of the slate, was a country of yellow and white limestone, opening up here and there in rifts and caves, porous, shattering from itself easily, overlaid by grasses, and containing shells and corals. Out of the walls of a cave I chipped specimens of *terebratulae* and other fossils similar to those I had once found at Chichester, and held them warming against the palm of my hand as with a feeling of familiarity, of return; a small, heart-shaped shell dark and with a surprising weight or solidity, seeming to dissolve into the dark of the shallow cave itself, and here a similarly darkened tooth of a shark, its point raised slightly from the piece of rock that it sat in, almost an inch in length. Also amongst this lime the structures of corals, branched and exposed porous surfaces that seemed to blend with the surface of the calcareous cementing material, which, sure enough, when inspected closely under a glass revealed hints of its intricate finer structure, built from the feathers and complexities of still smaller fossils, the *textularia*, *rotaliae* and so on. The whole formation had apparently been copied to the last detail from the rocks and fossils I had found in Sussex, so that, after spending some time collecting the specimens, after stepping into the light and turning the fossils over under the glass, I looked up and felt an instant of surprise, as if I had expected to see the town in the middle distance, the quarrymen, the fog and exhalations of life carrying on in the fields around and beneath me. Instead I was brought home quickly to the sweeping, empty country with, yes, a village in the distance towards the coast, but with its food platforms seeming to sway like the tips of grasses, the whole movement only emphasising the strange, windblown, cold of the land. We walked across it, coming and going, visiting the villages, negotiating and surveying, now with difficulty, as if we had grown heavy, as if the sand of the beaches to the north had remained under our feet. Towards the coast the limestone gave out again to layers of clay and volcanic grit, including a blue clay that contained numerous fossil specimens, and a sandstone also with fossils, and then, some way south, a collection of spherical boulders, septaria that had been washed from the clay by the action of the waves: some more than five feet in diameter, and entire or broken to reveal yellow and brown crystals of spar filling the rough geometrical cracks, and those that were hollowed out were filled with seawater from the high tide. I stepped into one, feeling the newly cold water seep into my already sodden boots, and the skin of my feet crawl and contract away from its touch—then, standing there, I had the sense of having emerged from its broken shell.

Wills was nearby. He said, A fine natural foot-bath, Mantell! If we could only heat water to put into them . . . Then, when I said nothing: But we have to take comfort when we can find it.

I said, I'm tired, Wills.

Yes.

How long since we've had any real comfort?

Yes. But our expectations change, don't they? Our view changes, and we start to see things differently, take comfort even in the smallest things, in the faintest hints . . . ?

I was still standing up to my shins in the cold water filling the broken septarium. I had sketched them—the whole specimens with a sort of radial zone of clay around a diameter, and the angles and surfaces of the interior of the fragments. The natives were now nowhere to be seen—or I had stopped seeing them, though the nearby village was visible as a collection of uprights fading into the sea's mist. Now, Wills and I stood and were given a strange pause by the heavy globular formations around us. Wills was right: I had begun to take comfort in different things; in the fossils I pulled from the chalk, in the sudden views and the notes and sketches about their geology that rendered them comprehensible, that provided a sort of genuine grounding for our activity, and made palatable for now the natives' sullen existence, their desperate cold lives, I couldn't help thinking, their strange ignorance—in the centre of one village, instead of cutting drainage channels, they had put up with water inches deep, and traversed this pool precariously on planks laid over it. Their looks, the efficiency with which they guided us, accompanied us, welcomed us, expected us, all with a shrug and a half-smile—was I imagining it? Were they eyeing us, performing something and tolerating our presence and our activity as if it were just a move in a game and nothing more, this making each of their actions a falsehood? When I dealt with them I kept my hand on the pebble of green quartz, or at least felt for it often, even for its shape against the cloth of my trousers, though now I had no need to think of the time I had picked it up, of the woman or girl whom I had met in the forest and who had talked briefly also to Wills. Feeling in my pocket again for it now, I wondered at Wills's behaviour, his times of quiet watchfulness, and now he was quiet but facing the ocean, away from me, his body hunched slightly against a cold wind and slight drizzle that blew across the beach in occasional bursts, hardly wetting the surfaces of things. Even in his companionship, in the times where he seemed at first genuine, hadn't there been something in his eye that raised my suspicions? It was hard to believe now, as he swayed slightly, seeming only vulnerable, as isolated here as myself.

Now a crowd of natives was approaching from the village along the beach, the individuals still undifferentiated in their distant mass. I closed my eyes. I started to talk to him, half under my breath.

I said, The thing is, Wills, I'm tired of constantly thinking of their motives . . . I said, I'm tired of thinking of what they might want, what Eyre wants, what Grey wants out of all this and how best to gain it, how to negotiate everyone's wishes, what moves to make. I don't want to think like this . . . I had no idea whether he was listening to me, but I carried on: I don't want everything I say or do under surveillance, everything watched from all quarters until I have no idea of anything. I can't help feeling that I've been forced into this. From the very start of this business, maybe from the start of everything, I've been forced to think only about what we and I might get out of it, and to be honest I think nothing, nothing at all—I've only got to think about how to survive and I'm tired of surviving. I'm tired of negotiating. I'm tired of feeling as if I'm a playing a game, and sometimes I feel as if I'm hardly even a piece in a game, a pawn—look at this place, its cold bare existence! I don't know if my legs will carry me any further, and I'm half-forgetting what it is to live in any comfort, to rest for a day without thoughts. Each minute there is some negotiation, but I don't know quite whether the language I speak is being understood, whether I understand his, their language, whether he—have they even seen a contract, prior to this, known what it means to sign? Well, I brought it on myself. To be fair, I chose to come here, but at the same time there was no other choice. But I don't know whether the arrangements and contracts I make are understood; I don't know whether—and God, I'd rather simply dig, hold onto something, avoid becoming simply the person who signs and contracts and negotiates and plays these games. Even the science is part of it, I know, but when I find something, when I look at it under the glass, that is

272

when I escape to an unreachable part of myself.

But you'll be sending it all back to him.

That's—that's the problem. It goes back to him. When he hit me I thought I'd bought something, traded something, allowing myself some time—even if I was bruised it allowed me some bruised, unreachable time when he could do nothing but look away and I was free to keep digging, and I understood that; it was my contract, my own deed or settlement, the thing I held back, and if it failed it's because it always came back to him, it got pulled into the same need for negotiation, the same constant difficulty, understanding, negotiating: how could I be sure that he even knew what it was we'd agreed to? Wasn't he oblivious, going about his business, unused to contracts and signatures, as if he'd never seen them in his life—well, I moved to the farm but on an understanding, bought and rebought; I never wanted him to hit me, but it was part of the deal, maybe a cruel one. Finally—oh great, what great freedoms I bought—I was free to imagine Mantell stuck standing in the middle of some half-filled septarium with a group of indistinct natives coming up on him and whispering while a heavy surf broke not far away, throwing up hissing mist over everything, obscuring everything slightly. It was only because he had once stood on a low rise that was still there on our farm, drawn the same view that I recognised, the son of Gideon Mantell *here*; that was why I wrote about him—but what use is a coincidence? Still, after I had seen it I couldn't help seeing the farm through new eyes, eyes that saw dusty surfaces, that saw the roots of plants clutching at soil, that saw the mountains washed down to the sea, that saw the survey poles with their shallow purchase, sometimes falling and taking up a divot of earth with them at their lower end, and didn't he, his vision, offer me something? Some way to stay at the farm, at least to be able to look at it, even if it meant removing myself from every aspect of the place's working life, and making the place itself in some way impossible?

Is that why you resisted? You looked at me with something like horror—I refuse to believe it. If it's a phase, why won't it pass? Won't you one day read this? I stopped writing for the world long ago. I was never writing for the world; I never wanted to. I never knew who I was writing for, but it's you.

At the funeral I was hardly able to speak; too much was strange, and I hardly knew my feelings—sad, devastated, of course, but nothing impacted on me for some time; I remember the heat and the people, the relatives. Her cousin, my nephew, was there, who is now a writer, standing as if to deflect attention away from himself; I noticed it because, like him, I wanted to be hidden away from the centre of things, and the condolences. Nothing really impacted on me until I saw her kiss him and overheard their conversation. I had noticed his stance and his attitude, but until then I had never really noticed him, that he was becoming an adult, as was my daughter, though on a second glance both of them seemed like children—with this kiss I saw the both of them newly, the boy I hadn't paid much attention to on his visits, except to see him as a child, and my daughter, who was both always noticed, always in my vision, then suddenly I would see her afresh and it would be as if I had been blind to her. This kiss was something new, and made my daughter into a stranger for a second. They were out the back of the house, where there was a small vegetable garden between the house and, to one side, the shed and, to the other, the old workers' quarters. They were alone there in the shelter from a warm wind that blew dust, as always, from the plains, that fingered at the soil and grasses, and each had a hand up over their eyes. I had been in the kitchen, where Peter's sister, who had been staying since he died, his cousin—the boy's mother—and a few other of his family were still gathered after most of the guests had departed, and I had left for my writing room, saying I wished for a few minutes on my own. In the room with its concertina window open, the desk, its papers, I shut the door, and then, seeing Meri just outside leaning on the wall, put out a hand to her but was stopped in my action—the boy was there too, and he leaned in to her, kissed her briefly before she pushed him away. This was only yards from me, and I stepped back. Her eyes had closed with this kiss, then screwed shut, and as she pushed him her face was tight before she looked quickly away.

She said, Not now.

He said, Oh, I know.

No, it's too strange.

I know . . . He was still looking at her, at the back of her head; a few paces forward and I could have leaned out slightly and touched their hair, or just leaned, and but for the kiss I had seen I might have done so. It seemed so unlikely that they hadn't heard me enter, hadn't heard me shut the door, with the windows wide open, that I felt at once as if this were a performance put on purely for my benefit, and at the same time as if I didn't exist, that even were I to lean out to them they wouldn't notice me. How had Meri become suddenly so distant? Or, hadn't she been distant now for years, and hadn't it just been brought home to me? It felt as if I didn't exist partly because I had no idea that this kiss could happen—had it happened before? I had no way of knowing, and I was unable to move. I had no idea of her life, her thoughts.

She said, It's so sudden, I don't feel anything yet.

I wanted to say, That's how I feel, Meri!

She said, I only feel as if everything is strange, and I don't quite get it. I don't quite believe anything.

I wanted to say, Yes! . . . It was as if she was speaking for me, had taken my voice, and I didn't mind it being taken—if I kept silent now, still because the image, the sight of the kiss was fresh in my mind, it was also because I wanted her to carry on, to keep speaking.

She said, Because it's so sudden I only know what I'm supposed to feel. I can't stand this, all these people watching to see how I feel—what am I going to say? What can I say? There's just nothing, nothing where I should be or, no, that sounds . . .

I wanted to spur her on—it sounds . . . ? It sounded like it made perfect sense, and if she was performing for me now, actually aware that I was standing there so close, closed off to them but able to hear every word, was this her demonstration that she in fact understood, that she wasn't making every struggling movement simply to escape from me as, for years, it had seemed, looking on with disgust when I felt helpless, disgusted at the helplessness that, yes, I was helpless to do anything about? Now she seemed as helpless herself, seemed in her words to be struggling, the way I struggled with my words, and not against me but against the wordless position she herself was in.

Now she began to whisper, and I had to strain to hear her more clearly: It's not fair. I'm angry, I'm just so angry. Why did he die? Why him?

I took a step back. No. After the whispered conversation, really a monologue, she ran. Her cousin had left already, stiffly, not looking over his shoulder, his face in profile and his eyes downcast, walking quickly into the wind and his eyes flicking against it until quickly he was out of sight. There was something deliberate in his movements, the same desire not to engage that I had seen in him earlier, the desire not to be seen—and this seemed to be bought with the agreement not to see, to keep his gaze fixed on the ground in front of him. At once I was sure: he knew, had known all along, that I was in the room, and was silently as he walked entering into an agreement with me, a sort of game: he would never mention that he knew, and would spare me the uncomfortable prospect of acknowledging what I had overheard. With his stiffness, the pointed manner of his movements, he was signalling to me, calling across to me in a language that I knew well. There was no need for anything further, and he seemed to step out of time as he left the frame of the open window, soundlessly moving around the house. I didn't see him again after that day, until today when I received his letter saying he would like to visit. Will the game finally be played out? Will I call back across to him?

She had whispered to him: Dad lived and breathed this place; he loved it. He was really happy and it's wrong that he should be taken away. This place makes no sense without him. Nothing, I—why wasn't it, it's stupid, but why wasn't it me?

The cousin inhaled.

I thought to myself: and why wasn't it me?

She said, Why wasn't it her? . . . She said, She hates everything here. She tries to sit me down and tell me about the farm and why it's stolen or something. She just sits inside with her history books deciding that everything here is wrong, that we shouldn't be farming here—she can't say anything positive . . . She was, wasn't she, tapping or slapping at the wall beneath the window with her hand as she talked, as if trying to hammer something out, or there was some noise, some other noise, and I fell sideways and remained standing, one hand now against the desk, its papers that in an instant I could have swept onto the floor, but I stood still, holding

my breath. She said, Everything secretly means something
. . . She was shaking, gentle movements that quickened and
it occurred to me that this was her tears, and still did I want
to put out a hand to her? Maybe I did, maybe leaning with
the other still on the desk I reached out into a space now full
with the distance between us: what, how had this happened?
It was an accident, it was an accident that she had said this
or felt this; it meant nothing, and still it repeated Peter's
acts of violence that came from nowhere. No, more, this
struck deeper, as did each petulant look throughout her long
teenage years, but this, deeper still, until, after the cousin had
silently left and she was left alone—she had stopped talking;
he had put his arm around her, sat for a second, then left—I
wanted to reach out further and touch her, and to stop her
turning, stop her seeing me, and I thought: don't turn . . .
I held my breath: don't turn . . . She turned, and her look,
teary, tear-streaked, the red from her eyes slipping into the
wet at the corners of her lips, turned out, recoiling—what
did I do? It's my fault, I could have held her look, looked
back differently, given her something, touched her, but she
was just out of reach, could have done something different
with my face, enveloped her or smiled and held her eye, but
I looked away as if caught eavesdropping, and looked down,
maybe dismissively, since in truth I couldn't bear to see her
now, and she shouted, something inarticulate, and ran. Then,
though she had gone, I heard from her, as if in replay: Why
wasn't it her? She hates everything here. She tries to sit me
down and tell me about the farm and why it's stolen, she tells
me about things that happened outside of time, things she
writes and dreams about, only dreams about how this place
was the scene of violence, and it *was* the scene of violence,
poles put in the earth, an unexpected violence, sometimes
gentle, unintended maybe.

In the days since he had died I tried to forget his violence, and her face now repeated it, impossibly repeated the violence, shattered the distance to it, made the thought of reaching across impossible, since there was no longer any across: she touched, struck, then ran. Like her cousin, she never mentioned it again, although later that day I still longed to touch her. As the guests were taking their leave, leaving me with her and Peter's sister, her eyes were fixed on the floor, signalling a retreat. The same look stayed with her, an avoidance, until, some torturous days later, taken up with silences, she left for her flat in the city.

Now, in London, there was a knock on the door; it would be him. I called out, then stood; it was always difficult to make myself heard through the heavy wood. The girl was upstairs already, and I had advised him to make his own way through to the waiting room, but I had neglected to leave the door ajar as I often did in such circumstances. The dark had grown imperceptibly and the knock had brought it to me that it was no longer light enough for reading, or for receiving my visitor, and, calling out again for him to wait, I lit the lamps. Then, opening the door to him, I said, Mr Wills, come in. I'm sorry to have kept you standing.

Thank you . . . He looked down, hesitated for a moment, his eyes, clearly despite himself, on the stick I held close to the side of my body, and on the hand I held it with.

I said, I need it most after sitting for a long time. The infirmity that comes in old age from an active earlier life, I'm afraid. You'll have to watch your own bones, no doubt, after your expeditions in New Zealand.

No doubt. But I shan't be returning to the colony. I think the life of a surveyor here is likely to be far easier . . . He followed me in, closing the door after him. He held in one hand an envelope, which, as he sat, he pushed across the corner of the desk to me. He said, From your son.

Is there news of him?

The news he will give himself, in the letter. But he seems to be fine, the last I saw him. He is doing an exemplary job for the government, and has been given work negotiating the purchase of further blocks of land from the natives.

I fear I'll never see him again.

I never saw him as one for the colony—altogether too rough a place for him, and no signs of improving. He's sure to return, sooner or later.

Later may be too late . . . There was a silence, and Wills looked down at the back of his hand, flicked his eyes to me once and then back. I said, Sorry, Mr Wills, this is no way to talk to a perfect stranger. But I have heard much of you from my son's letters.

Well, and I of you, of course. He was most anxious that the collections he sent should arrive safely with you.

As they did . . . Again, a silence. He appeared to be studying his hand, holding it in the other, bending each finger in turn gently back for a second. I was surprised at his demeanour, the half-frown of his forehead, and the somewhat lax slump of his body in the chair before me, hardly giving him the figure of the adventurer. His eyes, however, although turned down, had an intelligent look, a consideration and even humour to them, and something of a spark.

He said, Walter was collecting samples wherever possible. Even where it seemed there might be nothing other than bland infusorial earth he would scrape away at it—

What I received is most thorough.

And it seemed, as we proceeded down the length of the Middle Island, his enthusiasm grew, rather than waned.

Though it is always a matter of some deprivation, some exhaustion, on these surveys, he threw himself into his science each day. You can be proud—

Yes, of course. My presentation will be based entirely on his work. Tell me about the swamp collection? You were with him?

Yes . . . Now his eyes once again raised up to mine. He said, It is not the first excavation at the locality, though it is the most definitive, I am sure. There is no inch of the ground that has not been gone over already by fossil hunters excited by the high prices the bones can afford, and it leaves it somewhat—it is somewhat depleted. When told of this by one of the whalers, who himself had sold some pieces, Walter became quite wild, and insisted, though we were close to the end of our voyage south, that we look over it with complete thoroughness. I myself was resistant at first. I get to a state of utter distraction, when all I wish for is a comfortable bed. I'm afraid I gave your son little assistance at times. But—here, let me draw it for you?—in this small bay, under a point that runs out to the ocean, a swampy area sits against the water. The mission house is just above, and the native pa is only a short distance away. Some day, the water from the river will wash through a narrow strip of land to the point, and it will break away as an island. The coast is steep—spectacularly so. We were forced to scramble down a precarious, loose bank to reach the site, which the natives did as though it were second nature to them. But even if the point does not break away, leaving the site exposed to the river's full current, it is slowly eroding into the sea. A fine deposit is being lost to the elements and the greed of the fossil hunters . . .

While the room remained still, evenly lit and, to all intents and purposes, entirely removed from the outside world, he described the site in further detail, allowing me to write notes as he spoke, and going on to mention two further sites where the bones of *Dinornis* had been reported, though he and Walter had not been near them. He carefully answered my questions, pausing and closing his eyes as if to take himself back to the colony in his imagination. He seemed to be referring to a perfect mental picture, a memory so precise that, for a moment, it seemed as if he might be able to conjure up for me an image of my son much more detailed than I might guess at from the letter he had carried with him. However, what could I ask him about Walter? I almost wanted him to describe my son's face, a face that had surely changed in the years since he had left, and whose image was fading in my memory in any case.

After a time Wills said, It is possible that we found everything that was left to be found at the Waikouaiti site. I was taken aback at the sight of two of the natives lifting a heavy object from the earth, and the realisation that this was an enormous bone. Until then I must say I had been unconvinced. The image of the bird whose leg this had once been, upright, perhaps ten feet tall, hunted by the natives . . .

I said, They are astounding creatures.

It is only a shame that we shall never see one.

We can't be certain of that, Mr Wills. Science is full of surprises, and we shouldn't close our minds to what might yet be found. There is always some—some hope. It is easy to feel that the world is complete. Perhaps you will see one in your lifetime. As for me, I can be far more certain that I shall not live to see many new discoveries.

Doctor Mantell—

Yes, yes, forgive me. Or humour me, if you like. One spends one's life concerned with the mysterious extinction of entire races of highly organised beings, and can't help but focus on one's own extinction. When I think of what once was—entire worlds that exist now only in the imagination—it is sometimes a shock to open my eyes to what is around me: another world, quite uncaring, moving steadily on. It seems strange that it is the largest creatures that are driven to their extinction: the great lizards, the Irish elk, perhaps the moa—leaving us with only the small, the everyday. Could there be some principle there, do you think?

I'm sure I couldn't say . . .

The colony is a rough place?

Rough, yes. Desolate, windswept, far from anything. It will never take off. There are new settlements planned now in the Middle Island, but I can't see them succeeding. Maybe that is what stops me from returning—I am surveying land for new developments, but I am certain no settlement will last. The place will fall into ruin, and all my work will be wasted. The natives will continue to do what they want, and the government will lose any authority it has gained with them. They are much greater in number than the settlers, and have shown that they can resist if they wish . . . A melancholy air settled on the room as his voice faded; he made a gesture as if to try to illustrate his point further, but words seemed to elude him, and he seemed quietly frustrated at not being able to convey the full force of his meaning, the full detail and colour of his imagination. The picture was, however, clear enough: a colony on the edge of chaos, a brief experiment in governance quickly failed, where sickness and struggle would become the norm, where regression would rule, where life would be a desperate scramble for its necessities. Weren't the established orders everywhere beginning to fail? Didn't the situation in Europe signal the same thing, a breakdown, an extinction, a fall into anarchy that might well be final? The small uprisings could only grow, become general, spread and trigger more so that even here in Britain there could no longer remain an order to things. Could Wills see, as I did, an image of time that showed only decline, that showed complexity failing, that showed the ends of things and their transformation into static remains of themselves, excavated and studied but giving only hints as to their failed magnificence? He had stopped his gestures, and once again was looking down at his hands, which rested now, unmoving, on his lap. If we built walls, if we built science and industry, if we built great buildings now, it was only to put off for a little longer the inevitable rise of destruction, it was already to invite thought of their decay, to imagine them crumbling and to imagine them in thousands, hundreds of thousands of years, half-standing monuments. Time would turn its attention elsewhere. He looked down, perhaps, because in my train of thought I had been absently studying him, subjecting him for the length of his visit to a continuous gaze, and I suddenly became aware of it, and sorry for it. I myself looked away now, and at this he seemed to be freed. He stood, and said, Well, Doctor Mantell, I am sure I have taken enough of your time.

Not at all . . .

And in any case, I must be going. I hope what I have given you will be useful?

Yes, of course. Of course, it will be very useful.

Good . . . He turned, and turned again. He said, Don't get up; I will find my own way out . . . Instead, for a minute he stood over me, allowing himself to watch me. He said, Doctor Mantell, I'm sure your son is very well. And you will be able to judge his success for yourself when he returns.

Thank you.

I should leave the door shut?

Thank you. That would be good.

Goodbye, then.

Yes.

His few steps across the room were heavy, then, turning once more to grasp the door handle, he gave a last signal of farewell, and pulled it silently closed after him.